The couple was partially screened by a low hedge, but something in the girl's demeanor triggered a subconscious response and Sigrid hesitated at the top of the steps, her mother behind her.

"Is something wrong?" she asked, peering into the shadows.

"N-no," the girl stammered. "N-nothing!"

Her bloodless face belied her words. There was glittering hostility in the young man's upward glance and an even stronger impression of wrongness in the way he gripped the girl's arm.

Sigrid reached into her purse for some ID even as the man was saying, "You heard her, lady, so bug off, huh?"

"I'm a police officer," Sigrid told the frightened girl. "Are you sure there's nothing—"

The filthy obscenities that streamed from the youth's mouth startled her almost as much as the flickering switchblade which suddenly appeared in his hand.

She automatically flung her left arm out to deflect the slashing blade and as he crashed past her, her snub-nosed .38 came free. Deliberately aiming low, Sigrid sent him howling to the pavement with one shot.

Behind her in the shadows, the girl began to scream hysterically.

"Oh my God!" Sigrid's mother murmured.

Sigrid's left arm was still numb, but the streetlights revealed the dark stain that soaked through her sleeve. Blood also ran freely from a cut on the underpalm of her left hand.

"My radio," she told her mother as mounting waves of dizziness washed over her. "Tell them—officer needs assistance . . . assailant needs ambulance . . ."

"I don't believe this!" her mother cried. "Bleeding like a stuck pig and you still talk like a policeman!"

Bantam Books offers the finest in classic and modern American murder mysteries. Ask your bookseller for the books you have missed.

Stuart Palmer
THE PENGUIN POOL MURDER
THE PUZZLE OF THE HAPPY HOOLIGAN
THE PUZZLE OF THE RED STALLION
THE PUZZLE OF THE SILVER PERSIAN
Craig Rice
THE FOURTH POSTMAN
HAVING A WONDERFUL CRIME
MY KINGDOM FOR A HEARSE
THE LUCKY STIFF
Rex Stout
BAD FOR BUSINESS
BROKEN VASE
DEATH OF A DUDE
DEATH TIMES THREE
DOUBLE FOR DEATH
FER-DE-LANCE
THE FINAL DEDUCTION
GAMBIT
THE RUBBER BAND
SOME BURIED CAESAR
TOO MANY CLIENTS
Max Allan Collins
THE DARK CITY
William Kienzle
THE ROSARY MURDERS
Joseph Louis
MADELAINE
M. J. Adamson
NOT UNTIL A HOT FEBRUARY
A FEBRUARY FACE
REMEMBER MARCH
Conrad Haynes
BISHOP'S GAMBIT, DECLINED
Barbara Paul
FIRST GRAVEDIGGER
THE FOURTH WALL
KILL FEE
THE RENEWABLE VIRGIN

Benjamin Schutz
ALL THE OLD BARGAINS
S. F. X. Dean
DEATH AND THE MAD HEROINE
Robert Goldsborough
MURDER IN E MINOR
DEATH ON DEADLINE
Sue Grafton
"A" IS FOR ALIBI
"B" IS FOR BURGLAR
"C" IS FOR CORPSE
R. D. Brown
HAZZARD
A. E. Maxwell
JUST ANOTHER DAY IN PARADISE
THE FROG AND THE SCORPION
Rob Kantner
THE HARDER THEY HIT
Joseph Telushkin
THE UNORTHODOX MURDER OF RABBI WAHL
Richard Hilary
SNAKE IN THE GRASSES
PIECES OF CREAM
Carolyn G. Hart
DESIGN FOR MURDER
DEATH ON DEMAND
Lia Matera
WHERE LAWYERS FEAR TO TREAD
Walter Dillon
DEADLY INTRUSION
Robert Crais
THE MONKEY'S RAINCOAT
Margaret Maron
THE RIGHT JACK
Ross MacDonald
THE GOODBYE LOOK
SLEEPING BEAUTY
THE NAME IS ARCHER
THE DROWNING POOL
William Murray
WHEN THE FAT MAN SINGS

THE
RIGHT JACK

Margaret Maron

BANTAM BOOKS
TORONTO · NEW YORK · LONDON · SYDNEY · AUCKLAND

THE RIGHT JACK
A Bantam Book / December 1987

ISBN 0-553-26859-7

Published simultaneously in the United States and Canada

Bantam Books are published by Bantam Books, Inc. Its trademark, consisting of the words "Bantam Books" and the portrayal of a rooster, is Registered in U.S. Patent and Trademark Office and in other countries. Marca Registrada. Bantam Books, Inc., 666 Fifth Avenue, New York, New York 10103.

PRINTED IN THE UNITED STATES OF AMERICA

O   0 9 8 7 6 5 4 3 2 1

For David C. Brown,
who was born with a
deck of cards in his hand—
Shut up and deal!

My thanks to Carl Honeycutt,
Peter Klausmeyer and Harold Medlin
for their help with certain technical details.

THE
RIGHT JACK

PROLOGUE

In the main kitchens two levels below the Hotel Maintenon's glittering lobby, the midday rush was winding down. In the dessert and pastry kitchen next door, however, an orderly bustle continued as exquisite raspberry tarts, miniature eclairs, and tiny cream puffs were tucked into individual lace cups and arranged on large silver trays. Two almond cakes and a silver platter of thinly sliced fruitcake sat beside four dark chocolate multilayered tortes which awaited a final ribbon of buttercream icing across their satiny tops.

In less than half an hour, tea would be served in the beautiful Cristal Galerie just off the Maintenon's mezzanine, so the staff hurried with its finishing touches. Upstairs, the huge silver urns would already be filled with fresh boiling water and slender tea hostesses in white silk blouses and long black velvet jumpers would be giving the room a final check, assuring themselves that there were no smudges on any of the beveled mirrors that lined the walls between gilded pilasters, that none of the tall vases of cut flowers had dropped petals over the ivory brocaded chairs, and that the tins of tea—all twenty-two different varieties were full and lined up alphabetically beside the urns.

Trays of triangularly cut sandwiches filled with shrimp salad, watercress, smoked salmon and the Maintenon's special blend of herbed cream cheese had already been sent up to the serving pantry behind the elegant room, where hot buttered scones also waited in a specially heated basket. The cozy aroma of warm raisins permeated the area.

Downstairs, in the pastry kitchen, workers had begun to load the tea carts, frivolous-looking but sturdy contrivances of silver and glass, which would be wheeled through the Cristal Galerie for the teatime dessert course, tempting New York sophisticates and visitors alike to forget about diets and calories and give themselves up to sybaritic indulgences. Tiny silver *pots de crème* nestled beside a cut-glass bowl of *poires au gratin* and a woven silver basket of fresh strawberries.

1

At a nearby counter, a newly apprenticed assistant chef was so absorbed in his task of cutting a bunch of sugared grapes into individual clusters that he failed to notice when a sudden silence fell over the room.

"Gently, gently, *mon petit!*" said a sharp voice.

The youth turned, realized who had spoken and became so flustered that he dropped the scissors he had been using.

His fellow employees held their breath, watching the shapely blonde woman who had appeared seemingly out of nowhere.

To the uninitiated eye, there was nothing intimidating about the Maintenon's owner. To her guests, Madame Lucienne Ronay could be, and usually was, Gallic charm personified. Her staff, who knew a different side of the French coin, called her "La Reine" behind her back because of her regal off-with-his-head manner when any employee was caught debasing the impeccable standards she set for her hotels. And the guillotine blade could fall at any moment, since Madame did not remain safely aloof in her throne room on the thirtieth floor, where the executive office lay. She prowled her kingdom relentlessly, bestowing the largess of a radiant smile when pleased or, more often, slicing a malefactor into tattered shreds with her sharp tongue.

Today, it pleased her to be merciful and she stooped gracefully for the dropped scissors and gave the terrified youth a gentle reproof as she demonstrated the Maintenon way to snip sugar-coated grapes.

"*Regardez.* Thus and thus we do, *mon petit.* More gently so the sugar it does not shatter. *Comprenez-vous?* You see?"

"Yes, Madame," replied the chastened worker.

"*Bien!*" She returned the scissors and, with a benevolent smile for the rest of the staff, exited from the dessert kitchen. A palpable easing of tension swept over the room as Madame Ronay's employees returned to their preparations for high tea.

"Like so we do, *comprenez-vous?*" mimicked a pastry chef, twirling a tray of *petits fours* on fingertips above his head before depositing them safely on the glittering glass-and-silver serving cart.

The others laughed but there were several nervous glances toward the door, and the tea carts were fully loaded and on their way up to the Cristal Galerie before everyone felt free to relax.

CHAPTER I

As chairman and majority stockholder of Maritime National Bank, Zachary Wolferman commanded sophisticated global resources to keep him abreast of current economic trends. Reports came by teletype and satellite, came hour by hour, even minute by minute if he so desired, to tell him what was happening in the money markets of London, Bonn, or Tokyo.

Yet in times of real decision making, when storms of adversity threatened, Mr. Wolferman preferred to cast other straws upon the wind.

It was not enough to read *The Wall Street Journal* or *Economics Today,* Mr. Wolferman was fond of lecturing his fellow board members. Nor was it enough to study the four-color graphs and charts of which those energetic young chaps assigned to strategic planning were so proud. No, said Zachary Wolferman, gravely shaking his silvery head, to find out where the economy was really going, one must get down and rub elbows with the common folk, listen to what the man in the street was saying.

The thought of the fastidious and aristocratic Zachary Wolferman rubbing elbows with ordinary people amused the youngest member of the board.

And how, he was once audacious enough to inquire, did Mr. Wolferman go about meeting such people? Did he invite the paper boy in for a drink or leave his limousine and chauffeur at home occasionally and take a cab?

"Those are good possibilities," Mr. Wolferman conceded approvingly, "but cribbage is better. It's an old sailors' game, you know. My grandfather Augustus was quite fond of it. Learned it as a gunner's mate during the Cuban blockade back in 1898. Taught it to my cousin Haines and me when we were boys. As a matter of fact, it was his cribbage winnings that led him into banking."

Since Augustus Wolferman had parlayed a sailors' dime savings plan into one of the country's largest financial institutions, the newest board member wondered if perhaps he ought to look into the game.

At six-fifteen of that same Friday evening, Lieutenant Sigrid Harald was still at her desk. A slender, dark-haired woman with changeable gray eyes and erect carriage, she plowed steadily and efficiently through the paperwork which had piled up in the last three days.

Her small office was standard city issue: a square box painted off-white, a fluorescent light recessed behind frosted glass in the ceiling, two scuffed green file cabinets with bookshelves above them, a fairly new dark green steel desk, for herself a swivel chair with armrests, a couple of mismated straight chairs for visitors, wire In- and Out-baskets, typewriter, wastebasket, a clotheshook behind the door. Except for an administrative flow chart and a map of New York City, the walls were as bare of ornamentation as the lieutenant's ringless fingers. There were no plants on the window ledge behind her desk, no clutter of knickknacks. Instead, it held a neat row of police bulletins and manuals kept firmly in place by a no-nonsense metal bookend. The hard white glare of the overhead light was softened by a sturdy brass desk lamp with a green glass shade, the only nonstandard piece of office equipment.

There were no photographs on the desk, no whimsical paperweights or tooled leather desk sets. Other than the desk lamp, the only items that might have given a perceptive stranger some clue to Lieutenant Harald's personality were a magnifying glass, her coffee mug and a tangle of brass, steel and silver rings heaped in a small glass bowl.

The magnifying glass was used to study crime scene photographs in greater detail, but it was bound in nonutilitarian polished brass. The pottery coffee mug was cylindrical in form, more upright than squat, and glazed in a deep blue-green. A narrow band of slightly darker blue diamonds circled the cup an inch from the top. The diamond shapes were so closely toned to the mug's overall color that one had to look very closely to see them. Most visitors to Lieutenant Harald's office, even those who shared coffee, never noticed the subtle, inlaid pattern.

They did notice the little bowl of puzzle rings, however, and the lieutenant's habit of absent-mindedly fitting the interlocking circles of metal into a single band at times when her mind was focused elsewhere.

This evening, the puzzle rings were left untouched as she

completed the last entry on a particularly bleak case. A mother and three daughters, ranging in age from two to eight, had been found dead in a shabby TriBeCa apartment. All four had died of knife wounds, and the uniformed officers first on the scene had initially called it in as a homicide.

A few hours later, an autopsy told them that the mother, two days shy of her twenty-fifth birthday, had committed suicide. A reconstruction of events proved that she had carefully slipped the same sharp knife into each small body, then tenderly tucked them all into bed.

None of the neighbors could even begin to suggest a reason why. They said the mother was widowed and a loner. Kept herself to herself and was a conscientious parent. No child neglect there and no string of weekend "uncles" for her daughters, thank you. Maybe a little too strict with them, said her baffled neighbors, and always quoting the Bible to anyone who tried to strike up a conversation.

In the end, it was the Bible that answered their questions. It was the most expensive thing in that threadbare apartment: white leather, gold-edge pages, a red silk ribbon marker, and big enough to rest on a pulpit and preach the coming of Judgment Day. Passages from Jeremiah and Revelations had been heavily underlined and it was stuffed with scrawled slips of paper that precisely documented the deterioration of a mind.

Quite literally, she had killed her daughters to save their souls and then, unable to live on without them, had killed herself.

Sigrid Harald sighed, closed the folder and put it in the Out-basket. She covered her typewriter and neatened her desk; then taking a black-and-gray plaid jacket from the clotheshook, she switched off the light and walked out into the main office. To her surprise she found Tillie still at his desk.

Detective Charles Tildon was half a head shorter than she and a few years younger, a mild unimaginative man who had made plainclothes by sheer methodical attention to detail. He thrived on paperwork, something most officers avoided whenever possible, and could be relied upon to put down everything he'd seen during an investigation, no matter how trivial. There were times when his insistence upon the minute could be exasperating but, on the whole, Lieutenant Harald preferred his careful approach over some of the brighter but more lackadaisical officers. No criminal court case had ever been thrown out because Tillie broke the chain of evidence.

On the other hand, he was the archetypal family man and she

could count on the fingers of one hand the times she'd known him to stay late voluntarily on a Friday evening.

"Still working?" She paused at his desk and was puzzled to see he was only killing time with a deck of cards.

Tillie gathered in the two hands he'd dealt and began shuffling again, his round face hopeful beneath a mat of sandy brown hair. "You don't happen to play cribbage, do you, Lieutenant?"

Sigrid Harald looked at the unfamiliar board, a cheap plastic affair hinged in the middle so that it could fold into a box to hold a deck of cards.

"Sorry," she said. "Solitaire and bridge are the only card games I know."

"My father-in-law, Marian's dad—he's a nut about it. Every other Sunday when we go over to their house, he brings out the board and we have a go at it. He taught Chuck this summer. Chuck's good at it, too."

Tillie laid out another pair of hands and Sigrid sensed an air of gloom in his manner.

"You don't want your son to play cards?"

"It's not that. Cards are okay and cribbage is mostly addition anyhow. See, you score points by adding up runs and pairs and combinations of fifteen."

He pointed to the five cards in front of him: the jack of hearts, five of diamonds, the six and nine of spades, and, off to one side, the four of hearts.

"Face cards count ten, so the jack and five make fifteen for two points—" Tillie lifted a little peg on the plastic board and advanced it two holes. "The four, five, and six add up to fifteen for another two points; six and nine for two more; then the four, five, six make a run of three for three points. Finally, since my turn card was a heart and I have the heart jack that's another point."

He pegged the other eight points.

"You get two points every time your cards hit fifteen on the nose: seven and eight; two, three, ten; two sevens and an ace—"

To keep him from reeling off every combination in the deck, Sigrid nodded to show that she understood. "Chuck's what now? Nine? Third grade? This looks like excellent arithmetic drill."

"It is," Tillie admitted. "He got to be a whiz at factoring fifteens this summer. If your opponent misses any of his points you can peg them for yourself. Chuck never misses."

"So?"

"There's a cribbage tournament up at the Maintenon this weekend," Tillie explained glumly. "The first round starts at eight tonight. Forty dollars entry fee, ten thousand for first prize. Marian's dad's too old to play straight through two-and-a-half days and Chuck's too young. You have to be fourteen to enter. So they pooled their money and entered me instead. I don't even like the game that much," he concluded unhappily. "I just play because Walt and Chuck like it so much."

In Sigrid's estimation, bridge was the only card game that weighted a player's skill more heavily than his luck in the deal and cribbage certainly didn't look to be an exception. She said as much.

"You can't peg points if you aren't dealt any," she added reasonably.

"You only count those up after the hand's played," said Tillie. He launched into a complicated description of the strategy needed to play your cards so that you scored runs and pairs and fifteens off your opponent, yet prevented him from scoring off your cards.

Sigrid nodded and murmured in the right places, but her heart wasn't in it and she sneaked a glance at her watch.

"It sounds interesting, Tillie, but—"

"I could teach you," he offered eagerly. "I'm just waiting till it's time to catch the subway up to the hotel. Unless you have something else on?"

"Sorry," she said, thrusting her arms into the rumpled plaid jacket. "I'm afraid I do."

She was almost out the door when conscience overtook her. Tillie was usually so cheerful, but the possibility of letting his son and father-in-law down seemed to be making him edgy and unhappy. Someone had once accused her of insensitivity and cruelty to small furry creatures. Not that Tillie, even with his trusting blue eyes, was a small furry creature. All the same . . .

Sighing, she turned back and said, "I have to drive uptown. Why don't you let me drop you near the Maintenon? You could forget about cribbage for an hour, eat a good dinner, and then go in fresh and win."

Tillie's cherubic face brightened. "Great. And that'll give me time to tell you how the crib works. Each person is dealt six cards, see, and then you both contribute two to the crib, face down, and the dealer gets to count those when you've finished playing the first four and—"

Tillie's penchant for detail was an asset when investigating murder. As pure conversation, it could border on the tedious.

Resigned, Sigrid followed him from the office.

Commander T. J. Dixon, United States Navy, shucked her dark blue-black uniform with its neat gold stripes, crisp white shirt and dark blue tie and somewhat absent-mindedly considered what to wear that night. One could probably dress as for a civilian business event; on the other hand, the cribbage tournament was being held at the elegant Hotel Maintenon and surely the eight P.M. opening session argued for a dressier formality?

She stood before her open closet, barefooted, in an ice-blue satin teddy—once past boot camp, female personnel seldom followed the Navy's advice on lingerie, and Commander Dixon had a decidedly feminine streak. At forty, her hair was prematurely white, but the rest of her body was that of a younger woman. Every muscle was firm, every curve allured, nothing sagged.

While part of her mind weighed a dark red gown with a square neckline against a rich royal blue sari, the other part puzzled over the strange message that had been left on her answering machine.

It was the first communication with her only relative since their bitter quarrel last year, and Commander Dixon had played the message over several times, analytically dissecting the girl's words as thoroughly as any arcane code.

"Teejy? It's me." The use of that childhood name argued a willingness to let bygones be bygones, didn't it? *"I won't tell you where I am or what I'm doing right now . . ."* Beneath her young cousin's infuriatingly complaisant surface lurked a surprising amount of stubborn pride, Commander Dixon had discovered. This was another example. *". . . but we may run into each other soon."* Did that mean the girl planned to come to New York or did she think T.J. was due to visit Florida? *"Anyhow, if we do, please pretend you don't know me. It's very important. I'll explain soon, okay?"*

It was not okay, thought Commander Dixon and had immediately dialed the area code for Miami. After two rings, there was a series of familiar electronic tones and a pleasant mechanical voice said, "We're sorry. The number you have reached is no longer in service. Please consult your—"

Commander Dixon had hung up and replayed her cousin's message.

"Please pretend you don't know me."

There was a trace of urgency in the request, but she didn't sound upset or in trouble. In fact, thought Commander Dixon, for the first time the girl actually sounded as if she might have found a little backbone this past year.

Maybe she was finally growing up.

Pleased with that thought, the commander turned back to her closet. The sari was more flattering, she decided at last, but the gauzy blue stole had a tendency to slip. It might prove a distraction, and Commander T. J. Dixon was too competitive to let herself be handicapped by feminine vanity.

"—so that by 1969, the SDS, Students for a Democratic Society, was in disarray and ready for takeover by student activists who were more radical than the moderate pacifists or even the Maoists. They took their name from a line in Bob Dylan's song, *Subterranean Homesick Blues;* you know, that bit about not needing a weatherman to know how the wind blows. The Weathermen aimed to bring the war home to Americans and graphically demonstrate what it was like to live with violence and terrorism in their own streets."

John Sutton touched the pause button on his tape recorder and sat back in his desk chair to focus his memory on those tumultuous and exhilarating days.

In 1969, he had been a graduate student at McClellan State, one of the battlegrounds for the Weathermen. Now he was a professor of history at Vanderlyn College, a branch of the New York City University system, and, to his own bemusement, teaching a course on the Sixties and Seventies to kids who were in first or second grade when Richard Nixon was forced out of the White House.

The course was immensely popular and so was John Sutton. A local television station's evening news program had even featured him on one of their pop culture segments, belaboring the irony of a man just turning forty already teaching events in his own personal life as formal history.

Sutton pressed the record button. "The typical Weathermen were white, middle to upper-middle class, well educated, and in revolt against materialistic values. They tended to be idealistic and impatient with the very real, but very slow, gains the peace movement was making. Privileged themselves, they were deter-mined to extend those privileges to blacks, Hispanics, and the ghetto poor. These were terrific goals and I'm not knocking them. Hell! That's why I joined SDS in the first place. But the Weathermen—'' John Sutton's voice became wry.

"Many of the far-left leaders were subconsciously aping their own Establishment parents in thinking they knew what was best for the cause. They could be just as spoiled and willful, accustomed to getting their own way, and they didn't quite understand why the rest of us wouldn't fall right in behind their banners. And let's be blunt: not all radicals were in the movement for purely altruistic reasons. Some were grooving on the heady excitement of power for its own sake, for the thrill of being outside the law. They arbitrarily decided the student movement would either become confrontational and violent or it would cease to exist.

"In the fall of 1969, they destroyed all the SDS records and went underground. The bombings that followed that winter and—''

The door of Sutton's study swung open. "Come on, John," scolded Val Sutton. "Shake a leg or we're going to be late."

"Mm?" He switched off the tape recorder and peered at his watch. "Val? Do you remember Fred Hamilton and Brooks Ann Farr?''

"Personally or from afar?'' she asked, pushing back her chocolate brown hair so that she could fit a gold earring into her left earlobe.

"Either,'' he said, admiring the graceful swing of her hair.

It was thick and lustrous and absolutely straight. Until recently, she'd worn it shoulder length and combed away from her thin, catlike face, but the previous day she'd come home with a blunt cut that just brushed level with the line of her chin and half-veiled her face when her head tilted forward. He still wasn't used to the alluring novelty.

Val couldn't resist a small bit of preening. Clavdia's charged the earth for a new styling session but getting one's husband to look at one like that after ten years of marriage was worth every dime.

"No, I didn't know McClellan's most-wanted alumni personally,'' she told him affectionately. "You were the one in SDS, love, not me. I only marched or sat-in or sang. But I do remember them. Fred was dark and brooding, a smoldering sexpot; Brooks Ann was a lumpy sophomore, dreadful acne, and lank brown hair that always looked like she hadn't rinsed out all the shampoo. The original dishwater blonde. Meow.''

Val Sutton leaned across the desk and straightened her husband's tie. "Come on, love. Mrs. Herlbut's already in with the kids and we've really got to go. Now.''

He smiled and allowed himself to be coaxed from the chair. "I never knew you thought Fred Hamilton was sexy."

"Ravishing," she assured him as she handed him his jacket from the hall stand and slipped on her own, an intricately embroidered Chinese import of heavy gold satin. "If they hadn't gone underground when they did—"

"You'd have signed up for his bomb-making course?"

Their laughter muted as they abruptly remembered the bombs Fred Hamilton and his followers had planted that violent winter of 1970. The four children who were killed outright, the woman left blind, the man who'd eventually died after two years in a coma.

"Do you suppose they'll ever surface?" Val asked as John tried to flag a taxi in front of their Greenwich Village apartment.

"It's odd you should ask that," he frowned.

Val looked at him questioningly, but he was distracted by the balky door on the battered yellow cab that slid to a stop at the curb; and once they were both settled inside, their thoughts turned to the cribbage tournament ahead.

"Hotel Maintenon," Sutton told the cabbie, then reached for his wife with an exaggerated leer. She fluttered her eyelashes at him and slipped closer; but when his hand began to wander too freely, she clasped it firmly and said, "Now pay attention, class: how many points for three sixes and a pair of threes?"

CHAPTER II

After a comfortable dinner at their club, Zachary Wolferman and his cousin, Haines Froelick, entered Mr. Wolferman's limousine for the short ride to the Maintenon.

Mr. Froelick's mother had died shortly before he finished his first year at prep school and his aunt, Mr. Wolferman's mother, had instructed the boy to look upon her thenceforward as his own mother.

Some women have such generous hearts that each new demand merely enlarges their capacity for love. Fitting a second child into her crowded social calendar meant a halving of Mrs.

Wolferman's maternal devotion, but half of almost nothing made little difference to seven-year-old Zachary.

He was so pleased to acquire a live-in chum for the summer holidays that he barely noticed any diminution of his busy mother's affection. Lacking other siblings, the two boys grew up as close as brothers.

Mr. Wolferman, of course, had filled his appointed slot at Maritime National; Mr. Froelick, with a modest income from various family trusts and a disinclination for hard work, had devoted his life to photography and assorted charitable works. Both had remained bachelors.

They played cribbage with a zest unabated since old Augustus taught them the game the summer they were ten, and they began keeping a cumulative score their thirtieth summer. Mr. Froelick had enjoyed a run of luck lately so the tally currently stood at 8,132 to 8,105, but Mr. Wolferman had placed higher in last year's tournament, making one of the last thirty-six finalists before being eliminated by a pharmacist.

"By a pharmacist from somewhere in Brooklyn," he was reminiscing to his cousin Haines. "Flatlands? Flatbush? Flat-something. Interesting chap. He was the reason I took that flyer in Westmachter Pharmaceuticals."

"I believe I read that the trial begins next month," commented Mr. Froelick, still piqued because he'd been eliminated in the fourth round of play last year after being dealt three nineteen-point hands in a row.*

There was silence in the limousine.

"It wasn't his fault that Westmachter's quality control was so abominable," Mr. Wolferman said defensively. "They were doing quite well until that batch of tainted pills."

The gleaming limo pulled up at the East Forty-seventh Street entrance to the Hotel Maintenon.

"You needn't bother about later, Willis," said Mr. Wolferman. "Mr. Haines and I will take a cab."

He knew how much his cousin hated taxis. However, if one planned to venture among common people, one might as well make a thorough job of it. Haines could jolly well lump it, he thought,

---

* A cribbage hand may contain anywhere from 0-29 points with one curious exception: the cards never add up to exactly 19 points. Therefore, a hand with no points at all is ironically referred to as a "19-pointer."

nodding graciously to the uniformed doorman who held the polished glass slab open for them.

Lucienne Ronay would have been insulted had she known that Mr. Wolferman entered her establishment with a vague expectation of someone about to go slumming. Of her trio of beautifully appointed hotels, the Maintenon was Madame Ronay's favorite, the central jewel in the necklace of properties she had inherited from her late husband.

On the other hand, she shared something of Mr. Wolferman's ambivalence toward the cribbage tournament booked into her d'Aubigné Room this weekend. It was not the Maintenon's usual cup of souchong, but the room had been available, Graphic Games had not quibbled about the cost, and Lucienne Ronay was as pragmatic as any Frenchwoman when it came down to dollars and francs on her balance sheets.

From her observation post on the second-floor balcony, she viewed the main entrance and lobby and could not resist comment as tournament players began to straggle up the wide marble staircase.

"We might wish for more tweeds and silks," she told Molly Baldwin, one of her trainee assistants, "but polyester will buy our caviar this weekend, *ma petite*."

Her diamond and emerald earrings sparkled against the smooth line of her cheek as she glanced down complacently at the vibrant green of her silk taffeta. There was a lush Elizabethan feel to the gown. The tight bodice and shockingly low neckline made the most of her small waist and magnificent bosom, while the long full sleeves restored a semblance of modesty.

Molly Baldwin, dressed in a simple dark blue sleeveless sheath with crystal earrings, felt like a drab little mouse by comparison.

Of course, Lucienne Ronay's extravagant clothes and lavish jewels were part of her glamorous public persona. Her guests expected it and would indeed have felt slightly cheated if Madame Ronay suddenly began to dress like a denizen of Wall Street. Besides, gray flannel would ill-become someone so very blonde, so generously proportioned, who sprinkled even business conversations with intimate French phrases and who moved in a mist of fragrance created just for her by an exclusive *parfumeur*.

Skillful makeup widened her hazel eyes and lent an illusion of high cheekbones to a face that was basically round and might even have been ordinary had it not been for the personality that animated it. Makeup also hid any trace of wrinkles, even though Madame Ronay occasionally bemoaned the fact that she was only a year or so away from fifty.

Fifty! Molly Baldwin thought despairingly. She would gladly have doubled her own twenty-three years if she thought there was a chance that age would leave her with La Reine's poise and beauty.

Misinterpreting Molly's sigh, Madame Ronay smiled indulgently. "Nervous, *cherie?* Is not everything as the so handsome Mr. Flythe has ordered?"

Her tone was light, but the question was serious. And she expected a positive answer.

Coordinating the cribbage tournament was Molly's first solo assignment at the Maintenon. She wished it had been something else, but assistant manager trainees did not question La Reine's assignments. There had been a thousand details to oversee: the hospitality tables, the coolers of wine, the urns of coffee, trays of hors d'oeuvres, the fresh flowers, the scheduling of waiters and busboys for the weekend, the sound system, the proper number of linen-covered tables, sufficient chairs—the list seemed endless.

Fortunately, Theodore Flythe of Graphic Games had proved easy to work with (Madame was right: he was extremely handsome); but even if he'd been fussy and demanding, Molly would have risked displeasing him sooner than Madame Ronay, who possessed a regal intolerance for incompetence.

"No," she told her employer, looking down at the players who were now streaming through the lobby. "Everything seems to have fallen into place. It's always amazing that it does."

"Out of so much chaos, order?" The older woman nodded serenely. She had spent enormous amounts of time and money in assembling and training her staff, and when it did not move like well-oiled machinery, the balky cog soon found itself out on the street.

Molly Baldwin had learned this very quickly. She had also learned that what Madame Ronay didn't know couldn't be used against anyone. Especially since the only two times the imperturbable Mr. Flythe had been annoyed were both her fault.

The Maintenon provided a lavish setting, but Graphic Games saw to the actual tournament equipment: the boards, the playing cards, and the scoring sheets. Since the tournament was also an advertising ploy, three long display cases along the wide hall outside the d'Aubigné Room were filled with samples of Graphic Games products. There were exquisitely detailed chess sets, board games that could be stored on one's bookshelves and then unfolded into large intricate playing surfaces, old familiars like Chinese checkers whose marbles were subtly colored metamorphic rocks and quartzites, and, of course, each case featured one of Graphic Games' beautiful cherry cribbage boards.

Molly had ordered the cases brought up from storage. They were beveled glass boxes on mahogany legs, banded in brass, and the maids had polished them to the gleam of burnished gold and crystal. One of the seamstresses had produced some dark blue velvet that made an effective backdrop for the game pieces and Mr. Flythe had arranged everything to his satisfaction on Thursday morning.

On Thursday afternoon, it was discovered that one of the cribbage boards was missing.

Molly Baldwin was stricken. She hadn't thought to lock the cases and, conscious of her guilt, she listened to a mild lecture by Mr. Flythe and came away shocked. It had not previously registered that the hand-enameled chess set was cast in solid silver, nor that a Chinese checkers game could cost several hundred dollars. Chastened, she had hurriedly located keys to the cases, but when she returned to lock the barn doors, she found Mr. Flythe even more vexed than previously.

"Miss Baldwin, I'm certain I made it clear that the pairings were not to be posted until immediately before the room opened tomorrow night," he'd fumed.

The tournament was limited to five hundred players, and those names had been fed into a computer at Graphic Games for random pairing. Mr. Flythe retained a copy of the print-out and had given one to Molly, who had passed it on to the Maintenon's visual arts man. He, in turn, had drawn a seating diagram, mounted both the pairing list and diagram on velvet-covered tagboard, and set the board upon a delicate brass display easel just inside the ballroom sometime on Thursday.

Molly vaguely recalled Mr. Flythe's original admonitions, but she really didn't understand his insistence on such secrecy and said so. Besides, she added reasonably, the list was *inside* the ballroom, not out in the public areas where any passerby might read it. None of the staff could be interested in who played whom and at which table—staff members and their families were strictly barred from the tournament—so surely no harm was done?

Mr. Flythe had gazed upon her troubled blue eyes and earnest young face and his wrath had melted. Mr. Flythe was at least fifteen years older than Miss Baldwin, but he had been with

Graphic Games less than a year and this was his first solo
tournament, too—although he had no intention of letting Miss
Baldwin know that.

Instead, he had raked his dark beard into a neat point, smiled
at Miss Baldwin and invited her to dinner.

Now, as Lucienne Ronay swept along the upper hall for a final
inspection of the d'Aubigné Room, Molly followed like a nervous
shadow. La Reine would flit around the room to twitch a tablecloth
into smoother drapes or position a pink satin matchbook stamped
with the Maintenon's silver crest into the exact center of an ashtray,
but with a little luck that was all she would find to fault Miss
Baldwin with tonight.

CHAPTER III

Like the Cristal Galerie, the d'Aubigné Room was clearly designed
and furnished by someone enamored of the decorative arts which
had flourished under the Bourbons. Proto-baroque motifs first seen
under Henry IV were indiscriminately mixed with the *rocaille* of
Louis XVI. Florid paintings of Greek gods and goddesses *en
famille* alternated with mirrored panels, and both were framed by
fanciful scrolls, wreaths and shells carved of gilded plaster.
Nymphs in plaster relief sported chastely on the coved ceiling amid
dazzling chandeliers.

Heedless of the nymphs above, Mr. Wolferman was enjoying
the pre-tournament social hour immensely. He had taken a glass of
wine with a schoolteacher, a plumber and an insurance broker, and
had heard the president's economic programs lauded and damned
with equal fervor until the plumber tactfully insisted they change
the subject to cards; whereupon Mr. Wolferman slipped away to
replenish his glass and join a promising-looking group of hearty
outdoorsman types.

At the last moment, he recognized Sam Babcock, a piratical
old tycoon who had evidently sailed down from Newport for the

tournament with a contingent of fellow yachtsmen. He'd hear nothing from them he couldn't hear over lunch at any one of his clubs every day, so he veered off sharply before they recognized him and almost sloshed his wine on a very attractive woman.

"I do apologize!" he exclaimed. "It's crowded in here, but I should never forgive myself if I've spoiled your pretty red frock."

Commander T. J. Dixon smiled at his quaint turn of phrase and assured him that no harm was done. She glanced discreetly at his name tag. "No harm at all, Mr. Wolferman."

Her voice immediately charmed Mr. Wolferman. It was soft, but absolutely clear, with bell-like overtones that suddenly reminded him of childhood summers in Switzerland. He leaned forward to read her name tag. *"Commander* T. J. Dixon?"

"United States Navy," she nodded.

"And what does T. J. stand for?" he inquired.

"That, Mr. Wolferman, is a closely guarded military secret," she laughed, and the pure tones of her laughter tugged even more strongly at the fringes of deep-seated memory and made him helpless.

"Forgive my saying it, but you have the most enchanting laugh. Would you object to meeting my cousin Haines?"

He saw her give his wineglass a considering glance. "Forgive me again, Commander," he said hastily. "I assure you I'm neither inebriated nor a lunatic. My cousin is here tonight, also a contestant. He has a much finer ear than I and I'm sure that if he could but hear you speak or laugh, he'd be able to explain why your voice reminds me so clearly of our boyhood."

Intrigued, Commander Dixon agreed. "Only we have to wait until—" She stood on tiptoes to search the crowd, then waved to a tall bearlike man whose glowering face broke into a happy grin when he spotted her. He carried two brimming wineglasses, one of which he handed to her as delicately as if it were a stemmed eggshell, then beamed at Mr. Wolferman as the small woman said, "Mr. Wolferman, may I present Comrade Vassily Ivanovich of the Soviet trade delegation?"

"Charmed, charmed," said Mr. Wolferman and guided them through the crowd toward his cousin.

After an unobtrusive glance in one of the gilt-framed mirrors to reassure himself that his tie was knotted properly, Detective Tildon joined the crowd gathered around the list of pairings. He saw the figure 102 beside his name and scanned the placard for his

opponent. He might have known: the other 102 was a Commander
T. J. Dixon. He'd be sunk by the Navy before the evening even
began, he thought gloomily. Probably some grizzled old mustang
who'd come up through the ranks and polished off amateur
cribbage players like him before morning chow.

He tugged at his tie again. It was a rich brown rep, heavier
than his usual workday ties. The kids had given it to him on his last
birthday and they'd made him wear it today for good luck. Tillie
miserably decided he'd rather be home reading them a bedtime
story right now.

As he stood there contemplating disaster, he heard the woman
beside him say, "I've got an Eisaku Okawara. What about you,
John?"

"Zachary Wolferman," he replied. "As in hungry as a. He'll
probably swallow me whole."

"Don't be such a pessimist," said the woman. "And no fair
playing to lose just because you want to get back to your lecture
notes. We both stay till we both lose, agreed?"

"Agreed. Now let's go see if their wine's worth drinking."

The couple moved off and Tillie suddenly wished Marian was
here tonight, too.

"*Sprechen Sie deutsch* by any chance?" asked Haines Froelick
when his cousin presented him to Commander Dixon and Comrade
Ivanovich and invited him to listen to her musical voice.

"Only enough to say *nein*," she smiled, revealing an unexpected dimple in her left cheek.

Mr. Froelick was even more charmed than his cousin.
"Fraulein Schlaak!" he exclaimed. "Remember, Zachary? When
we were eight? Higgins broke her leg and couldn't come to Europe
that summer, so your parents engaged Fraulein Heika Schlaak as
our nursemaid and she used to take us on picnics up to an Alpine
meadow near a little waterfall. We've never again had such
wonderful cream puffs."

"There." Mr. Wolferman nodded his dignified silver head
emphatically at Commander Dixon. "I knew he would remember.
Fraulein Schlaak," he murmured blissfully. "She was young and
gentle and she told us the most blood-curdling fairy tales in a voice
just like yours while water gurgled down on the stones behind her
like the chuckles of a dreaming giant."

Mr. Froelick and Commander Dixon were unprepared for Mr.

Wolferman's sudden excursion into poetry. Even Vassily Ivanovich looked respectful.

Mr. Wolferman blushed. "That was what Fraulein Schlaak used to say. That the river giant was laughing at her stories."

The gray-haired Comrade Ivanovich remembered something similar from his own childhood and had begun to share the memory in somewhat awkward English when he was interrupted by the public address system. Turning expectantly toward the podium, they heard Theodore Flythe say, "Ladies and gentlemen, please take your places so that we may begin."

Ten long tables, each seating fifty players, had been arranged in a double row. Tables 1 and 6 were nearest the podium, Tables 5 and 10 were at the rear.

"I'm back there at Table 5," said Commander Dixon, offering her small hand to Mr. Froelick and Mr. Wolferman. "Good luck to you, gentlemen. Perhaps we'll meet again."

"I'm at Table 5, too," said Mr. Wolferman as the other two men turned away. "Number 101. Are we opponents?"

"No, I'm number 102. Against a Mr. Tildon, I believe."

As they started down the wide central aisle between the two rows of tables, the crowd parted briefly and Commander Dixon came face to face with a taller, younger woman who gave her a startled look, then quickly moved away through a swirl of people.

"A friend of yours?" inquired Mr. Wolferman.

"I must have been mistaken," said the commander, but the expression on her face was puzzled.

At Table 5, Tillie had located board number 102, the second position at the rear corner table. Each long table was set with twenty-five ashtrays, twenty-five new decks of cards, and twenty-five cherrywood cribbage boards, each of whose six pegs were in starting position. Across the aisle from Table 5 was Table 10; beyond 10 was another wide space and then, perpendicular to the playing tables, was the refreshment table, which ran the length of the room's side wall.

With ten years of police experience behind him, Tillie had automatically taken the chair with its back to the wall so that he could look out across the crowded ballroom. He recognized the player already seated at 101, diagonally across the table from him, as the man he'd seen earlier up by the seating chart. A John Sutton, according to the man's name tag.

He was disconcerted when another couple approached their end of the table and the woman smiled at him pleasantly. "Mr. Tildon? I'm Commander Dixon."

Tillie jumped to his feet. "Commander? I was expecting—" He hesitated, patently embarrassed.

"Someone with anchors tattooed on his forearms?" she dimpled, which made him abruptly conscious that her forearms were nicely rounded and absolutely bare of any tattoos.

Before he could answer, Ted Flythe was requesting their attention again.

As everyone settled in their seats, busboys in short green jackets swept through the aisles with their trays, clearing away abandoned glasses under the watchful eye of the room steward, who was very much aware of La Reine at the front of the room. Her attention seemed focused on the speaker, but he knew that if any of his people made the slightest slip, he'd get the cutting edge of her tongue before the night was over.

Pernell Johnson resisted tugging at his short green jacket. If anyone looked at him, he wanted them to think, "Look how sharp that kid moves. Look how smooth he is with the tray."

From dishwasher to busboy in two months. Not bad. Next stop, dinner waiter in the hotel's fancy Emeraude Room. That's where the good money was. Even after splitting with the busboys, bartender, and headwaiter, those guys went home with a wad of bills every night and it was going to take money, lots of money, to finance his new dream.

Scared the bejesus out of him when the Dade County police caught him boosting hubcaps off Ferraris. Scared Granny, too. "I'm too old for this mess, boy," she'd told him. "Ain't no way I'm gonna let you turn into jail meat." She'd shipped him right up here to Aunt Quincy, who spent the weekend putting the fear of God in him and then brought him down to work with her on Monday morning and talked to them about giving him a job in the kitchen.

Aunt Quincy'd gone from maid to assistant housekeeper at the Maintenon, so they'd taken him on. She had made a comfortable life for herself and when she saw that her nephew wasn't afraid of hard work, she'd immediately tried to open his eyes to bigger possibilities. She watched his growing fascination with the workings of the hotel, the smoothness with which the many operations meshed; and she casually planted in the boy's mind a vision of the small hotels all over Florida that were just waiting for a young black man with ambition and determination.

The seed had taken root. He worked diligently at the hotel and he'd even begun a night school course in hotel management. When an extra busboy was needed, she'd spoken the right words in the useful places. It wouldn't be long now before he'd be wearing one of those dark green jackets in the Emeraude Room.

Even La Reine knew who Pernell Johnson was. Scared everybody to death she did whenever she came poking and prying around the kitchens, but he just smiled and yes ma'am'd her like all bosses expected the help to do and she said, "You're Quincy Johnson's nephew, aren't you?"

At first he'd thought the others were calling her La Wren behind her back; and from the way she looked at the sinks and opened cabinet doors and fussed about grease on the floor, it had seemed apt. Just like one of the wrens on his granny's back porch, she was. Nosiest bird God ever made. Always sticking its beak in every nook and cranny, pulling clothespins off the line, hopping in and out of the wash pans, chirping and tweeting the whole time. Same bright eyes. Wasn't anything got by her. Look at old George and Ms. Baldwin—both of them standing there like they had corncobs up their asses just because Madame Ronay was up there at the front with that games man, looking at them . . . looking at him, too, he remembered, and gracefully swung through the open service exit with his tray balanced on his fingertips.

Lucienne Ronay stood to acknowledge Flythe's introduction and the great chandelier overhead caught every facet of her emerald and diamond jewels and made her taffeta dress smolder with green fire.

Tillie heard a feminine sigh several seats to his right and a whispered, "Isn't she gorgeous? Can you believe she's almost as old as I am?"

In charmingly accented English, Madame Ronay welcomed them to the Maintenon, hoped they enjoyed the tournament, and graciously wished everyone success. *"Bonne chance!"*

While most of the eyes at his table were on the Maintenon's glamorous owner, Tillie noticed that Commander Dixon's attention kept straying to the hospitality table off to the right, or rather to the tall girl in a dark blue gown who seemed to be conferring there with a man Tillie assumed was a headwaiter.

Lucienne Ronay retired from the room in a flurry of applause and Ted Flythe reclaimed the microphone. For the next half hour, he reviewed the rules of cribbage and reminded them that a player must win four out of seven games to advance. "Double elimination. Those of you who have played our tournaments before know it takes skill, luck and stamina to play for two straight days. We'll begin with two rounds tonight and pick it up tomorrow morning at nine o'clock sharp."

The bearded young man next directed their attention to several men and women positioned around the room. All wore navy blue blazers with Graphic Games logos on their breast pockets and toothpaste smiles of helpfulness on their youthful faces.

"If there's any discussion or misunderstanding, just raise your hand and one of our referees will come over immediately. And now, ladies and gentlemen, you may cut for the deal. Low card deals first and may the best player WIN!"

Amid the flurry of applause, Tillie shyly offered their deck of cards to Commander Dixon. She cut the three of clubs, but he turned the deuce. When he'd finished dealing and their crib cards were lying face down off to the side, she cut the deck again. Tillie turned over the top card. It was a jack.

"His nibs," he murmured happily and pegged the first two points. Maybe he wouldn't get blown out of the water so quickly after all.

The large room settled into a low murmur of voices, the riffle of cards, an occasional burst of laughter, or a smothered oath as the right—or more often wrong—card was cut before the play of each hand.

After two hands, Tillie began to relax. Commander Dixon was a skillful opponent and he sensed that she was probably a better player, but as Lieutenant Harald had noted earlier, luck was a big part of the game and luck was keeping him slightly ahead of her skill.

Play was brisk and after only five deals, they were heading down the homestretch. She would be ahead of him when she finished pegging this hand; but he'd have first count on the next and if his luck continued, he'd win.

"I'm afraid you have position on me," Commander Dixon said ruefully as she started to peg her points.

Somehow the wooden peg slipped through her fingers,

dropped on the lap of her scarlet gown, and skittered under the table.

"I'll get it," Tillie said, pushing back his chair.

Commander Dixon peered beneath the table and nudged the peg toward him with the tip of her neat satin slipper.

At that exact instant, Zachary Wolferman pegged across the finish line with a double-double run and complacently inserted a peg into the game hole to mark his win.

There was an immediate, blinding flash of blue light. The board exploded with a horrendous bang. The table splintered with the impact and Tillie was buried beneath it. Stunned silence gripped the room for an instant and then the screams began.

CHAPTER IV

It was a little past nine and Sigrid and her mother were already late when Anne Harald finally located her airline ticket jumbled into one of her camera cases. The editor of a large magazine was gambling that a certain elderly Peruvian poet would finally win a Nobel prize in literature and had made arrangements for Anne to do an extensive photo-interview with him before he dropped dead of old age.

They came rushing down from Anne's apartment, Sigrid feeling guilty because she'd taken advantage of her NYPD tag and parked in front of a fire hydrant. As they hurried from the bright lobby down a sidewalk shadowed by oak trees that still held their leaves in mid-October, Sigrid noticed a young couple standing just below street level in one of the unlit areaways.

They were partially screened by a low hedge, but something in the girl's demeanor triggered a subconscious response and Sigrid hesitated at the top of the steps.

"Is something wrong?" she asked, peering into the shadows.

"N-no," the girl stammered. "N-nothing!"

Her bloodless face belied her words. There was glittering hostility in the young man's upward glance and an even stronger impression of wrongness in the way he gripped the girl's arm.

Sigrid reached into her purse for some ID even as the man was saying, "You heard her, lady, so bug off, huh?"

"I'm a police officer," Sigrid told the frightened girl. "Are you sure there's nothing—"

The filthy obscenities that streamed from the youth's mouth startled her almost as much as the flickering switchblade which suddenly appeared in his hand. Before her own hand could disengage the ID and close around her gun, he had darted up the shallow steps.

She automatically flung her left arm out to deflect the slashing blade and, as he crashed past her, the snub-nosed .38 came free. Deliberately aiming low, Sigrid sent him howling to the pavement with one shot.

Behind her, in the shadows, the girl began to scream hysterically.

With a startled cry, Anne Harald dropped her cases on the sidewalk and ran toward Sigrid, who clutched the iron railing feeling curiously giddy and light-headed.

"Oh my God!" Anne murmured and Sigrid followed her mother's eyes to her own left arm. It was still numb, but the streetlights revealed the dark stain that soaked through the thin sleeve of her jacket and dripped onto the steps. Blood also ran freely from a cut on the palm of her left hand.

All stiffness drained out of her legs and she sank down on the steps. "My radio," she told Anne as mounting waves of dizziness washed over her. "Tell them—officer needs assistance . . . assailant needs ambulance . . ."

"I don't believe this!" Anne cried. "Bleeding like a stuck pig and still you talk like a policeman."

She whirled and ran for Sigrid's car; but for once, as if on cue, a patrol car appeared when needed.

As the uniformed officers fashioned rough tourniquets for her arm and for the wounded man's leg, Sigrid tried to hold onto consciousness, but the girl's terrified cries turned into low sobs that were rather lulling against the street noises and Sigrid lost her tenuous thread of awareness before the ambulance arrived.

As the anaesthesia wore off, there was a memory of violence and pain, then an uneasy disoriented feeling of being in an unfamiliar place.

Even more disorienting was the sound of her mother's voice, angry and intense.

Her eyelids still felt too heavy to open, but returning alertness brought with it the smell of antiseptic and alcohol, so she must be in a hospital. But who else was in the room and why did her mother sound so awkward and harsh? Fear, yes. Sorrow and anger, too; but Sigrid had never heard this particular quality in her mother's voice before.

Even past fifty, Anne Lattimore Harald remained petite and slender. Short hair almost untouched with gray covered her head in a soft cap of dark curls; her skin was still soft and smooth except for the laugh lines around her luminous dark eyes and generous mouth, and thirty-five years in the North hadn't been enough to erase all the magnolia from her voice. Flirting was second nature to her. Women's Lib arrived too late to persuade Anne Harald that vinegar could be as potent as honey or that a woman shouldn't use feminine wiles to get whatever she needed.

Certainly it had helped her get her foot in the door after Leif Harald was killed, when she had struggled to support herself and her toddler daughter with camera and typewriter. These days Anne could afford to pick and choose assignments—several of her critically acclaimed photojournal pieces had won national awards —but that easy, laughing charm was still part of her professional technique. Her warmth could thaw the frostiest politicians, and the resulting photographs often revealed more than her subjects intended, to the great delight of her editors.

Sigrid had been too young at the time of her father's death to remember him clearly. She had only unconnected memories of a tall uniformed blond man who'd swung her up on his shoulder, his laughter. She had never been jealous of the men with whom her mother flirted so openly, precisely because Anne *was* open, her flirting never quite intimate; her quicksilver elusiveness kept men her friends and nothing more.

If there had been truly romantic entanglements since Leif Harald's death, Sigrid was not aware of them.

As she grew into gawky adolescence, Sigrid had watched her mother with despairing envy, wishing over and over that she had inherited some of Anne's graceful Southern poise, something her Grandmother Lattimore kept insisting was Sigrid's natural birthright. "All the Lattimores have it, honey, and I'm sure you do, too, if you'd just sit back and let it flow."

Although no longer as tongue-tied as in childhood, Sigrid knew she still seemed stiff and cold in social situations; almost as cold and stiff as Anne's voice was now in this hospital room.

Sigrid struggled to focus on their words as her grogginess

lifted. The man's voice was a placating rumble under her mother's ragged tones, but there was something familiar about it. A doctor? Sleep pulled at her, but she resisted.

"She could have been killed," Anne was saying angrily. "And she wasn't even on duty."

"A police officer's never completely off duty, Anne. You know that."

Startled, Sigrid's eyes flew open. "Captain McKinnon!" she said hoarsely.

Anne pushed past the big man who stood at the foot of Sigrid's bed and touched her daughter's hair. "Oh, honey, you had me so scared. Are you okay? How do you feel?"

Captain McKinnon gave her an appraising smile. "Finally with us, Harald? I was beginning to wonder if they'd knocked you out for good."

McKinnon had never seen his buttoned-up and normally efficient subordinate looking this vulnerable. Her dark hair had loosened around her thin face and those wide gray eyes held bewilderment and uncertainty. "How's the arm feel?"

Sigrid looked down at her left arm. It seemed to be tightly taped now from shoulder to elbow. Another sterile bandage was wrapped on her hand, which ached dully and more painfully than her arm. An IV drip was attached to her right arm. There had been a man, she thought, and a knife. Reality wavered, then she remembered that he'd slashed her arm.

"How bad is it?"

"You lost gallons of blood," said her mother. Anne's words faded and Sigrid struggled to hold on to them. "I forget how many stitches they said."

"No permanent damage," the captain assured her easily. "I asked the doctor."

Sigrid's boss was built like an overgrown teddy bear, but his tongue could be sharper than a grizzly's claws when he chewed someone out. In the time that she'd worked under him, Sigrid had come to respect the big rumpled man, yet he made her uneasy and she didn't know why. He was scrupulously fair and treated her like his other officers. Still, he seemed to expect something more of her. An indefinable tension crackled in the air whenever he called her in to discuss a case, more tension than her own prickly nature usually elicited. It wasn't because she was a female officer, she'd decided. There were other women in the department and she hadn't noticed that vague air of expectation when McKinnon dealt with them.

Even more puzzling was her mother's present reaction. Anne had many virtues, but they were certainly not domestic. Her apartments always looked as if they'd just been ransacked by burglars, nothing matched or was color-coordinated, yet here she was straightening Sigrid's sheets, aligning the water carafe with its drinking glass on the nightstand, twitching the curtains. Sigrid almost expected to see her whip out a dustcloth and start polishing the headboard.

First anger and now this fidgeting self-consciousness from a woman who'd learned how to twist men around her little finger before she started kindergarten?

"That was good work tonight," McKinnon said.

"Is the suspect okay?" Her throat was dry.

"He'll survive. Probably even be break-dancing next month. You shot him through the calf."

"Good."

"Dear God in heaven!" Anne exploded. "A crazy man almost cuts your arm off and you worry if you've hurt *him?*"

McKinnon's attention flickered to the woman and back to Sigrid. "We're pretty certain he's the perp who's raped at least seven women in the last three months. This one we'll nail so tight no lawyer'll get him off. I'll want your report tomorrow afternoon."

Sigrid nodded, but Anne blazed up again. "Tomorrow?"

"Mother, please."

"No, maybe she's right." The big man nodded. "Day after tomorrow will be soon enough. You take it easy tomorrow."

He hesitated, then spoke again. "I might as well tell you. Somebody set off a bomb in the Hotel Maintenon tonight."

At first it didn't register. She looked at Captain McKinnon apprehensively. "Detective Tildon—?"

McKinnon nodded grimly. "Two people DOA, two more hanging on by a toenail. Tildon's over at Metro Medical Center. I stopped in on my way here."

White-faced, Sigrid held her breath until McKinnon added, "He's still in surgery but they think he'll make it."

Anne abruptly turned her back on them and went to stare out the window.

McKinnon's face betrayed his exhaustion. "I'd better get back up to the Maintenon," he said. Had Lieutenant Harald been any other of his officers, the captain would have stooped over and given her hand a clumsy, reassuring pat. Yet even wounded and sedated, her habitual reserve made his own hand hesitate until the moment passed.

As if sensing his ambivalence, Sigrid detained him with anxious eyes. "Who's going to handle it, Captain?"

"Me, right now." He looked down at her. "You want this one, don't you?"

"Yes."

There was nothing declamatory or dramatic in her simple affirmative, but the resolution in her tone was unmistakable. McKinnon glanced at Anne's back uneasily. "Let's wait and see how quickly you get back on your feet."

As he moved to go, Anne remained rigid by the window. He paused in the doorway. "I'm sorry it had to be like this, Anne, but even so, it was good to see you again."

She turned and faced him coldly. "Good-bye, Captain."

In the split second before the door closed behind McKinnon, Sigrid could have sworn she saw his shoulders droop beneath the whiplash finality in her mother's words.

She looked up at Anne curiously. "I didn't realize you two knew each other."

"We don't."

"Oh, stop it, Mother," Sigrid said wearily. "I'm a police officer, a trained observer, remember?"

"He and Leif used to be partners."

Sigrid was stunned. "And?"

"And nothing. They were partners and your father was killed and this is the first time I've met him since the funeral."

"But you *hate* him. Why? Was it something to do with Dad's death?" Abruptly, Sigrid realized she'd never been told many of the actual details. "What really happened? Was it the captain's fault?"

"I don't *know* what really happened," Anne said raggedly. "I wasn't there." Sudden tears misted her thick eyelashes. "All I know is that your father was killed and McKinnon wasn't even wounded." She ran a tired hand through her curls. "Honey, I'm bushed. Home to bed for me."

"What about El Diego?"

"He'll just have to wait. I can't go jetting off with my only child slashed to ribbons."

"Don't be dramatic, Mother. I'm perfectly capable of managing."

"Oh Lord, don't I know it!" Anne sighed. How very apt that

old tale of a hen's bafflement when she discovered she'd hatched a duckling. . . .

Since infancy, Anne had known how pretty she was. It was a matter of record and not conceit. All the Lattimore women, sisters, mother, aunts, and cousins were beauties: in that family, mere prettiness was taken for granted. Therefore, when she went north to study photography and almost immediately married a stunningly handsome New Yorker who looked like a direct throwback to Viking forebears, everyone assumed their child would be something special.

Yet even a geneticist couldn't have predicted Sigrid's rearrangement of parental genes. She had Leif's height, nearly six inches taller than her mother, but her skinny angularity lacked his athletic gracefulness. She had also inherited his thin nose and high cheekbones, and her wide eyes were shaped like his blue ones, but their changeable gray color came from Anne. Her hair was dark like Anne's, yet absolutely straight and so silky fine that Sigrid had long ago quit trying to do anything with it. She kept it braided into a severe knot at the nape of her neck and could put it up in two minutes flat without the aid of a mirror.

In fact, Sigrid seldom looked in mirrors. She well knew that her neck was too long, her mouth too wide, her chin too strong. By the age of thirteen, she'd decided once and for all that she would never be attractive. From that time on, mirrors had stopped being important.

Of course, thought Anne, none of this would have mattered if only her daughter had caught the Lattimore knack of easy self-assurance. At least half the famous women she photographed every year had serious beauty flaws, but they believed themselves lovely and a willing world accepted their own valuations.

She blamed herself for Sigrid's lack of physical self-confidence. In those first few years after Leif's death, she'd moved around so restlessly, changing apartments the way other women change furniture, too unhappy to see what her frenetic lifestyle was doing to an already introspective child.

"I should never have sent you off to that boarding school when you were so young," she said mournfully. As if to compensate for past maternal lapses, Anne poured a fresh glass of water from the carafe and held it to Sigrid's lips.

Sigrid sipped obediently and then lay back upon the pillow. "It didn't hurt for you to leave me then and it's not going to hurt now," she said, following the main points of her mother's illogical thought processes with the ease of long practice. "Go home, Mother. Get some sleep and then get on a plane. I'll be fine."

Her arm throbbed and she was too tired for more talk. "If you really want to do something for me, just get my car away from that fire hydrant and don't forget to leave a note telling me where you've put it."

"I'm not *that* disorganized," Anne protested and they both smiled, remembering.

"Good night, honey," Anne said softly and Sigrid smelled the familiar scent of jasmine as her mother bent to kiss her, then left.

Pain stabbed her left arm, her hand burned, and her right arm was beginning to hurt, too, from the intravenous apparatus. To complicate matters, Sigrid realized that she was going to have to sleep on her back, a thoroughly disagreeable prospect for one who always slept on her stomach.

She delayed the ordeal for a few minutes, replaying in her mind the scene that had just taken place between her mother and her boss.

What an odd coincidence that she should wind up working for her father's onetime partner. That at least explained the tension she'd always sensed with him, his air of undefined expectation. He must have thought it strange that she never mentioned her father to him, but why had he waited for her to bring it up first?

She scrunched her shoulders deeper into the pillow, trying to get comfortable as she considered her relationship with Detective Tildon. She was shaken and angered that he'd been hurt tonight, but although they worked well together they knew almost nothing about each other's personal lives. She was sure it would have been different with her father and McKinnon.

Anne never talked about those days, but relatives who enjoyed telling Sigrid what a love match her parents' marriage had been had also described Leif Harald as possessing a genial friendliness as open and spontaneous as his wife's. Those two would surely have made McKinnon a part of their lives; yet she, their daughter, had grown up with no recollection of ever having heard McKinnon's name. Nor, in that handful of snapshots her mother kept, had there been a picture of the two men together, although Sigrid seemed to recall half a picture of her young father laughing into the camera and someone's hand on his shoulder. McKinnon's?

What really happened, she wondered, that day her father died? Why had Anne cut McKinnon out of their lives as neatly as she had scissored him out of that picture?

Both arms hurt badly now and Sigrid began to long for sleep's release. She tried naming the fifty states in alphabetical order and when that failed, she began a chronological listing of presidents and vice-presidents, a proven soporific. She had just reached Ulysses S. Grant and Schuyler Colfax and was drowsily fumbling for Grant's second vice-president when the door to her room whooshed open on pneumatic hinges and a young Asian nurse entered to remove the IV needle from her right arm.

Sigrid gratefully flexed it and the nurse smiled sympathetically. "Feels better, yes?"

"Yes."

"And your other arm, please? Your doctor, he has left pain medicine if it hurts too much."

"Not yet," Sigrid said stoically, easing onto her stomach.

The nurse tucked in the blanket and rolled the IV stand out while Sigrid gave up on Grant's second term and moved on to Rutherford B. Hayes and William Wheeler . . . James A. Garfield and . . . Chester A. Arthur. No vice-president for Arthur and then came Grover Cleveland and Henderson? No, Hendricks. Thomas Hendricks . . .

The throbbing of her arm took on its own metronomic rhythm and she fell into an uneasy sleep.

CHAPTER V

Sigrid awoke in a pale gray dawn to the trill of the telephone beside her bed. An incautious movement sent such pain lancing down her arm she could hardly concentrate on Anne's breathless words.

"—and Charlie's simply having kittens! He keeps raving about how his father went completely gaga after fracturing his hip and he's sure El Diego's going to break out in waves of senility just because he twisted an ankle yesterday. Charlie says I have to be on the next plane or he'll send someone else. Now, honey, I can tell him what to do with this assignment, but it's such a plum. I mean, what if El Diego actually gets the Nobel after all these years of being kept out of the running? So if you're really sure you can manage—"

"I can manage," Sigrid reiterated patiently, wishing Anne would just say good-bye and *go*.

"Okay. Anyhow, Roman's promised to take care of you and the car and I'll send you over some fresh clothes and, Siga, honey,"—Anne's voice dropped into a confidential, all-us-girls-together tone—"why *didn't* you tell me? We've really got to sit down for a long talk when I get back."

With those alarming words, she clicked off. Sigrid was filled with foreboding. Mother-daughter talks always left her feeling guilty and depressed.

She lay back on the lumpy pillows and tried to imagine what Anne had seen in her apartment that could possibly make her think she had girlish secrets to confide. It certainly couldn't be Roman Tramegra, the man with whom Sigrid shared the roomy garden apartment.

An odd assortment of people wandered in and out of Anne Harald's slapdash life and Roman was one of them. Sigrid first met him when she mistook him for a burglar in Anne's apartment last spring while her mother was on a European assignment. A large, soft, slightly pompous man with thinning hair and a never-ending, monkeylike curiosity, Tramegra had been insulted by her suspicions because he had Anne's invitation to use the apartment until he found a place of his own.

His natural inquisitiveness had gotten the better of him, however, and upon learning that Sigrid was a homicide officer he was entirely captivated. He had always wanted to write a best-selling whodunit and immediately decided she would act as his technical adviser.

Roman Tramegra's age and self-absorption quickly overcame Sigrid's usual awkwardness in making friends. Indeed, the avuncular manner with which he treated her made his presence comfortable enough so that after her apartment building went co-op, she agreed to a trial lease on a larger apartment which Tramegra, through arcane family connections, had located on the lower West Side.

When she returned from Europe, Anne had not approved. If Sigrid wished to share an apartment, her mother had hoped it would be with someone romantically interested. "Where's the future in this?" she scolded when Roman had tactfully retired after dinner to his refurbished maid's quarters beyond the kitchen. "I know you two are supposed to overlap only in the kitchen, but he'll always be in and out if you have visitors. It's worse than a chaperone. It's like living with your grandmother."

"Not really," Sigrid had smiled, scraping the remains of Roman's eggplant parmesan into the garbage disposal. "Grandmother's a good cook."

"You know what I mean," Anne had said darkly.

But Anne was accustomed to Roman's presence now, so what could have set her off this morning? Time enough to worry when Anne returned from South America, Sigrid decided.

With that, she sat up, swung her legs off the bed and was halfway across the room before dizziness overtook her. Sheer willpower got her to the bathroom, where she splashed cold water on her face, but her head was reeling and her legs wobbly before she made it back to bed. Her arm throbbed torturously now and willpower no longer helped.

Disgusted with herself for being so weak, Sigrid pushed the call button.

The nurse who promptly responded was the same young oriental woman from the early morning hours. "Awake so soon?" she asked cheerfully, then moved to check Sigrid's pulse and temperature. "Your arm, it hurts very much now, yes?"

"Yes," Sigrid admitted.

"You are very silly not to call me sooner," the nurse reproved. "The doctor would not leave the medicine if he did not think you needed it."

Still scolding, she expertly rolled Sigrid over, swabbed her hip with alcohol, and inserted the hypo so deftly that her patient barely felt it.

By eight, breakfast and bath were concluded and the doctor, a man who seemed to have modeled his bedside manner after Genghis Khan or Ivan the Terrible, had retaped her arm, pronounced it satisfactory, and given her some pills to keep the pain in abeyance.

"And take 'em," he'd snarled. "They're nonaddictive, so you don't get any Brownie points for a stiff upper lip."

By eight-thirty, rain was sluicing down her window and she'd begun to give up on whomever her mother had sent out with her clothes. There was no television in the room, but an aide brought in a newspaper which had the Maintenon explosion all over the front page and Sigrid quickly skimmed the scanty details.

The blast had occurred shortly after nine P.M. at the rear of one of the ballrooms where, according to the paper, a cabbage tournament was in progress.

(Irritably and half-subliminally, Sigrid noted that proofreading seemed to be a dying craft.)

Those dead at the scene were Zachary A. Wolferman and John Sutton; in critical condition were T. J. Dixon and Charles Tildon; five others were listed as serious but stable.

No motive for the bombing had been advanced and, except for the usual crazies, no one had claimed credit. Police refused to speculate whether it was politically motivated or inspired by purely personal animosities.

There were side stories on Wolferman's considerable financial holdings and on Sutton as a former SDS activist and contemporary historian. It was reported that Sutton's wife and Wolferman's cousin were among those also present at the tournament. Mrs. Sutton had collapsed upon seeing her husband's body and was currently in seclusion with their two children, ages four and seven.

As the clock ticked toward nine, Sigrid impatiently tossed the paper aside and examined once more the clothes she'd arrived at the hospital in. The jacket was impossibly stiff with her dried blood, but the gray slacks and black print shirt merely looked oil-stained. There was no way she'd be able to hook her bra or put her hair up unaided; still, if she could get someone downstairs to flag her a cab, she could probably make it home without any help from Anne's unreliable courier.

She eased out of the hospital gown and was reaching for her shirt when the door swooshed open and a tall lean man whose thick white hair stood up in angry tufts stopped in her doorway to glare at her with piercing blue eyes.

"What the hell kind of Valkyrie theatricals were you trying to pull last night? Wrestling with knife-bearing madmen! You idiot—you could have been killed."

The exasperated, warring emotions which this man could arouse in her held Sigrid speechless for a moment, then abruptly realizing her nakedness, she pulled a sheet around her thin body.

Her gesture increased his fury, and he slammed her own overnight case down on the hospital bed.

"I'm here to *bring* you clothes, dammit, not strip you," he snarled. As he turned and stomped out of the room, he flung over his shoulder, "I'll wait at the front entrance. Ten minutes."

And *that*, Sigrid realized wryly, explained why Anne had gone all chirpy and twittering earlier. Awkwardly getting to her feet, she opened the case and found a knit suit in autumn shades of rust and gold.

For years Sigrid had owned two sets of clothes: the serviceable, severely cut and neutrally colored suits she invariably chose for herself and the brighter, more feminine things Anne chose for her to wear whenever they made duty visits south. Sigrid had never enjoyed clothes, but it was easier to wear Anne's selections than listen to Grandmother Lattimore's complaints that "Sigrid simply isn't trying."

"Gilding the turnip" had always been Sigrid's private feelings on the subject and Anne usually bowed to the inevitable, but Oscar Nauman's appearance that morning seemed to have impelled her to pick from the Carolina side of her daughter's closet.

Why he should have been at her apartment that early in the morning, Sigrid had no idea. Nothing about the man was safely predictable anyhow, except that if a panel of randomly selected art critics or scholars were asked to list America's top five artists, one could be sure that Oscar Nauman's name would appear on every list. His paintings were so eagerly snapped up that he could have long since resigned his position as chairman of Vanderlyn College's art department and lived on the proceeds; but money slipped through his fingers and he loved teaching too much to give it up even though he grumbled considerably about the time it took from his painting.

And time was passing, Sigrid would occasionally remember. The thought gave her inexplicable regret. Oscar Nauman must be nearing sixty, yet he retained the vigor and virility of a much younger man. Indeed his freewheeling spirit frequently made Sigrid feel ages older than he.

They had met last spring during a homicide investigation at the college when there was a possibility that Nauman had been the intended victim. The end of the case had been the beginning of their prickly relationship. She did nothing to encourage him, nothing of which she was conscious, yet he kept turning up at odd times, keeping her emotionally off-balance, poking and prodding until she felt like a science fair project while he endeavored to change her dress, her palate, and her taste in art. No matter how rudely she resisted, he refused to be driven away and kept walking in and out of her life as if it were simply an extension of his own.

She wasn't quite sure why she permitted it.

Slowly, she dressed herself in the rust and gold suit, repacked the drab bloodstained things, and was waiting under the hospital canopy when Oscar Nauman splashed up in his yellow, much-abused MG.

The morning was still gray with rain so he had the top up. The inside of the car smelled of damp leather and the clean blend of turpentine, cologne and pipe tobacco that she had come to associate with him.

"Sorry about this damn top," he apologized.

"I like it. You don't drive like Richard Petty when it's up."

She hated his competitive driving, especially since Manhattan's streets belonged mostly to kamikaze cabbies, cumbersome busses and lane-hogging delivery vans. How Nauman hung onto a driver's license was something she'd quit wondering about. She had personally been present at four separate issuances of careless-and-reckless citations. Either the computer hadn't yet tagged him as a scofflaw or someone in DMV kept cleaning up his record for him. Probably the latter, since Nauman's circle of acquaintances was even wider than her peripatetic mother's. ▬▬

Nauman seemed to have forgotten his earlier anger. On good behavior now, he drove at a moderate speed, obeying all the laws. At the first stop light, he twisted in his seat to study her.

"How bad is it really?" he asked, turning her bandaged left hand gently in his.

"Not bad," she answered, reclaiming her hand. "There's no nerve damage. The knife cut into some arm muscle, but they've stitched it all up and if I keep it in a sling, it's supposed to stop hurting in four or five days."

The light changed and Nauman allowed a cab to cut in front of him unchallenged.

"Your mother exaggerates a bit, doesn't she?" He smiled. "I expected black eyes, bruises, and slash marks all over."

"Mother enjoys dramatics."

"And you didn't actually wrestle with that guy?"

"No."

"But you *did* shoot him." Nauman had been truly shocked the first time he realized that she always carried a gun.

"Yes."

"That doesn't bother you?"

"It's the first time I've ever shot someone," Sigrid said slowly. "I always wondered how I'd feel if I ever had to. Now that it's happened, I don't know."

The windshield wiper on her side swished back and forth erratically, smearing raindrops, and she stared blankly through the obscured glass.

"I guess I'm glad I didn't kill him."

"But you would have?"

"Yes."

They'd had this discussion before.

"He may have been poor and he may not have a father, but that boy wasn't looking for food or love or even money to feed a drug habit last night, Nauman. It was violence pure and simple. He was there to rape that girl and he was ready to knife anyone who got in his way."

She leaned back against the headrest wearily. "Do me a favor, will you? Swing past Metro Medical?"

"What's wrong?" The little car swerved as Nauman's attention swiftly shifted to her pale face. "Are you bleeding? Your stitches come loose?"

"No, it's— Look out!" she cried and braced herself as the left fender kissed the side of a passing van. The driver gave them an obscene gesture and roared ahead while Nauman sheepishly wheeled back to the center of his own lane.

"Sorry about that, but why Metro Medical?"

"My partner's there. Tillie. He was nearly killed in that explosion at the Maintenon last night."

"That's why I tried to find you this morning."

Sigrid was puzzled. "Because of Tillie?"

"No, John Sutton. He was killed in that blast. He teaches— *taught* at Vanderlyn. He and Val—his wife—met in a seminar I gave one summer at McClellan. I've known them for years."

"I'm sorry, Nauman."

"Just the damn waste," he said, showing his anger and grief. "John was one of the best. Genuine idealist. Intelligent. And Val—I went as soon as I heard. Falling apart. Told her you'd, but your mother said slashed and anyhow so crazy."

When upset or distracted, Oscar Nauman's speech became almost telegraphic as his mind raced ahead, forcing his tongue to omit words in order to catch up.

"SDS, of course, but that was *years*. He's teacher. Real teacher. So why?"

By now, Sigrid could follow his words with a fair degree of comprehension. "Maybe he wasn't the intended target," she suggested. "Don't forget that a man named Wolferman, a banker, was killed, too. And others are in critical condition."

"Somebody killed him without *caring?*"

That would be the sticking point, Sigrid knew. Nauman was an old-style liberal with a touching belief that, given adequate housing, full bellies, and meaningful work, mankind would automatically live the Golden Rule. The existence of pure amoral evil was not something the liberal mind liked to admit.

"The police care," she reminded him quietly.

CHAPTER VI

Metro Medical Center was one of the city's newer hospitals, with shiny scrubbable polymer surfaces, bright colors, and, judging by the flow of people through its halls, a user-friendly attitude toward visitors. While Nauman circled the area to look for a parking space, Sigrid was directed up to a waiting room on the eighth floor where she found Marian Tildon surrounded by her sober-faced parents and several friends.

Normally Tillie's wife was a vivacious redhead, with an aura of wiry strength to her small-boned figure; but after a night in and out of the intensive care unit, where tubes and electronic monitors held her husband's life together, there was no sparkle left in her face and her green eyes were dull as she stared in bewilderment at Sigrid's bandaged hand and arm sling.

"Were you there, too, Lieutenant?"

Briefly, Sigrid explained she'd acquired her wounds elsewhere. "How is he?"

"They've been letting me go in for ten minutes every hour," Marian replied, automatically glancing at her wristwatch. "He opened his eyes when I was in last time, but I'm not sure he recognized me."

"I think he did, Mare," soothed her mother.

Marian Tildon stood up. "They allow two of us in at a time, Lieutenant. Would you like to see him?"

They walked down a hall painted melon and turquoise to a pair of bright yellow double doors. Marian took a deep breath and pulled one open.

Sigrid had never been inside an intensive care unit before and her first thought was how mechanized it seemed. It reminded her of the modern diagnostic garage where she had her car serviced occasionally—the semicircle of bays around a central console, with a snarl of tubes and hoses hanging down. The tubes and hoses at the garage held oil, air, and brake and transmission fluids, while here the tubes carried oxygen, saline solution, or hemoglobin.

Two nurses sat inside a hollow circular counter at the center of the large room with an uninterrupted view of the electronic monitors connected to each of the fourteen stations radiating out from the middle. A strong medicinal odor hung in the air.

There were no regular hospital beds. Instead, patients lay on what looked like armless lounge chairs upholstered in creamy yellow plastic, extended to semi-reclining position and elevated so that the nurses could work on each without bending.

· Sigrid followed Marian across the room to where Tillie lay swathed in so many bandages that she did not at first recognize him. His face was discolored, his lips swollen, his eyes half-open but unfocused.

Marian leaned over and kissed his bare shoulder gently. "Charles, darling, Lieutenant Harald's here."

There was no change in Tillie's expression, but Marian whispered that the nurses had told her that surgery patients could often hear and comprehend even if they couldn't respond, so Sigrid drew nearer and tried to keep her voice brisk and matter-of-fact.

It was a very long ten minutes, made more difficult by watching the other woman attempt an upbeat manner while her voice trembled and tears spilled down her cheeks.

Through it all, Tillie did not move or react.

When their time was up and they were back out in the hall again, Marian's composure crumpled. She rested her head against the cool wall and fought against sobs that wracked her trim body while Sigrid stood paralyzed by the awkwardness that always seized her whenever raw emotions were laid bare.

Her mother or grandmother or any of the Lattimore women, for that matter, would have automatically gathered the grieving woman in their arms and made soothing, comforting noises. Sigrid had seen them do it as effortlessly and naturally as they breathed, but she could only stand frozen.

"Can I get you a damp towel?" Sigrid asked, gesturing toward a nearby door.

Marian choked back a final sob. "No, it's all right now. I'll come."

Inside the tiled restroom, she splashed cold water on her face, then rummaged in her purse for a comb and lipstick. "I'm sorry," she apologized, slashing bright orange onto her lips. "I know crying doesn't help, but—"

"You probably need sleep," Sigrid said pragmatically. "Weren't you awake all night?"

"It's not just that." Marian stared at Sigrid's reflection in the mirror over the pink washbasins. "I mean, I can accept what Charles does. How he makes our living. He's a policeman. Policemen lay their lives on the line every time they go to work. Okay, I accept that. I've even learned to live with it. But this? No. No, I can't! He wasn't even on duty last night. He was just an ordinary citizen minding his own business and he was almost killed."

"You sound ' e my mother," Sigrid said. "That's what she told Captain McKinnon last night."

"And he told her a cop is never off duty, right?"

Sigrid nodded.

"Well, he's wrong!" Marian said fiercely, turning to face her. "Is Charles a good detective?"

"Yes."

"Well, he's an even better father. And husband. When he's with us, he could be an insurance salesman or a dry cleaner or a—a *plumber* for all we hear about police work. When he's with us, he *is* off duty and I don't give a damn what McKinnon says. It isn't fair!

"That bomb last night," she asked. "Did they mean to kill Charles?"

"I don't know," Sigrid answered. "I'm sorry. At this point, all I really know is what was in the paper."

"But you'll be working on it? Or will your arm—?"

"I'll be working on it," Sigrid promised grimly.

Oscar Nauman was not in the lobby when she got back downstairs, but through the front glass doors Sigrid glimpsed his yellow sportscar creeping past the hospital. She hurried down the rain-soaked sidewalk and caught up with him at the corner light.

"Have you been circling all this time?" she asked, sliding in beside him.

"This was only my second trip around. I figured you'd be up there a few minutes so I stopped off at the deli and got some kaiser rolls and cold cuts for lunch. My place or yours?"

"Mine, but I'm not hungry."

"Yes, you are," he told her. "You just don't realize it yet."

There was no sign of Roman Tramegra when they reached her apartment on the westernmost edge of Greenwich Village. At least no sign of Roman in the flesh. He had been there recently, witness the fresh bouquet of herbs on the counter; and he planned to return soon if the hunk of frozen veal thawing in the sink could be trusted.

By tacit agreement, the cheerful green-and-white tiled kitchen was primarily Roman Tramegra's domain and that would-be gourmet chef had indulged his love of gadgets and appliances. Birchwood counters topped mint green cabinets and held Roman's mixer, food processor, blender, coffee grinder and coffee maker, each ready to whir into action at the flick of his pudgy fingers. Pottery jars bristled with wooden spoons, wire balloon whisks, ladles, spatulas and various utensils whose purpose Sigrid couldn't begin to guess. Opposite the enormous white refrigerator stood a six-burner chrome and porcelain range with an oven big enough to roast a young pig. Copper pots and iron skillets depended from a rack overhead and copper wire baskets filled with onions, peppers and lemons hung above the stainless-steel double sink. A dozen different knives were racked beside the thick wooden chopping block and a four-shelf spice cabinet was jammed with jars of exotic spices and herbs.

Roman's denim apron had been tossed across one of the tall white bar stools. Oscar Nauman added his own raincoat to the heap and began to cut the rolls. He planned to slather them with a concoction of mustard, olive oil and freshly chopped rosemary that he and Roman had invented one afternoon when Sigrid was late getting home.

While Nauman rummaged in the refrigerator, Sigrid went through the dining and living rooms and down the hall to her bedroom. This part of the apartment reflected her own taste. The clean-lined furniture was comfortable to use, if bland to the eye: a white linen couch, oatmeal-colored chairs, uncluttered surfaces. Little by little, though, Roman Tramegra was sneaking in a few softening touches.

Arguing that the dining room was an extension of the kitchen, Roman had felt justified in persuading Sigrid to buy the refectory table he'd discovered in a secondhand thrift shop. "It's perfect for your chair," he'd told her.

The chair in question was a massive carved affair with handrests formed of small wooden cat heads which Sigrid had unaccountably lugged home last spring when she found it abandoned on the sidewalk near her old apartment building. Roman had reupholstered the back and seat in a dark red velvet and that made a perfect excuse for bringing in two room-sized oriental rugs in soft red tones.

Behind the couch, a row of windows looked out into their

small courtyard and Roman had filled that space with ferns and palms and a baby Norfolk Island pine. It was nothing to do with her, Sigrid warned him. "I've murdered my last plant. Either I water things too much or not enough and I'm tired of throwing out pots of dead vegetation."

So far the plants seemed to be flourishing.

Through the years, Anne had given her several framed photographs and Nauman had recently presented her with a playful sketch done in vivid gouaches, and these added vibrant color to the rooms.

Her bedroom, however, remained free of anyone else's touch. Except for a floor-to-ceiling bookcase and a dark green carpet, no brilliant hues had crept in here. Her comforter was off-white, as were her lampshades. An armchair near the bookcase was an indeterminate beige, and on a nearby wall hung black-and-white line drawings, reproductions from the Morgan Library's collection. Sigrid did not believe in yoga or meditation, yet there were times when she retreated to this bare room and sat looking into those ascetic late Gothic faces until her own calm was restored.

While Oscar busied himself with lunch, Sigrid changed into more suitable working clothes of gray slacks, white shirt, and a baggy off-white corduroy blazer with deep pockets that had seen her through several springs and autumns. With her left arm out of commission, she decided to dispense with her shoulder bag; so that meant a gun harness worn under her jacket with the rest of the items she normally carried stuffed in her pockets.

Getting dressed was difficult enough; doing anything with her shoulder-length hair was impossible, for she could not reach behind with both hands. She wound up carrying a blue scarf out to Oscar, who had unloaded a tray of sandwiches onto her dining room table.

"Would you mind?" she asked, trying to gather her hair into position with her right hand.

"Sit down. I don't know why you don't just leave it loose," he grumbled. He liked her hair and thought it a waste that she kept it so confined. "What's the point of long hair the way you treat it?"

"It's easier to take care of." She bent her head so he could get at the job better. "I don't have to keep getting haircuts every two weeks or worry about it flopping in my face. I can braid it, pin it back, and forget it."

She did not like to be touched, so Oscar resisted kissing the vulnerable nape of her slender neck, but he stubbornly took his time tying the scarf. "There's more to hair than just keeping your neck warm."

"A woman's crowning glory?" Sigrid gibed.

"Something like that," he said, fluffing up the bow loops of the silk scarf.

"Haven't you learned by now that I'm never going to turn into a sex object, much less a swan?" she asked and reached back to flatten some of the bow's exuberance. Oscar's face as he sat down across the table from her was so exasperated that Sigrid couldn't help smiling.

"Poor Nauman. Why do you keep bothering with me?"

"Damned if I know," he smiled back. "Want some ale?"

"Yes, but I'd better not mix alcohol and whatever's in this painkiller."

Her arm had begun to throb again and she went back into the kitchen for a glass of cold milk to wash down the tablet. She found that she was as hungry as Nauman had predicted and for a few minutes they devoted their attention to the food.

"Tell me about John Sutton," she demanded when the first edge was off their hunger. "What were you doing out at McClellan?"

"It was one of those interdisciplinary seminars, a sort of academic happening in support of the peace movement. John was president of McClellan's SDS that year; Val was a cute little undergraduate full of innocence and optimism. Flower children hoping to better the world. I was old enough to know better, but I was just as naive. We thought we could make a difference."

"And you did, didn't you?" She took a second sandwich and cut it in half. "The war ended."

"Not soon enough," he said and sat lost in dark memory until Sigrid pushed half her sandwich at him. He looked at it, then began to munch absent-mindedly.

"John Sutton," she prodded.

"Bright. Wacky sense of humor. Played the guitar. Used to make up parodies of Bob Dylan songs—the whiney ones. Val played the autoharp. Quick ear. They hadn't met before, but one night when he played for us, she started echoing his tunes, then embellishing them. Solemn as a churchwarden the whole time. Her face—" Nauman took another bite of his sandwich, waiting for the right words to convey the odd attraction of Val Sutton's face. "What are those cats that look like Siamese except they're all brown? Burmese? Abyssinian?"

Sigrid shrugged, not being a pet owner.

"Think of a triangular face that's a cross between Nefertiti and an Abyssinian cat, with sleek brown hair falling to her waist. That was Val. You'll see. Not beautiful. Men don't notice her right away; but once they do, they don't forget her. John never had a chance."

He grinned, describing how artfully Val had managed John's wooing; how John, if he had been aware of her wiles, hadn't struggled against them.

Sigrid, who had never so far as she knew turned any man's head but Nauman's, listened and briefly wondered how it must feel to have such power over someone's heart.

"John loved to argue. We had several all-night sessions that summer, but I'd almost lost touch with them when he and Val came east four or five years ago. Vanderlyn's history department offered him an associate professorship and Val audited some of my classes. She's one of the curators at the Feldheimer and a pretty fair Sunday painter herself. I've lent them my place up in Connecticut several times and John and I've served on some committees together. The Mickey Mouse ones. They don't think we take the so-called important ones seriously enough. Administration usually does what it wants anyhow and why the hell they have to waste our time—"

"John Sutton," Sigrid interrupted, having heard tirades against Vanderlyn's administration before. "Who were his enemies?"

"I never heard that he had any. John was bright and opinionated, but not mean. Like last Wednesday when the CCC met and—"

"The what?"

"The Condensed CUNY Committee. That's what John called us. I've told you how the university tries to promote the idea that the different branches around the city are one big happy family?"

Sigrid supposed so. She couldn't work up much interest in the politics of the City University of New York. Keeping up with politics within the NYPD was tedium enough.

"So CUNY subsidizes faculty dinners at one of the big hotels and we have to shell out some of our own money to break bread together and pretend we know each other. Except that the combined faculty's so large that it gets boiled down to senior members and one year it's for liberal arts and the next for the sciences, that sort of thing. This year it's the arts and John and I were sent to meet with delegates from the other schools at the Maintenon on Wednesday to set things up and there was this jackass from Brooklyn College who—"

"Wait, wait!" Sigrid thumped the table gently. "The Maintenon? John Sutton was at that hotel two days before he died?"

"Right, but it's not what you're thinking. The guy from Brooklyn was mad, but I can't see a linguistics professor going back to Brooklyn, whipping up a bomb, and sneaking back to plant it."

"Forget about the linguistics professor. Just tell me everything about Wednesday, from the moment you and Sutton stepped into the place until you left."

Sigrid procured a note pad while Oscar obediently cast his mind back to Wednesday morning.

"We met in the lobby of the hotel shortly before ten. There were about fifteen of us. We met with a Ms. Baldwin, who looks about twelve but had all the facts and figures. Told us how much it would be with cocktails before and wine during, and the difference in price if we had vichysoisse instead of fruit compote with *crème fraîche*—you sure you want to hear all this?"

Sigrid nodded.

"After the menu was settled, we all trooped up to have a look at the rooms available that weekend. The first would have been too crowded, the second was okay. Typical Cool Whip on the walls."

"Cool Whip?"

"Well, Sutton called it whipped cream. *I* thought it was more like the imitation stuff: you know, huge pictures of wistful dandies in lace pushing swings full of eighteenth-century airheads in an atmosphere of giddy abandon. Gods and goddesses. Lots of frothy pastel colors. The sort of things decorators drag in to go with the gilt and red velvet." His voice became mincing as he spoke into an imaginary telephone. "I need two and a half dozen *fêtes galantes* and six *billets doux*. Cool Whip," he repeated firmly.

"So what happened next?"

"There were guys bustling around, setting up long tables, and Ms. Baldwin asked if anybody played cribbage because this was where some games company was holding its tournament Friday night. Sutton said yes, he was a contestant; and about that time the man who was running the tournament came in with Lucienne Ronay, so Ms. Baldwin introduced him to Sutton—Flit or Flyte or something like that—and presented the famed Madame Ronay to the rest of us. She informed us how honored she was that we'd selected the Maintenon and that was when the jerk from Brooklyn unctuously piped up and said, 'It seems we've also selected a very charming corner of the eighteenth century as well, Madame Ronay.

We've been admiring your pictures. Are they the originals they appear to be?'

"And John said, 'Appearances can be deceiving. This one's still wet.'

"And everybody laughed."

Nauman drained his glass. "Then Madame Ronay and what's his name went on about their business and we took another vote on whether all the arrangements were approved and the committee adjourned. That was it."

Sigrid leaned back in her chair with her elbows on the armrests and started to tent her fingertips before her as she usually did when concentrating, but the position was uncomfortable with her taped arm and she had to rest it on the table instead.

"Did you hear any of Sutton's conversation with the man from the games company?" she asked. "Did they seem to know each other?"

"Wasn't much of a conversation. What I heard of it seemed to be the usual—'How are you? Looking forward to Friday night. How many players do you expect?' That sort of thing. But you know," he mused, "it was odd."

"Yes?"

"After he and Lucienne Ronay moved off and all the time Ms. Baldwin was babbling on about how the hotel would arrange the tables for the CUNY dinner, John kept glancing over toward him, like there was something about the guy that puzzled him."

"Did he say what?"

"No. He finally shrugged as if it wasn't important and started trying to be nice to the linguistics jerk from Brooklyn College."

CHAPTER VII

An explosives expert was summing up as Sigrid entered the conference room at headquarters and Captain McKinnon waved her to an empty chair near his while the expert continued.

Judging from the crumpled napkins, soda cans and coffee

cups, and the deli smells of pastrami and onions and mustard still redolent in the air, this session had begun with lunch.

Elaine Albee and Jim Lowry were among the dozen officers seated around the long table. Sigrid had worked with the two younger detectives before and had watched with a slightly jaundiced eye the more-than-professional relationship developing between them. Lowry discreetly pantomimed that he'd get Sigrid a cup of coffee if she wished, but she shook her head and turned her attention to the bomb expert.

He had covered a chalk board with diagrams of possible ways the bomb had been wired. Precisely how the detonation had been accomplished appeared open to question, since only slivers of wires, cherry wood, and battery fragments remained after the violence of the explosion.

On the table before her lay one of the cribbage boards which the bomb squad had picked up at the Maintenon. Milled from heavy closegrained cherry, it was twelve inches long by four inches wide by three-fourths inch thick, divided lengthwise on top by a curving pattern of two parallel rows of pegging holes. One row for each player, thought Sigrid, recalling the details Tillie had told her about the game. Each row contained one hundred twenty pegging holes so that whichever player pegged a hundred and twenty-one points first would win.

The hardwood must have been difficult to work, but with a fine drill it would have been possible to hollow out quite a nice-sized chamber on the bottom. An hour or so of painstaking effort and the chamber would have become roomy enough to hold a small wad of explosive and some sort of trigger mechanism.

When everything was taped into place, a piece of cardboard was probably cut to cover the hollow and the green felt backing neatly reglued. To the casual eye there would have been nothing to distinguish that cribbage board from the one Sigrid was holding.

"No traces of radio or clock components," the bomb expert was saying, "so we don't think it was detonated by remote control or timer switches. Witnesses say play had begun about twenty minutes before the blast, so it was probably a switch that closed a simple circuit from batteries to the explosive itself. It takes about twenty minutes to play a game—in fact, some of the contestants were already beginning their second—so the switch probably involved a game-marking peg. Pull it up and zing went the springs of his heart. Or, just as easy, push it into the hole that stood for the first win and he turns out all his lights."

"Any ideas about who?" McKinnon's face was grim.

The expert shrugged. "Anybody who wants to spend an hour with a couple of technical encyclopedias could pick up the theory. And any bright ten-year-old could make the stuff with the right chemicals.

"One thing, though," he added. "Whoever did it has probably done it before. There's a certain finesse here. This bomb wasn't meant to kill more than the one or two people in direct contact with this particular cribbage board. I don't care how many nuts call in and claim to have struck a blow for the freedom of caged canaries or death to all cribbage players—"

"A private kill?" nodded McKinnon. "I wondered why the Feds weren't busting down our doors."

"He could just as easily have blown up the whole ballroom if he'd wanted to," the expert hedged.

"And you think he's done it before?" asked Elaine Albee, a fragile-looking blonde who'd made detective last year after bringing in three Central Park muggers single-handedly.

"Look, people, this stuff packs a hell of a wallop. More than an amateur realizes, so amateurs always wind up with overkill. This guy used just enough to do the job. I don't say he's a professional killer, but I do say he's experienced."

"Like a demolition worker," suggested Lowry as he doodled an exploding cribbage board on his note pad.

"Or an ex-frogman," said the expert, who'd helped mine Haiphong Harbor.

"Or one of those Mideast crazies," someone contributed.

"Or maybe," suggested someone else, "a disgruntled bank teller with a grudge against Maritime National."

"I'll run my data through the FBI's computers," said the explosives expert. "Maybe we'll get lucky."

"In the meantime," Captain McKinnon told his troops, "we do it the old-fashioned way, people—shoe leather and interviews. Peters, what've you got on Wolferman?"

"Wolferman, Zachary Augustus, of Central Park South," said Detective Peters, reading from his notes. "Caucasian male, age sixty-one, unmarried. Chairman of the board and principal stockholder in Maritime National Bank. According to his lawyer, after all the debts and some hefty bequests to distant relatives, servants, and various charities, the residual beneficiary is a cousin, Haines Froelick. The lucky Mr. Froelick will probably wind up with around six million."

With two pre-school daughters and a third child on the way,

Bernie Peters was lucky if he had six dollars left over between paychecks and his wistful sigh echoed around the room. Almost palpable in the air were visions of Caribbean resorts, sleek cars, and expensive baubles.

"The cousin was at the Maintenon last night, too, wasn't he?" asked McKinnon.

"Yes, sir. Mr. Wolferman's housekeeper said they spent a lot of time together. Met for dinner and played cribbage two or three nights a week. They were in last year's tournament out on Long Island and the year before that at one down in Raleigh. Housekeeper says they bickered a lot but that they were as close as brothers. Mr. Froelick's parents died when he was a kid and his aunt, Wolferman's mother, sort of adopted him."

"What's Froelick's financial standing?"

"I haven't gotten that far on him yet, but he has rooms at the Quill and Shutter Club about two blocks from Wolferman. I figure he's not living on food stamps."

"Quill and Shutter? Is he a writer?"

"Amateur photographer. Putters around in the club's darkroom and gets some of his pictures in group exhibitions once in a while."

Mr. Wolferman's housekeeper had proudly shown Peters a collage of hand-colored Polaroid prints of herself in her best black silk with her grandmother's cameo at her neck, a collage that had won Mr. Froelick first prize for best nonprofessional work in the club's annual exhibition four years ago.

The housekeeper was younger than her late employer and his cousin, yet she seemed to look upon them both with a sort of maternal indulgence. "Not a bit of harm in either of them," she had told the detective, wiping away genuine tears. "Who could have done such a wicked thing?"

"The housekeeper can't name a single person that didn't like him. Chauffeur says the same. Ditto the lawyer."

"Everybody has enemies," rasped McKinnon.

"Maybe the cousin was in a hurry to inherit," said Jim Lowry.

"And what does an elderly Park Avenue club man know about building bombs?" Albee objected.

"The battery for that bomb could have come from one of those instant cameras," the explosives expert reminded them.

They grudgingly agreed that Haines Froelick should receive further attention.

"What about Sutton?" Captain McKinnon asked Elaine Albee.

"Not too much yet," she answered, absently pushing a pencil through her blonde curls. "His wife's really torn up about it. She's on a heavy guilt trip because apparently she's the one who signed them up for the tournament. He taught modern history over at Vanderlyn College; she's a curator at the Feldheimer Museum up near Lincoln Center. Two kids."

"Money?"

"Just their salaries, as far as I can tell. They were out at McClellan State before coming here and I got a printout of their rap sheets."

"The protest movement," explained Albee, seeing their surprised expressions. She shuffled through the papers before her and read off some of the main dates and places: the sit-ins, unlawful assemblies, and marching without permits; more than a dozen incidences of civil disobedience on John Sutton's part, fewer by Val Sutton. Mrs. Sutton had been fined twice and acquitted of any serious charges. John Sutton had spent fifteen days in a Chicago jail for assaulting a police officer during the 1968 Democratic Convention. Their records were not unusual for committed campus activists of that period in American history, she summed up. "Both were questioned after something called the Red Snow bombing, but no charges were filed."

The bomb expert's head came up. "Red Snow? Were they involved with those bastards?"

"What's Red Snow?" Albee asked, who was in grammar school in the late Sixties.

"One of those violent underground groups that splintered off SDS around sixty-nine or seventy," he replied sourly. "Sometime in early 1970—"

"January ninth," Elaine Albee interposed from her printouts.

"January ninth," he nodded, "a group of radicals bombed a draft board in Chicago. What they hadn't bothered to check was that the draft board only took up part of the building. The other part opened onto a side street with just a flimsy wall between. Draft board on one side, day-care center on the other. Four little kids were killed outright, along with one of the teachers and a couple from the draft board. It had snowed that morning and kids were blown out into the street, mangled and bloody in the fresh white snow.

"That's what I mean about amateurs," he said grimly. "They always use too damn much. Anyhow, that's supposed to be where they got the name. Red Snow. The papers had another version, though. Said the leader, Fred Hamilton, was a Ho Chi Minh sympathizer hooked on cocaine at the time.''

"Yeah, I remember now," said one of the older detectives. "Weren't they the ones that blew themselves up in a fancy fishing lodge up around the Finger Lakes?''

"Yeah, that *was* Red Snow," McKinnon rumbled reminiscently. "Funny how you forget about things like that. It was a seven-day wonder with the papers. Beautiful young debutante.''

His younger officers were looking blank again, so he refreshed their memories.

"One of the Red Snow members was the only daughter of a wealthy stockbroker who owned a twelve-room vacation cottage on Cayuga Lake.

"He knew she'd been a member of a radical SDS chapter at college that winter, but he thought she'd broken with them and joined some sort of back-to-nature outfit. At least that's what he told the FBI and the state troopers later. I guess granola and free love sounded so much better to him than riots and sit-ins that he let them use the place that summer while he and his third wife went off to Europe for a couple of months.''

"She'd left SDS all right," said the bomb expert, picking up the story, ''but Red Snow was no love-happy commune. They'd begun to stockpile weapons and explosives and they must have had several hundred pounds of the stuff because somebody got careless one August night and the place went up like Nagasaki. They say you could see the flames as far away as Syracuse, a hundred miles away.''

"When the ashes cooled, seven bodies were found, but they were so badly burned that four of them were never positively identified. The house was built out over the lake and a couple of canoers swore they saw three people dive off an upper balcony with their clothes afire. The debutante's burned body was floating in the lake the next day, but they never found the other two.''

"Red Snow had a meltdown," someone quipped.

McKinnon scowled. "And the Suttons were mixed up with them?''

"They were questioned," said Albee. "In January and again in August of that year.''

"Probably because Sutton was active in SDS at McClellan State," said Sigrid, entering the discussion for the first time.

The others looked at her curiously. "You knew Sutton?'' asked the captain.

"A friend of mine over at Vanderlyn first met them when John Sutton was head of McClellan's SDS. As I recall, Fred Hamilton was from McClellan, too. That's probably why the Suttons were questioned."

"So Sutton's wife might know how to make a bomb," said Peters.

Albee shook her small blonde head in vigorous denial. "No way. That was no act that lady put on last night. Besides, Sutton's not the one with the six-million estate."

"Keep an open mind," growled the captain. "He could have been carrying insurance. Check it. And check what the marriage was really like before you say 'no way' again. We're looking for somebody with bomb-making experience and for my money, an SDS background puts Mrs. Sutton on the charts. You've already said the tournament was her idea."

"My friend says he and Sutton were at the Maintenon on Wednesday," Sigrid said quietly. "They were actually in the same ballroom."

A babble of questions erupted just as a uniformed sergeant put his head in the door. "Captain? There's some guy here from the Navy to see you about the Maintenon bombing."

The captain heaved himself to his feet. "Take over, Lieutenant Harald," he said and went out to see what the Navy wanted.

CHAPTER VIII

For the next quarter hour, Sigrid passed along to her colleagues the background information Nauman had given her about Sutton's McClellan days, his current standing at Vanderlyn and his brief visit to the Maintenon Hotel on Wednesday. In return, she heard from them the mostly nonconclusive findings the various forensics teams had delivered earlier that morning.

The sling on her arm elicited questions, and she briefly described her confrontation with the assailant she'd shot the night before. It was the first time any of them had ever seen the austere lieutenant without her hair severely bound. The blue scarf did not restrain her hair as tightly as bobby pins and already a few stray tendrils had feathered around the strong lines of her face.

Some of the older men still had residual misgivings and resentments about a female lieutenant working homicides; but Tillie was universally liked and, as his partner, Sigrid was the automatic recipient of spontaneous condolence. Their warmth and sincerity made Sigrid momentarily tongue-tied, but for once— perhaps influenced by the sling and the blue scarf—they seemed to attribute her stammering acknowledgments to depth of feeling and not to the coldhearted detachment most tagged her with.

Tillie was one of their own, and since Sigrid was the most directly affected by his injury, it was taken for granted that she'd be running this case.

Whom she'd be partnered with until Tillie's recovery was another matter.

Depending upon whom you asked, Tillie was either a saint or a simpleton and not just because he worked with Lieutenant Harald without complaint, but because he also insisted that the lieutenant had a sense of humor and a human side somewhere under all that ice and efficiency. But Tillie could say what he liked: it had not gone unnoticed that Lieutenant Harald's frozen reserve seemed to make even Captain McKinnon uncomfortable at times.

Before anyone was forced to throw himself on the barbed wire, the captain returned with a young naval officer in a dark blue uniform, his black-billed white cap tucked under his arm.

He was not tall, an inch or so short of six feet in fact, but he was well-built: wide shoulders, slim hips, and an easy way of carrying himself that blended military discipline with athletic vitality. In his late twenties, the young officer had deep-set brown eyes, a lopsided smile, well-defined jaw and straw-colored hair a few shades darker than the bright gold stripes on his uniform.

An electric awareness immediately flickered through the other four women seated at the table.

"This is Lieutenant Alan Knight of Naval Intelligence," said McKinnon. "He'll be sitting in on our investigation because of Commander Dixon."

An attractive young man, Sigrid noted clinically, and was amused to see a slight scowl appear on Jim Lowry's face as he became aware of Elaine Albee's cuter than usual friendliness when the captain introduced her to the newcomer. In addition to Albee's flashing dimples, Sigrid noticed that Detective Urbanska was smoothing her curls and that the two women from the bomb squad sat just a shade more provocatively in their chairs.

Her inner amusement deepened as Lieutenant Knight shifted his hat to his left hand and a broad gold wedding band gleamed on that all-important third finger. A nearly inaudible female sigh swept the room and suddenly everyone settled back to normal. As hormonal tensions eased, they were replaced by the ordinary wariness that arises whenever a different authority meddles in what is perceived to be NYPD affairs. It was bad enough that the explosion had the FBI waiting in the wings. Who needed the Navy as well?

Lieutenant Knight seemed to sense their wariness and tried to ~sure them that the Navy did not mean to interfere with civilian ~atters.

"Frankly, Commander Dixon doesn't appear to be the bomber's target," he told them, with a slight drawl. "All the same, she *does* carry a high security clearance. It's probably sheer coincidence and plain bad luck for the commander that the bomb went off so close to her, still—"

He shrugged and flashed that boyish, lopsided smile again. "The Navy sure would appreciate it if you'd let me tag along."

"Shucks, gee willikers, yes indeedy," Jim Lowry mimicked softly, under cover of the captain's rumbled acquiescence.

Elaine Albee kicked him.

"What's the commander's condition this morning?" she asked.

"Not good. She's still in critical condition. Her right side caught the main force of the blast. If she lives—" Knight shook his head pessimistically. "I never met her, but they say she was real attractive."

Elaine Albee, who knew she was pretty and enjoyed that knowledge, suppressed a superstitious shudder, imagining what a bomb could do to smooth skin and fragile bones.

"Lieutenant Harald will coordinate our investigation," McKinnon said, making it official. "We're shorthanded right now, Knight, so as long as the Navy wants you to look over our shoulder, why don't you work with her?"

"Fine with me," nodded Lieutenant Knight, grinning at Sigrid.

Briskly, Sigrid ran down the list of priorities, noting which ought to be followed up on immediately and which could wait. "We need a list of everyone connected with the tournament," she told Albee. "Get enough copies so that Mrs. Sutton, Marian Tildon, and—does Commander Dixon have any immediate family here?" She turned to Knight.

He shook his head. "According to her file, her next-of-kin's a cousin in Miami."

"It's unlikely he can help—"

"She," Lieutenant Knight corrected. "The cousin's a woman, as I recall."

"In any event, we might as well mail her a copy, too. See if she recognizes any of the names."

Peters and his partner, Matt Eberstadt, were told to continue looking into Zachary Wolferman's life with an emphasis on his cousin, Haines Froelick. Albee and Lowry were to return to the Maintenon and continue questioning the staff and anyone connected with the cribbage tournament who might still be there.

"Don't forget your report on last night," McKinnon reminded her as the meeting broke up. "They got a fistful of positive IDs on your assailant."

Sending the others on ahead, Sigrid returned to her own office to fill out the report required every time an officer discharged a weapon. She was struggling to insert the form into her typewriter with one hand when Lieutenant Knight appeared in her doorway.

"Can I help you with that?"

"I thought you went with Albee and Lowry," Sigrid said inanely.

"Didn't Captain McKinnon mean for me to stick with you?" He watched her clumsiness with the return mechanism. "I'm a right good typist. Why don't you let me do that?"

Without waiting for permission, he swung the typewriter around to his side of the desk, seated himself in the nearest chair and rollered the forms into the machine with a businesslike air.

Bemused, Sigrid leaned back in her own chair and gave him her name, rank, and all the other required data. Observing the tilt of his fair head, she realized again how handsome the Navy officer was and, almost against her will, found herself comparing him with Oscar Nauman.

Half as old and probably half as bright, she thought loyally, subconsciously defending Nauman against nebulous threats, completely unaware that loyalty was in question.

In a clear crisp voice, she dictated her account of the previous night's shooting, signed the forms in triplicate, and dropped them in her Out basket. At least Knight hadn't asked a lot of dumb questions about the shooting incident. Did that indicate tact or apathy?

"I'll have a car sent around," she told him crisply. "You do drive, don't you?"

"Sure, but that won't be necessary," he said. "I've got a driver waiting."

The baby-faced young sailor who hopped out from behind the wheel of the black Chrysler and held the rear door for them looked barely old enough to steer a homemade go-cart, much less hold a legal driver's license. He saluted smartly and sir'd and ma'am'd them when told where to go, but it was immediately apparent by the way he inched out into it that New York's free-wheeling traffic intimidated him dreadfully. He tried to hug the curb, ran afoul of a compulsory right-turn lane before he'd gone two blocks, and was freshly surprised each time his lane was blocked by double-parkers. Instead of swerving to the left as everyone else did, he would put on his blinker and wait hopefully for someone courteous enough to let him in. Since double-parkers were as plentiful as courteous drivers were rare, it began to look like a long trip up to the Maintenon.

"Try not to watch," Lieutenant Knight advised Sigrid in a low voice as the timid yeoman flinched from one speeding cab perilously into the path of another. "My regular driver's on liberty this weekend. Sorry."

"Quite all right," Sigrid said through gritted teeth and tried to find humor in the irony that made a slow and supercautious driver infinitely more terrifying than Nauman's breakneck recklessness.

"What can you tell me about Commander Dixon's background?" she asked.

"Born in Florida, daughter of a deceased Navy chief, graduated from college there," he answered promptly. "OCS at Newport, tours of duty in Japan, San Diego, Norfolk, and D.C. Stationed here in New York a little over two years."

"No, I meant her work. You said she holds a high security clearance. What's her field?"

This time the answer came less promptly. "Communications."

"Communications?"

"Messages from various commands back and forth," he said vaguely. "That sort of thing."

"In code perhaps?" she probed.

"Cryptography, yes," he admitted.

Sigrid waited in silence. She had found that as a rule most people felt compelled to fill an expectant silence and certainly became ill-at-ease if it stretched out too long. Lieutenant Knight merely smiled and returned her cool-eyed gaze with bland serenity until a raucous car horn behind cursed their young driver for drawing to a stop while the traffic light ahead was still yellow.

"You wouldn't care to elaborate on exactly what Commander Dixon does?" Sigrid asked, nettled.

"I don't think so. After all, it isn't important, is it? She was injured last night by sheer coincidence."

"So far as you know," she gibed.

He nodded agreeably. "So far as we know."

"Escorted there, I'm told, by a Russian."

"A superannuated, lower-echelon member of a trade delegation, Lieutenant. The Walker case notwithstanding, we *do* keep an eye on these things," he said lightly. "Which is why I'm along today."

Unnerved by all the horns that urged him not to block the lane before a light was actually red, the yeoman misjudged a yellow and edged into the intersection on the bumper of the car ahead. The light changed to red; the car in front did not move; crosstown traffic entered the fray and soon the intersection was so jammed that it took two more greens for traffic to sort itself out. By the time they drew up to the entrance of the Maintenon, the sailor's baby face was drenched in perspiration and he was somewhat wobbly on his legs as he opened the door for them.

"That'll be all for the day," Lieutenant Knight told him kindly.

"Oh thank you, sir!" he said with such fervent gratitude that Sigrid thought he was going to shake the lieutenant's hand.

CHAPTER IX

Inside the Maintenon's spacious lobby, all was discreet serenity. Guests came and went beneath the enormous crystal chandelier, apparently unaffected by the violent tragedy which had struck the previous night on the next floor. It was a tribute to the professionalism of Lucienne Ronay's staff. Fire trucks, ambulances, and a dozen or more police cars had responded to the alarms and after the dead and wounded had been removed and the emergency personnel departed, her housecleaning crew had swooped down upon the scene and labored through the remainder of the night to tidy away all traces of the disaster.

They were not allowed to touch anything in the d'Aubigné Room itself, of course. Cooperating with the police, Madame Ronay had personally ordered the blue velvet rope that now looped through brass stanchions and blocked the hall that led to the devastated ballroom. A few feet beyond, folding wooden panels decorated with frothy pastoral scenes screened the entrance to the room from casual view.

Molly Baldwin was passing near the main desk as Sigrid inquired directions and she introduced herself and escorted them upstairs. Madame Ronay's young assistant looked her full twenty-three years this afternoon. Her face was pale and drawn and there were dark circles under her eyes.

"Guess you didn't get much sleep last night," Lieutenant Knight said.

"Only four or five hours," admitted Miss Baldwin, leading them past the velvet ropes, past the ornate screens, and down the wide hall to the d'Aubigné Room. "It was hectic but I suppose it could have been much worse."

Indeed, the actual damage to the elegant ballroom was minor, considering the carnage the small bomb had wreaked. Except for the rear quarter of the room, in that corner surrounding Table 5, the room showed only the usual morning-after ravages: the empty glasses, dirty ashtrays, lipstick-smeared napkins and other detritus that a large crowd always leaves behind.

There were signs of panic and confusion, however, in overturned chairs and in the playing cards scattered over the deep plush carpet.

Table 5 itself was charred and splintered and Sigrid gazed in silence at the dark splotches where torn bodies had lain bleeding—Zachary Wolferman and John Sutton on the end nearest the corner walls, she had been told; Tillie and Commander Dixon next to the dead men. The long linen cloth that had covered their table was bundled into a scorched and sodden heap upon the floor.

"We were lucky about fire," Miss Baldwin told them softly. "One of our busboys put it out with a hand extinguisher, so there was no water damage."

"Where were you when the bomb exploded?" asked Sigrid as she began to orient herself in relation to the events of the previous evening.

"Over by the far table where the refreshments were."

"Were you looking in this direction at that moment?"

"Not really. I guess I was trying to watch everything and make sure it all kept moving smoothly."

Sigrid walked over to where Molly Baldwin had stood last night and examined the room from the new perspective. "And you don't remember anything out of the ordinary about Table 5?"

"No," the girl said quickly, "not at all."

"What about John Sutton?"

Miss Baldwin's face went blank. "Who?"

"One of the men killed last night. You had met him on Wednesday. Don't you remember?"

"I had?" She tugged at a short brown curl behind her right ear, a nervous mannerism probably left over from childhood; then her face brightened. "Oh yes! One of the professors from the City University. I had forgotten. *That* was why his face looked familiar!"

"When?"

"Why, when I saw him again last night," she said slowly.

"At Table 5?"

"I'm sorry, Lieutenant, I just don't remember. There were so many people here. Over five hundred. You know how it is—you see a face and there's something familiar about it, but heavens! It could be a bus driver or a bank teller—someone you recognize but that you've never actually talked to, you know?"

"And you must meet lots of people, working in a big hotel like this," Lieutenant Knight encouraged.

"Yes, I do," she said, turning to him gratefully from the more intimidating Lieutenant Harald.

"How long have you lived up North?" he asked.

"Why, just since Christmas." She smiled at him and her fingers twined around that same brown curl. "I thought I'd lost all my accent."

Sigrid began to suspect that Lieutenant Knight was going to be a distinct handicap in their investigation if every woman they questioned reacted to him like this. She curtly broke in to ask Miss Baldwin to describe preparations for the cribbage tournament.

Her professional capacity required, Molly Baldwin gave a fairly concise recap of the last three or four days, including her mix-up with the pairings and the cribbage board stolen from the display case on Thursday. Young and inexperienced as she might be, Miss Baldwin was quick enough to grasp the significance of both incidents.

"Which happened first?" asked Sigrid, clearing a space at one of the cluttered tables for her notebook. Her bandaged arm made simple actions difficult.

"I'm not sure. Gus— He's our calligrapher and visual artist, whatever we need in the line of place cards and posters and things like that. We can ask him when he sent up the pairings display, but I think it was sometime before lunch. Mr. Flythe didn't notice it right away and I'd forgotten it was supposed to be confidential. We set up the display cases on Thursday morning and a few hours later—about three o'clock, I think—we noticed the missing board."

"The pairings were where? In here or out in the hall?"

"In here. If you like, I'll get you a list of all the staff who worked in this room on Thursday. That's what's important, isn't it? You want to know who could have read where Mr. Wolferman or Professor Sutton were supposed to sit, don't you?"

"It's a place to start, Ms. Baldwin." Sigrid flipped her notebook shut and thrust it into her jacket pocket.

By now, the forensic crews had taken away everything of significance in the way of splintered cribbage board, bomb fragments, and the like, so Sigrid saw no reason to object when Madame Ronay appeared in the doorway with one of her accountants and a claims investigator from the hotel's insurers and requested permission for the two men to assess the damages. She did find it interesting that Madame Ronay, a female executive accustomed to male underlings, should automatically address her request to Lieutenant Knight.

Just as automatic, too, were her flirtatious manner, the way she gazed up at him through lowered eyelashes, her light touch on his sleeve, and the delicate perfume that enveloped them both when she murmured, "It is barbaric to think of money when so many were hurt last night, but a great hotel is like life, *n'est-ce pas?* And life also goes on, no?"

"Yes, ma'am. But I'm afraid you've confused me with Lieutenant Harald," said Lieutenant Knight, gesturing toward Sigrid with his hat. "She's in charge here. I just represent the Navy's interests."

Beautiful, self-assured women always made Sigrid sharply conscious of how little she knew of clothes and cosmetics. She stiffened as Lucienne Ronay's hazel eyes swept over her, coolly assessing her thin figure, her shapeless slacks, her scruffy corduroy jacket, her Woolworth scarf.

Their eyes met briefly, but before Sigrid could make her own assessment, the lovely Frenchwoman exclaimed, "But how silly of me! Always the uniform makes me think this one is in charge."

A bewitching Gallic shrug of her shoulders invited them to share her amusement over minor failings.

Young Molly Baldwin smiled dutifully, as did the cowed accountant; the insurance adjuster and Lieutenant Alan Knight were indulgent.

"A natural mistake," Sigrid said dryly. "And to answer your question, we've almost finished here. In fact, as far as I'm concerned, your people can come in—shall we say tomorrow?"

"Je vous dis un grand merci, Lieutenant. See to it, please, Molly. You cannot *know* how unhappy it makes me to see my poor d'Aubigné Room so *dérangé."* She turned back to Alan Knight as to the sun. "But what you said before, Lieutenant, I do not understand. Why has the Navy an interest in our bomb?"

Knight explained. Madame Ronay clicked her tongue sympathetically upon hearing that the wounded commander was a woman who might be permanently maimed if she survived, and Molly Baldwin paled when he told them grimly that the doctors were pessimistic about saving Commander Dixon's right arm.

"Were you here when the bomb went off?" Sigrid asked Madame Ronay.

"Alas, *non!* I welcomed everyone. I wished them all *bonne chance* and then I left. The Contessa di Biagio had arranged a small dinner party in her suite and I was expected there. But when they came and told me what had happened, I returned at once. *Quel dommage!* They told me that two were dead and many hurt."

"Did you know either of the dead men?"

"Monsieur Wolferman, only slightly. You understand, Lieutenant, three hotels keep me most busy. I have little time to play. Yet there are parties to which I must go, dinners I must attend, and Monsieur Wolferman also, I think. Two years ago, at a dinner for the governor, we sat next to each other. Since then, I see him here or there at similar places and we speak, but I do not say that I *know* him."

Her words were for Sigrid, yet her beautiful eyes kept straying to Lieutenant Knight. If the columnists could be trusted, Lucienne Ronay was at least twenty years older than he. Sigrid had heard that skillful makeup, careful hairdressing, and well-designed clothes could take years off a woman's appearance; but looking at Lucienne Ronay's ash-blonde hair, her flawless skin, the lush curves subtly enhanced by a designer dress of off-white cashmere, it was hard to realize that the hotel owner was almost as old as her own mother. Anne was unquestionably attractive, but no one would underestimate her age by fifteen years.

"What about Professor Sutton?" Sigrid asked.

Madame Ronay started to answer negatively, but Molly Baldwin tactfully reminded her of the CUNY group's Wednesday morning visit.

"Ah, was *that* Professor Sutton? But what a loss! So young and so handsome."

Molly Baldwin looked slightly shocked and the Frenchwoman gave a self-deprecating smile. "When you approach the half-century, *ma petite*, you will understand better that the loss of any handsome man is always reason to mourn."

Her eyes swept over the accountant and the insurance adjuster and rested provocatively on Alan Knight's clean-cut features. It was like seeing all those gossip columns come to life before his eyes and he laughed outright at this sample of the famous Lucienne Ronay outrageousness.

"No, no, no," she scolded, although clearly pleased by his pleasure. "We are very naughty to make light at such a time. Lieutenant Harald is not amused and she is right. And now, *mes amis*, I must fly. Already I am late for a meeting at my Montespan. Lieutenant Harald, Lieutenant Knight—please, whatever you wish, do not hesitate to ask. I have told my staff they are to give you all the assistance you need. And Molly, too, will—ah, but no! Molly must go straight home and go to bed and not get up till all those horrid circles are gone from below her pretty eyes."

With a word to her accountant, another to the adjuster, and a dazzling smile for Lieutenant Knight, Lucienne Ronay swept from the room, off to the smallest of her three Manhattan hotels where she intended to learn precisely why the Montespan had received two letters of complaint in the past month. Heads would roll.

As the victim in the last nine months of similar interrogations, Molly Baldwin did not envy her Montespan colleagues; and, her employer's words to the contrary, she knew she was expected to remain at the Maintenon this afternoon for as long as Lieutenant Harald needed her. No matter that her nerve ends were screaming for release or that her body felt as if she were moving through deep water. Instead, she must force herself to smile pleasantly at the two investigators, to wait expectantly until they had finished poking and prying.

"We'll check with Lowry and Albee, see what they've come up with so far," Sigrid told Lieutenant Knight, "and then I want to have a talk with this Ted Flythe of Graphic Games. If Ms. Baldwin can give us his address . . .?"

"Certainly," Molly replied, "but you don't need his address. He's just across the landing. In the Bontemps Room. Didn't someone tell you? They decided not to cancel the tournament."

CHAPTER X

"It surprised the hell out of me, too, Lieutenant," Ted Flythe admitted frankly. He sat on an imitation eighteenth-century settee upholstered in mauve silk and gazed at the nearly four hundred people engrossed in their cards and hunched over their cribbage boards.

According to a small plaque near the gold-and-white enameled double doors, the Bontemps Room was named for one of Madame de Maintenon's godparents. It was slightly smaller but just as ornate as the damaged d'Aubigné Room. The walls were covered with murals meant to depict the court of Louis XIV at play; elaborately bewigged and silk-suited courtiers sported beneath the trees with equally bewigged and lavishly dressed ladies. The ceiling far overhead simulated a celestial blue sky enhanced by puffy white clouds and interspersed with golden sunbursts from which depended brass and crystal chandeliers.

It was a room meant for formal music, for dancers in tuxedos and jewel-toned taffetas, for the discreet clink of champagne glasses and witty repartee. It was not quite the setting for these cribbage players casually dressed in corduroy or plaid wool slacks and autumn-colored sweaters, who kept the ventilating system busy dispersing clouds of cigarette smoke, and who broke the room's pastel serenity with smothered laughter and occasional raucous cries of "fifteen four and there ain't no more!"

"I held a meeting with the players this morning, told them I was authorized to refund all the entrance fees, but they wanted to go ahead with the tournament," said Mr. Flythe. "Not everybody. Not those who were hurt, of course; and a good number were too frightened to stay, but look at this!"

He gestured toward the tables. "Over three hundred and fifty people! Hell of a note, isn't it? You'd think they'd be afraid their board might be next."

The mauve silk couch and several matching side chairs formed a separate sitting area near the front of the large room. With the table and extra chairs Detectives Albee and Lowry had rounded up, it made a suitable place to winnow out and question witnesses.

They had just begun on Mr. Flythe when Sigrid entered with Lieutenant Knight and Molly Baldwin. Handing Flythe over to her, they had plunged back into the crowd, using newly revised seating charts to locate promising witnesses of last night's events.

"I suppose some of the contestants came a long distance," suggested Sigrid. "Perhaps had hotel or plane reservations they couldn't change easily?"

"Partly that," the tournament director conceded, "but I think it's mainly that they like the excitement. Most of the players are from the metropolitan area. They can go home by bus or subway. It's not as if they have to stay; but damned if they didn't want to, even though I made it clear that we'd have to reduce the prize money in proportion to how many pulled out.

"We've had to cut back on how many games they'll play, too. Instead of best out of seven, it's now three out of five to advance. That should finish us up in time."

While Mr. Flythe spoke of the procedural changes made in

order to bring the tournament to a close on schedule tomorrow evening, Sigrid studied him unobtrusively, remembering Nauman's account of John Sutton's puzzled glances back at the man he'd met on Wednesday.

There was more than a suggestion of a traveling salesman on the lookout for a likely farmer's daughter about Mr. Flythe, a slight arrogance in his lazy way of assessing every woman as if she wore no clothes. In his late thirties or early forties, Sigrid judged. No gray in his dark hair or beard but his hairline was receding a bit at the temples and there was a slight puffiness beneath his sleepy brown eyes. Bedroom eyes, her Grandmother Lattimore would have called them. If his chin line had begun to blur, that was hidden by the short beard which was clipped into a modified Vandyke point.

His clothes fit well, too: there was no tightness in the collar of his crisp blue-striped shirt, no straining at the waist of his custom-tailored navy blue blazer or gray wool pants.

If Alan Knight embodied the all-American lustiness of sunny haystacks and bosky dells, Ted Flythe was the *comme ci comme cq* of a sensual blues piano in a cocktail lounge on a rainy night; and his vibrations were just as strong as Knight's.

And he knew it, too, Sigrid suspected, noting how Molly Baldwin had instinctively chosen the empty space on the settee and how she sat closer than was required, just as the female members of the Graphic Games crew seemed compelled to consult their superior more often than one would have thought necessary.

"Perhaps we should finish this interview somewhere quieter," Sigrid suggested, when a blazered girl approached for a third time since they began talking.

"Sorry, Lieutenant. This is her first tournament, too." He beckoned the girl nearer. "Look, Marcie, I can't answer your questions right now, but I tell you what: you have any problems, you ask Barbara over there. She's an old pro at this, okay?"

"Okay," the girl pouted.

Sigrid was interested in Flythe's unexpected revelation. "Your first tournament, Mr. Flythe? You haven't been with Graphic Games long?"

"Only since the end of the summer," he admitted, watching Marcie's sulky retreat.

"And before that?"

"You name it, I've probably done it," he answered easily. "From waiting tables in high school to selling refrigerators to Eskimos."

"And in any of your varied jobs, had you ever met John Sutton before?"

"Who?"

"One of the men who died in last night's explosion," Sigrid said sharply, wondering why no one connected with the hotel seemed willing to admit having met Sutton. "You saw him, you even spoke with him in the d'Aubigné Room on Wednesday morning."

Ted Flythe stroked his beard into a sharp point; the lids of his sleepy eyes drooped lower. "I didn't realize it was the same man," he said. "No, if I ever met him before, I don't remember. Why?"

"No reason, really," she said. "Someone in the group thought that Professor Sutton seemed to have recognized you from a previous meeting."

"It's possible, I suppose. I've been all over. West Coast, East Coast, and everywhere in between, including a few years after college when I led tour groups around Europe. Maybe he was on one of those tours."

"Maybe," Sigrid conceded and made a mental note to mention that point when she spoke with Mrs. Sutton. "What college, if I may ask?"

"Oh, a little denominational school out in Michigan that you probably never even heard of. Carlyle Union. It's defunct now."

Lieutenant Knight had listened quietly until then and now leaned forward to ask, "Excuse me, Mr. Flythe, but were you ever in the military?"

"Nope. That's one experience I missed."

Sigrid paused, expecting Knight to pursue his question. When he settled back in his chair without doing so, she said, "For the record, Mr. Flythe, had you met any of the other victims? Zachary Wolferman, Commander Dixon, or Detective Tildon?"

"For the record, no, Lieutenant." He hesitated. "I heard that one of those seriously hurt was a policeman. Did you know him?"

"Yes," she said tightly and the curtness of her tone froze the conventional expressions of sympathy Flythe started to voice. "Ms. Baldwin has told us about the seating chart being brought up early from the calligrapher's. How did you arrive at those pairings?"

"Not me," said Flythe. "It's all done by computer. There's a space on the entry blank where a contestant can list anybody he doesn't want to play against—his wife, say, or a friend—whoever he's traveling with. That's so both of them have an equal chance of staying alive." Hearing what he'd just said, Flythe grimaced. "Bad choice of words. Sorry. What I mean is, if two friends play each other, one of them is definitely going to be eliminated, right? Whereas if each plays a stranger, there's a good chance, or at least a possibility, that both can advance."

Logical, thought Sigrid. "So your computer ensures that spouses or friends don't play each other."

"At least not in the early rounds. Towards the end it can't be helped. Of course, we have consolation games, too. The main tournament will go on until tomorrow night, but in another hour or so we'll begin a sort of mini-tournament for people who've been eliminated so far. Tonight we'll start a couple of smaller pools where losers can buy in for five or ten dollars. Our policy is to let as many people keep playing as long as they want to."

"When were the first pairings made?"

"The deadline for entries was two weeks ago. Our corporate office handles all that. I got the printout Monday and sent it over to Miss Baldwin here—was it that afternoon, Molly?"

The girl had been following his every word and Sigrid noted how she colored faintly at the intimacy of his smile, recovered quickly, and said, "The messenger brought it Tuesday morning and I hand-carried it straight down to our graphics studio with a rush order. They sent it back up sometime Thursday morning because it was there in the hall when I came by after lunch and that's when I set it inside the d'Aubigné Room."

"Which means that anyone passing through the hall could have seen it and learned who was to sit where for the opening round," Sigrid mused.

"Yes," Molly Baldwin nodded. "Ted—Mr. Flythe *told* me it was to be kept confidential, but I forgot to tell them downstairs and—"

She looked so miserable that Flythe reached over to pat her hand consolingly. "Don't blame yourself, Molly. For my money, the bomber probably didn't know where to put it till just before we started last night."

"Why do you say that, Mr. Flythe?" Lieutenant Knight asked.

In answer, Flythe caught the eye of one of the Graphic Games crew and signaled for her to come over.

"This is Kelly Underhill," he told them. "Keeper of our cribbage boards. Now, Kelly, I want you to tell Lieutenant Harald exactly what you told me this morning."

"Sure, Mr. Flythe," beamed the freckle-faced youngster, thrilled to be in the spotlight. Stretching out her shining moment as long as possible, she told her audience that she was entrusted with keeping tabs on the expensive cherry cribbage boards. "The losers can keep the cards if they like, but they have to return the boards because they cost too much to give away."

Graphic Games had provided two hundred and seventy-five boards packed in eleven boxes. That was twenty-five to the box, she explained, and they were packed in five rows with five boards to each stack so it was easy to keep a running count.

"I gave Mr. Flythe three boards on Thursday to put in those glass display cases and when one of them got stolen, I gave him another board to make up for it; so that left me with two hundred and seventy-one.

"Then last night, we had two hundred fifty set out to play with, which left me with twenty-one boards, see?"

She waited for their confirmation, and receiving Knight's nod, went on eagerly.

"Well, this morning, when the players decided to go on with the tournament and the policeman in the other room said we could move our stuff, we packed up all the boards and brought them in here. Some of the pegs got lost—we had to send over to the office for extras—but I found two hundred and seventy boards. Of course two of them were broken—from the explosion, I guess.

"I didn't think anything about having that many because I knew one of them'd had the bomb in it; but Nancy Kaiser knew I was worried about keeping up with all the boards—anything missing comes out of my pocket, see?—and she told me that the police had taken one of them for comparison tests or something."

She held out the crumpled receipt her friend had been given by someone in Forensics. Sigrid examined it and then handed it back.

"Well, don't you *see?*" said the girl. "After one board got stolen, I had two hundred and seventy-four. There're three on display, one board blew up and the police took one, so I should have only two hundred and sixty-nine." She stopped triumphantly.

"I do see," said Sigrid, leaning back in the gilt-legged chair, conscious of pain returning to her wounded arm. "Whoever stole the first cribbage board brought it back again. Undoubtedly with the bomb inside."

"And switched boards *after* the tables were set up," concluded Ted Flythe.

"Which was when?"

"Late Friday afternoon," Kelly Underhill replied, hurt by Lieutenant Harald's lack of response to her clever discovery. "We finished around five."

"Then I locked the doors myself," said Molly Baldwin, "and they weren't unlocked until I opened the service door at seven so the stewards could prepare the hospitality table."

"When were the hall doors unlocked?"

"At seven-thirty."

"So it would appear that the switch was made sometime between seven and nine," said Sigrid.

"Assuming no one from Graphic Games was involved," observed Lieutenant Knight.

Before Ted Flythe could take exception to his insinuation, Sigrid felt someone touch her on the shoulder and heard a merry voice say, *"Ciao*, Sigrid! I *thought* that was you."

CHAPTER XI

Despite a round face, blonde bob and frivolous rhinestone-studded, harlequin-shaped, turquoise eyeglasses, Jill Gill was a serious entomologist. She wrote successful, respected children's books; had provided Roman Tramegra with enough material on caterpillar life cycles to write two articles and six fillers; and was, if one could judge by her presence here in the Bontemps Room, a dedicated cribbage player. She was also irrepressibly interested in the personal lives of her friends and artless enough to beam at Sigrid and ask, "Why hasn't Oscar brought you to see me lately? He's not sulking because you and Roman have moved in together, is he?"

Alan Knight's eyebrows lifted in amusement and Elaine Albee was fascinated.

The police detective had approached Dr. Gill routinely, solely because the woman had played at the far end of Table 5 the night before. That she had also netted someone personally acquainted with Lieutenant Harald was totally unexpected.

The lieutenant was something of an enigma to Albee. Harald was known to be dedicated and efficient, with a cool, logical approach to her work and an unemotional detachment that discouraged any feminine confidences. She was also known to be unmarried and it was assumed in the department that she led a chaste and probably profoundly dull existence. Detective Tildon seemed to like her, but then Tillie liked everybody. Yet even he could add nothing to their pool of common gossip the few times Lieutenant Harald's name came up in idle discussion.

Driving up to the Maintenon earlier in the afternoon, Jim Lowry had expressed the usual judgment: "When Harald got cut last night, what do you think they found—blood or ice water?"

Elaine Albee, warm and lively and full of youthful charity, had defended the older officer. "I think she was upset about Tillie. She just doesn't parade her feelings."

Now, as the ramifications of Dr. Gill's words sank in, Albee found herself looking at Lieutenant Harald in a different light. She doesn't have to be that plain, Albee realized. With a good haircut, makeup, a few bright colors . . . I bet her figure's not all that bad in better clothes and—

Lieutenant Harald's slate gray eyes met her speculative stare and Elaine flushed as guiltily as if the lieutenant could read her thoughts.

Now the tall officer stood up and said, "Hello, Jill."

Dr. Jill Gill was another of Oscar Nauman's unexpected, wide-ranging friendships and Sigrid Harald generally enjoyed the entomologist's sunny, good-natured prattling. But not on duty. And certainly not with Alan Knight here to draw unwarranted assumptions or Albee to gape at her as if she suddenly suspected a secret life of wanton debauchery.

"Oh my dear! What's happened to your arm? A break? How awful!" exclaimed Dr. Gill. Her eyes narrowed with concern behind the rhinestone-encrusted glasses.

"Nothing serious," Sigrid replied evenly, even though her arm throbbed wretchedly now and she knew she should look around for some water to take another pain tablet. "Detective Albee, why don't you and Dr. Gill sit over at the table and begin on her statement," she directed frostily. "I'll be right there."

"Certainly, Lieutenant. Dr. Gill?"

As they moved away, she heard Jill ask anxiously, "Was Sigrid shot? Stabbed? Have you worked with her long?"

She could only hope that Elaine Albee would remember this

was a witness to a crime and confine her own questions to events of the previous evening.

Before following, she turned back to Ted Flythe and Molly Baldwin. "We'd like a few copies of your original pairings and the seating chart, Mr. Flythe. We'll need to ask the victims' survivors if they recognize any of the names."

"Sure, Lieutenant. Molly, could you Xerox the one on the display easel?"

"I'm afraid it got knocked over and stepped on," Miss Baldwin answered doubtfully. "Detective Albee has it right now, but it's awfully torn."

"No hurry," said Sigrid. "We'll work with it for now and perhaps you can supply us with fresh copies tomorrow?"

Flythe nodded and Sigrid asked Molly Baldwin, "Is your calligrapher here today?"

"Yes, he's in the studio. I'll have him come up."

"Why don't I go down?" offered Lieutenant Knight. "It'll give me a chance to look over the hotel, trace the board's route back up, see who had access."

"That might be helpful," Sigrid agreed crisply, obscurely relieved that he would not be sitting in on her session with the very talkative Jill Gill.

"I can only stay a minute," warned Dr. Gill as Sigrid approached. "We finished our round early, but they'll be starting again soon." She smoothed her long red-and-black striped skirt around her short legs. "Five minutes late and it's an automatic forfeit."

"I won't keep you," Sigrid assured her. "Just tell us what happened last night."

"Okay, but if you expect the trained-scientist-notes-all shtick, forget it," she said, brushing back the blonde bangs that threatened to flop over her turquoise glasses.

"I was a little late getting here. You know me. Missed out entirely on the hot canapés and barely had time to grab a glass of wine and find my place before La Ronay gave her little welcome speech and left."

"Did you pay any attention to the people at the far end of your table?"

"Not really. I looked them over, of course. Recognized Professor Sutton. Couldn't put a name to him, but I remembered his face from seeing him interviewed on television last spring. Sounded intelligent. Shame to lose him. Vanderlyn College, wasn't he? Do you suppose Oscar knew him?''

"They were friends," Sigrid said, without expression. "Did you notice anything out of the ordinary? Anything at all?''

"Not really. Well, yes, come to think of it. The woman sitting beside him—Commander Dixon? Very attractive. Her hair was completely white—bleached, do you suppose?'' she wondered aloud. "Because her face was very youthful. At that distance anyhow. I noticed because she kept looking in my direction instead of at the front.''

"You thought she knew you?''

"Oh no, she wasn't looking *at* me. Merely in my direction. Past me, in fact. Toward the refreshment table. But the only people down toward this end were the busboys, the head steward, and that tall, brown-haired girl who just left with that absolutely gorgeous Navy officer. Is he a hare or one of your hounds?''

"He's working with us," Sigrid nodded, "but—''

"My dear, if I were twenty years younger!'' Her blue eyes twinkled at Elaine Albee behind the rakish swoop of her glasses. "Now *you're* young enough to set your cap for him,'' she grinned.

Albee grinned back at the bubbly scientist. "I'm afraid he's already taken, Dr. Gill. You missed his wedding band.''

"A bad sign,'' Jill Gill agreed. "Men who wear their wedding rings always feel married. Too bad.''

"Could we get back to last night?'' Sigrid asked patiently. "Commander Dixon kept looking toward the refreshment table and Ms. Baldwin, and then—?''

"Or the head steward,'' Dr. Gill reminded her. "He was there, too. Steward . . . Navy? Perhaps he was a mess steward on her ship once. Or do women officers serve on ships yet?''

"Jill, please?''

"All right, all right,'' the older woman laughed. "Keep to the subject. La Ronay finished welcoming us. I won't waste a single minute describing how it feels to see a woman the same age as me looking that smashing,'' she said mischievously. "Even Liz Taylor had the grace to start showing her age when she hit fifty. Not Lucienne Ronay, though. Isn't it disgusting?

"Anyhow, after she left, Mr. Flythe—who's not exactly Homely Henry either, is he?—he reviewed the official rules and then we started to play. I had fantastic luck: three double-double runs in a row! We'd finished our first game and my opponent was shuffling when I glanced down the table and saw that Commander Dixon had pushed her chair back and was looking under the table as if she'd dropped something. That's precisely when the bomb went off. After that, it was merry hell for a few minutes."

All laughter had faded from Jill Gill's plump face. "I'm not a medical doctor, but I've had first aid training, of course. There were a pediatrician and a chiropractor in the room. We did what we could until the ambulances came—made a tourniquet for Commander Dixon's arm, lifted the table off that police detective, put a pressure bandage on another man's head—but those two at the very end of the table, Professor Sutton and Mr. Wolferman—they must have died almost immediately. It was hours before the ringing in my ears went away."

She took a deep breath. "Anyhow, your people arrived soon after, so you know the rest."

"Thanks, Jill," said Sigrid. "Too bad you didn't get here when the doors opened. You might have noticed someone changing the boards at your table."

Sigrid had known Jill Gill long enough to discount her disclaimers about her powers of observation. She had learned, to her occasional discomfort, that very little went on in front of those absurd glasses that the scientist didn't notice.

"I've never been early for anything in my entire life," Jill Gill said regretfully.

A small hand bell tinkled at the front of the room to signal the beginning of a new round and she stood reluctantly. "Better go now. Why don't you and Oscar come for dinner next week?"

"You're going to be late for your next deal," Sigrid said.

Dr. Gill laughed. "You don't get out of it that easily. I'll call Oscar tonight."

She trotted away on bright red high heels, her long wool skirt twirling around ankles surprisingly trim for such a plump woman.

Elaine Albee promptly assumed her most professional attitude and tried to look as if she hadn't found Dr. Gill personally interesting as she summarized for the lieutenant the statements she and Jim Lowry had collected in the last few hours.

The smudged seating chart lay on the table before them. Albee had highlighted with a yellow marker the names of everyone questioned thus far.

A contestant near the end of Table 5, on the opposite side from Jill Gill, had noticed that Tillie had bent down under the table immediately before the explosion.

"That's probably what kept Tillie from being killed outright," Albee speculated. "The table was between him and the bomb when it went off."

So far, no one seemed to have seen the cribbage boards switched.

They had located Haines Froelick's opponent, though, a young electrician who spoke of the older man's politeness and told the detectives that nothing in Mr. Froelick's demeanor had indicated nervousness or jumpy anticipation. The electrician was of the impression that Mr. Froelick had not immediately realized his cousin's proximity to the blast, but admitted that once the explosion occurred, he hadn't noticed Mr. Froelick again. Everything was too chaotic.

Val Sutton's opponent, a Japanese businessman named Eisaku Okawara, offered similar testimony when Jim Lowry brought him over to the witness table between rounds. Mr. Okawara spoke excellent English and conscientiously tried to answer their questions, but confessed that occidental facial nuances were a mystery to him. Mrs. Sutton had played skillfully; she had been friendly and smiling. When the blast occurred, she had immediately jumped to her feet and cried, "John!"

Mr. Okawara thought she had rushed toward the back of the room. He himself had prudently made for the main doors and was standing just inside when Madame Ronay and other hotel staff arrived. There had been much screaming and confusion. Madame Ronay had tripped over the little gilt tripod that held the seating chart. Busboys had rushed past, trampling it beneath their feet as they hurried with fire extinguishers to put out the flames. Then had come the firemen, police, and medical personnel, and Mr. Okawara had slipped away to his room on the sixth floor without seeing Mrs. Sutton again.

He had been distressed this morning to read in the papers that her husband was one of those killed in the blast.

They let him return to his cards. In the lull, Sigrid caught the eye of one of the busboys and requested a glass of water.

"I could bring you juice, coffee, or tea if you'd rather," offered the slim young black man in a soft Southern voice.

"No, thank you, water's all I want," she said, and when he returned with it, she asked, "Were you on duty here last night?"

"Yes, ma'am. In fact, I was the one that put out the fire. I was just coming in the door when it happened and as soon as I saw the smoke, I grabbed the fire extinguisher there beside the door and ran right over."

"That was quick thinking."

"Well, it was just a small fire," the youth said modestly.

Sigrid shook a tablet from the bottle in her pocket, washed it down with the water, and returned the glass to the young black man. "Before they started playing last night, did you see anyone moving the cribbage boards at Table 5? Picking them up or anything?"

"No, ma'am. They already asked us that. Most folks were up at the front or standing 'round the hospitality table eating and drinking. 'Course, I wasn't watching every minute because I had to take out dirty glasses and bring in clean ones, so I guess somebody could have. I didn't see 'em though."

Sigrid thanked him again for her water and turned back to answer a question from Jim Lowry. Beyond his shoulder, she saw Lieutenant Knight re-enter the Bontemps Room, closely followed by Molly Baldwin. The assistant manager looked exhausted and Sigrid decided she'd settle the point Jill Gill had raised and then let the girl go home before she fell asleep on her feet.

As the busboy moved away, he remembered how old George had praised him for acting so quickly and how the boss lady would likely give him a bonus. And he remembered something else as well. He turned back, but that police lady was already busy with other people. Besides, he thought, it was such a little thing. She probably already knew about it anyhow.

He hesitated and the room steward appeared at his shoulder. "Over there, Johnson. Someone's spilled a cup of coffee. Step to it!"

"Yessir, Mr. George," he said smartly and hurried off.

CHAPTER XII

Only a few minutes had passed since Sigrid swallowed the pain tablet, but already she could feel its effect. The ache in her arm hadn't yet begun to diminish, but at least it had stopped building. In the meantime, she tried to ignore her discomfort and listen intelligently while Lieutenant Knight perched on the edge of a gilt and purple silk chair and described his visit to the graphic studio down in the hotel's lower levels.

It was near the secretarial pool, he reported, that service area provided as a courtesy for business travelers who required light typing or access to a computer terminal or a Xerox machine during their stays in the city; just down the hall and around a corner from the barber shop and valet services.

"The calligrapher, a Mr. Gustaffason, says they finished matting the seating chart Wednesday afternoon. It sat on that tripod-easel doodad at the front of their studio all evening and was sent upstairs around eleven-thirty Thursday morning. The studio isn't locked and this Gustaffason seems like a popular, loosey-goosey character, so there's probably a steady stream of people in and out. Dozens could have seen it."

It was no more than she expected, Sigrid told him, and beckoned to Molly Baldwin, who stood wearily before one of the more exuberant murals. She looked as if she longed to step inside its meadowed depths and curl up on the grass beside one of those fat sheep around whom giddy shepherdesses frolicked with their serenading swains.

"I know you're tired," Sigrid told her, "so I won't keep you much longer. I forgot to ask you before: do you know Commander Dixon?"

The girl looked at them stupidly.

"The female naval officer who sat next to Professor Sutton," prompted Lieutenant Knight helpfully.

"Oh." Her voice was flat. "Sorry. My mind's almost quit functioning. No, I thought I told you. I didn't know any of the contestants. Unless it was like Professor Sutton; somebody I'd met in the course of my work and whose name didn't register. I don't remember meeting her here, though. Or Mr. Wolferman or that policeman or any of the others either.''

"One of the players thought that Commander Dixon kept looking at you last evening as if she knew you," said Sigrid.

"Really?"

"It was during Mr. Flythe's discussion of the game rules after everyone was seated.''

The girl's fingers began to twine around the same brown curl as she struggled to remember where she had been at that point. "I must have been on the far side of the room then, going over arrangements with the room steward. There were dozens of people between us. Are you sure your witness wasn't mistaken?''

"She could have been," Sigrid conceded. "Or perhaps Commander Dixon was interested in the steward or another of your people. From the angle, though, it would almost have to be someone standing up, wouldn't it?''

The girl shrugged listlessly and Sigrid accepted the inevitable.

"That will be all for now, Ms. Baldwin. Thank you for your help today. We'll probably talk again another time.''

"You're sure there's nothing else I can do right now? I don't mind, Lieutenant. Really I don't.''

Even as she spoke, she had to stifle an involuntary yawn.

"I'm sure," said Sigrid.

As Molly Baldwin left them, Lieutenant Knight looked at Sigrid critically. "Didn't you just get out of a hospital this morning?''

Sigrid nodded stiffly.

"Then shouldn't you take a break? If you don't mind me saying, you look like you're pushing the edge.''

"I'm quite all right," she told him. But she did stand to flex her neck and shoulders and, as long as she was up, she decided to call Metro Medical and check on Tillie's condition.

The telephone was at the end of the hall in a secluded alcove. Awkwardly clutching the phone with her wounded hand, she inserted coins and punched out the number she had hastily scrawled on a scrap of paper that morning. The hospital switchboard passed her from one extension to another until at last she was plugged in to the intensive care waiting room and heard Marian Tildon's voice on the other end of the wire.

Tillie's wife sounded tired but bouyant with relief. "You caught me on my way home for a few hours' sleep," she told

Sigrid. "Oh Lieutenant, it's wonderful! Charles is out of the coma! He said my name. He knew who I was!"

Until that moment Sigrid had not realized how worried she had been about Tillie. Hearing Marian's report, she felt some of the day's tension drain away.

Up in Zachary Wolferman's comfortable Central Park apartment, Haines Froelick was succumbing to the housekeeper's care. A hot cup of tea and then straight to bed had been Emily's motherly decree.

Outside the tall narrow windows, October seemed poised to jump from Indian summer to true autumn. Curtains of rain swooped across the park below and sheeted the gold and scarlet leaves with cold water.

It had been a horrid day, Mr. Froelick thought, splashing in and out of the limousine in the rain, making arrangements for Zachary's body. The conference with the undertaker and another later with the minister, the notices to the papers, and the telephone that never stopped ringing. Fortunately, good old Emily had sensibly suggested that he ask Maritime National to send someone up and now a capable young lady, a Miss Vaughan, sat in Zachary's study and listened to their friends' condolences and courteously promised to relay them to Mr. Froelick.

Then after lunch had come those two awful police detectives in their damp wool jackets with so many questions: Who hated Zachary? Who wanted him dead? Whom had he recognized at the Maintenon last night? And then their interest in his photography: What sort of cameras did he own and didn't one almost need a degree in chemistry to develop one's own film? And each of his answers had been greeted with such skepticism . . .

Now he lay awake in the guest bedroom. Emily had tearfully offered to put fresh linens on Zachary's bed, but he wasn't quite ready for that yet.

It would come, of course, thought Mr. Froelick. Zachary had made no secret of his will. This was all his now. Zachary's apartment, his housekeeper, his chauffeur, his limousine, his villa in Florence, his chalet in Switzerland, his money. Zachary had been more than generous, but accepting his generosity had sometimes chafed.

No more of that. No more worrying and watching the dwindling buying power of his own tiny trusts.

No more long walks with the man who'd been a brother to

him, though. No one to share childhood memories or match wits with over a cribbage board either.

He sighed and buried his head in the lavender-scented pillow and as he fell asleep, he told himself philosophically that every silver cloud had a dark lining.

On the Upper West Side, in an apartment she shared with two other young women, Molly Baldwin hung up the telephone and finished toweling her short brown hair. She'd gotten soaked in the downpour, but that was the least of her worries. She had learned nothing from the call and would probably never learn anything if she didn't go over and identify herself.

But if she did that—

What would Ted Flythe say? He might not make an issue out of it, but Madame Ronay would. If La Reine found out, she would probably fire her and then it would all have been for nothing and how could she stay in New York?

On the other hand, how could she explain? Much less justify?

Almost whimpering with indecision, Molly Baldwin did what she'd been doing for most of her twenty-three years when faced with a dilemma: she crawled into bed and pulled the covers over her head.

The parade of cribbage-playing witnesses continued through the afternoon in the Bontemps Room. Two more besides Jill Gill had noticed Commander Dixon's wandering attention during Flythe's lecture on cribbage rules. The room steward, Raymond George, was questioned at length, but denied knowing her.

Vassily Ivanovich, however, was quite another matter. Not only did he admit knowing Commander Dixon when they spoke to him during a break in the competition, he insisted upon it. "Since T. J. Dixon is a little girl I am knowing her."

"Would you like an interpreter or someone from your legation here?" they asked.

The big Russian was scornful. Did they doubt his linguistic abilities? "Me, I speak very good the English," he informed them proudly.

Ivanovich was the embodiment of the Russian Bear: big, burly, and expansive. He had small bright blue eyes, short gray hair, and a flat, florid face. He wore American style clothes—a dark tweed sports jacket, a green wool shirt buttoned to the neck,

no tie, and brown corduroy pants—but something about their fit
gave them a vaguely Slavic cast.

"Her papa and I are good friends from the war. We are all
Navy together," he said, including Alan Knight in his statement.
"You are working with her, Lieutenant Knight?"

"Not exactly with her," Knight hedged.

"ONI?" Ivanovich guessed shrewdly, revealing an unexpected familiarity with the Office of Naval Intelligence.

For a moment, various possibilities seemed to give him pause,
then he shrugged broadly. "What the hell? My people know and
your people know we are friends. They know we do not talk
secrets. Me, I have no secrets."

In heavily accented English, Vassily Ivanovich described how
he had met Commander Dixon's father during World War II.

"He is on minesweeper in the North Atlantic; I am on little
ship blown up by German U-boat. They stop for us."

Chief Dixon had shared his quarters, his tobacco, and his
cribbage deck with the young Russian sailor; and by the time the
minesweeper reached Murmansk, they were warm friends. A
chance meeting a few months later in Reykjavik, followed by a
riotous shore leave of mythic proportions in New York, sealed the
friendship in blood.

Not to mention scotch and vodka, gin and slivovitz, and a few
margaritas that got mixed in by mistake.

They had somehow managed to keep in touch through the war
years, but the various thaws and freezes of postwar Soviet-
American relations eventually made their friendship impractical, if
not dangerous. After 1948, they ceased to correspond.

Ivanovich pulled out a plump plastic folder of photographs
and showed them the son who was an agricultural minister near
Minsk and the son who was a rising member in the Party. That was
the one who had pulled a string or two to get his father attached to a
Soviet trade delegation so that the long-retired Ivanovich could
enjoy one last American fling.

There were pictures of his deceased wife, the sons' wives,
himself surrounded by four baby-bear grandchildren, and, stuck
between several family pictures, one of his old friend Dixon with
his pretty little daughter on his lap—Commander T. J. Dixon at
the tender age of two.

Sigrid was inexpressibly touched by the child's beauty,
knowing that the small right arm which lay so confidently on her
father's might soon be lost.

"So," Vassily Ivanovich was saying, "last winter, before I

come to America, I write to my old comrade and after many weeks, little T.J. writes back he is dead twenty-six years in boiler explosion, but she is commander now and also in New York. We meet, we talk about what hell-raisers are her papa and me when we young. She is like daughter to me here and she is also very good cribbage player. One day each week we take lunch together and we play. Just like in old days with her papa.''

"Whose idea was it to enter this tournament?" asked Sigrid.

"Little T.J. Someone shows her in *Daily News* and she says, 'We are both so good, Vassily. Let us go and win lots of capitalistic dollars.' ''

He looked at them doubtfully. "This is joke. She calls me big socialist bear; I say she is little capitalistic pig.''

His broad face clouded. "I love her very much, Officers. They do not let me see her at hospital so I am staying here and I am playing cards but also I am watching. Yet here are so many! Tell me what to watch for," he entreated. "Let me help you catch who hurts my comrade's little girl.''

They thanked him for his offer but admitted they weren't sure what to watch for themselves.

"We aren't even certain whom the bomb was meant for," said Sigrid. "Did she ever speak of any enemies? Any problems with her work or in her personal life?''

"Work we do not talk about," Ivanovich stated flatly. "It is not proper. Sometimes she does say how busy day it is, like I say how is weather, but no more. She very much likes her Navy job and wishes she can go to sea or have ship, but never will they let her.''

"Is she bitter about that?" asked Lieutenant Knight.

"Sometimes, you bet! More times, she accepts. You ask of personal life, Lieutenant Harald. She is knowing I am old-fashion about women.''

"So she didn't go into detail about the men in her life?"

Ivanovich nodded. Delicately, the big Russian explained that he knew T. J. Dixon was a normal woman with the usual appetites. But her career meant more than marriage, and she discreetly embraced the old sailors' tradition of someone in every port. Currently in New York's busy harbor were a Dave, a Judd, and an Eli.

"We know about those," Lieutenant Knight told Sigrid. "Incidentally, there's a Bob, too. She must be some lady.''

"She *iss* lady!" growled Ivanovich, ready to defend the injured T.J.'s honor. "And she is gentleman, too, when comes the end. Someone start to love her too much, someone marriage speaks—'' His large callused hand made a swift chopping motion. "She cut it off clean! Always I say to her, sure you good officer, but you are woman, too. You need someday a home, a husband, babies. And she laugh and say she have little Molly, but now she and Molly fight and—''

"Molly?" exclaimed Sigrid and Knight in one breath.

"Daughter of her dead cousin," said Vassily Ivanovich. "In Florida she is living."

"Molly Baldwin?"

"Da, da. You are knowing her?"

"That's why her name sounded familiar this afternoon," groaned Alan Knight. "I'm a dunderhead! I read it in Dixon's file last night but it never sunk in."

"Tell us about Molly Baldwin, please," said Sigrid.

"What is to tell?" asked the bewildered Ivanovich, cocking his grizzled head at their interest. But he complied.

Molly Baldwin was Commander Dixon's much younger cousin, orphaned six or eight years earlier, he told them. T.J. had been close to Molly's widowed mother and took a great interest in the child. After the child's mother died, T.J. had sent her to prep school and then college.

Each was the other's only relative and Ivanovich thought Molly had satisfied any maternal yearnings T.J. might have possessed.

"Yet you said they fought?" probed Sigrid.

Not really fought, Ivanovich quibbled. With much gesturing of his beefy hands and with their assistance on various idiomatic English phrases which escaped him, he managed a picture of the usual mother-daughter generation clash. On the one hand was T.J. Dixon, career-oriented, purposeful in her goals, her personal life separate from her professional.

On the other hand was young Molly, pretty and loving but also weak willed and indecisive. And not very industrious. She had drifted from one major to another through college, from chemistry to biology to history, no career in mind, her grades barely sufficient to earn a degree in sociology at the last minute. Once out of school, she seemed to expect her older cousin to continue her allowance as she took and lost a succession of modest jobs.

Finally last summer, Commander Dixon had thrown up her hands in exasperation. "In a dress shop Molly is working and one time too many she comes late, so they tell her to leave and T.J. gives her money enough for one month to live and says, 'No more,

kiddo. This is last red penny you have from me as long as I live.'
Then Molly says ugly things and they finish.'' Ivanovich shook his
head meaningfully.

"They aren't in touch now?"

"Only yesterday T.J. is thinking maybe she is too hard on
Molly. She is still little girl, says T.J. Since they fight, she is not
hearing from Molly and this hurts T.J. very much.''

"Have you ever met Molly Baldwin?''

"No. Pictures I see, but Molly real, never.''

He was astounded when Sigrid told him that Molly Baldwin
worked here at the hotel and had, in fact, been present last night
and again today.

"You're sure Commander Dixon didn't know?'' she asked.

"No. This I swear.''

He wanted to thresh out their revelation detail by detail, but
Sigrid patiently led him back to the night of the explosion.

Grudgingly, Ivanovich told of meeting Commander Dixon at
a nearby restaurant for a light supper, then on here to the
Maintenon. He told of her chance meeting with the banker Zachary
Wolferman, of their subsequent conversation with his cousin
Haines Froelick, and Mr. Wolferman's beautiful memory of a
young German governess with a voice exactly like T.J.'s.

"Was there anyone else she knew here?''

"No one, Lieutenant. We talk, then they say for everyone to
sit down, so we do. Then we play and then *Boom!*''

At a hospital several blocks away, the surgeon pushed back
from the conference table. The charts and X-rays only confirmed
what he'd earlier feared.

The grafts weren't taking. Blood had quit circulating, oxygen
was no longer reaching Commander Dixon's arm.

The best space-age microsurgical procedures had failed and
the only alternative left to them was but a couple of levels up from
the sort of butchery practiced in the Stone Age.

"No point letting it go gangrenous,'' the surgeon told his staff
grimly. "Might as well get it over with.''

CHAPTER XIII

By four-thirty, Elaine Albee's yellow marks on the pairings lists indicated that they had seen and spoken with everyone in the Bontemps Room who had been anywhere near Table 5 the night before. They had even spoken to several from the front tables who hadn't come close but who wanted to go on record as being opposed to terrorist tactics and personally outraged that such things could happen here. The detectives had listened to a dozen different theories of how the boards were switched and when and why, but no one said, "Yes, I saw it happen."

Someone would have to chase down the tournament contestants who hadn't returned today, listen to more theories, and hope that one of the missing had witnessed something tangible. In the meantime, Lieutenant Harald was ready to call it a day.

"Unless something unexpected turns up, I'll see you nine o'clock in my office Monday morning," she told Lowry and Albee. "We'll compare notes with Peters and Eberstadt. Will you have anything from your people?" she asked Lieutenant Knight.

"Probably," he answered. "What about Molly Baldwin? Want me to contact her?"

"No, I'd like to see her face myself when we tell her we know she lied."

From across the ornate room, Jill Gill waved good-bye to Sigrid as they left the cribbage players in the midst of the afternoon's final round before the supper break. They walked down the Maintenon's wide graceful staircase. Jim Lowry and Elaine Albee offered lifts back downtown. When Sigrid shook her head and Alan Knight drawled a vague refusal, the detectives headed across the lobby for the elevator to the hotel's basement garage.

Outside, the slashing rain made the hour feel later than it really was. Sigrid sheltered under the Maintenon's canopy to get her bearings, unsure of the nearest subway entrance.

"Buy you a drink, Lieutenant?" asked Alan Knight.

Across the street a comfortable looking tavern promised a warm dry interior with wide oak tables and man-sized drinks. The offer was tempting.

"A nice tall Dickle-and-Coke would be welcome right now," she told him regretfully, "but I can't mix alcohol with the stuff I'm taking for my arm."

"A raincheck then," he said with one of his appealing lopsided smiles. "I'm sure there must be a long story to explain why a Yankee cop drinks bourbon and Co'-Cola."

"I have a Southern grandmother, that's all. It's in the genes. See you Monday, Lieutenant Knight."

He touched the brim of his white cap in a half salute and darted across the street alone, dodging curbside puddles.

By the time Sigrid splashed the short distance to Grand Central Station, her blue scarf was sliding down, so she tugged it off and crammed it into the pocket of her jacket, letting her hair hang loose. A seat near the rear wall of the crosstown shuttle kept her arm away from traffic and the downtown train wasn't very crowded either, so she made it to her stop on the lower West Side without getting jostled. There, she climbed the damp and dirty metal steps up to street level to find the rain had slackened to a misty drizzle.

No sign of the sun though. If anything, the leaden skies looked as if they were only catching their second wind and would soon pour down even more rain. She knew she ought to call Roman, ask if there were groceries she should pick up on her way for supper tonight or tomorrow, but the apartment—she still thought of it as the new apartment—was several blocks from the subway, tucked among the commercial buildings near the dilapidated piers that lined the Hudson. She was afraid that rain would arrive before she did if she lingered along the way.

As it was, she had just unlocked the tall wooden street gate when the heavens opened and a new flood descended. She splashed across the flagstones to the sheltered doorway.

Sigrid was no gardener, but Roman Tramegra fancied himself a Renaissance man on a modest scale and would enthusiastically turn his hand to any task. ("Renaissance man indeed!" sniffed Grandmother Lattimore when she swept into town for one of her semiannual trips north. "More what we always called a jackleg, if you ask me, which you won't, I suppose.") At any rate, Roman had transformed the tiny courtyard into a formal herb garden. At least it started out formal. By October the scented geraniums had grown tall and leggy, the borage and bee balm flopped, and the purple basil and coleuses Roman had stuck in for color were tattered and going to seed.

Not that Sigrid cared. Nature in any form seldom interested her except as it interfered with her normal routine. As she fumbled for the door key, it did occur to her that the marble Eros that Roman had lugged home in late August looked a bit uncomfortable standing there naked in this first chill rain of autumn.

She was a little chilly herself but as she opened the door, she saw a light in the kitchen, heard Roman banging saucepans and cutlery as he unloaded the dishwasher, and best of all, she smelled the homey aroma of his most successful soup.

Roman Tramegra aspired to gourmet chefdom. He bought the freshest raw materials and would spend hours slicing, peeling and dicing. But he chased a will-o'-the-wisp of creativity around the kitchen with Portuguese wines, Chinese herbs, Greek cheese, or French mustards, constitutionally unable to follow a recipe without yielding to the temptation to improve it.

Few of his creations were totally inedible and over the course of time Sigrid had learned to be diplomatic. She did not like to cook and possessed an undemanding appetite. Before Roman Tramegra entered her life, she either stopped by a take-out place, fished something from the grocer's freezer, or opened a can of soup. There were times when Roman's culinary excesses made her long for those simpler meals—she would never get used to his broccoli-and-chutney curry for instance—but she usually repented when he miraculously came up with something absolutely delicious.

Such as the mushroom and barley soup she could now smell simmering on the stove in the green-and-white tiled kitchen they shared.

"Is it soup yet?" she asked from the doorway, shaking the rain from her soft dark hair.

"Sigrid, my dear! How *are* you? How is your arm? Why didn't you call? I've been so *worried* about you! Anne said you were simply slashed to *ribbons*."

His voice was several tones deeper than anyone's Sigrid had ever heard, yet he still managed to talk in italics half the time.

"I'm okay," she said. "A little tired, though. And ravenous."

"Then sit, sit!" Roman boomed, clearing a space at the breakfast counter with one swoop of his arm. He wore a long white linen shirt over tailored gray denim slacks with rolled cuffs and a heavy silver and turquoise necklace that clanked against the ceramic topped counter when he bent across to lay out a bowl and spoon. He was a large man, in his mid-forties. Not fat exactly, but with an aura of softness about him akin to that of a large pampered Persian cat. He moved like one, too, with a certain finicky grace and deliberation.

His sandy hair was thinning on top and the high dome of his hairline was echoed by the arch of his eyebrows and the curve of his hooded eyes.

"Let me wash up first," Sigrid told him and strode down the hall to her room, where she eased the jacket off over her bandaged arm and unbuckled the gun harness. She brushed her hair, freshened up in the bath, and returned to the kitchen in time to watch Roman ladle the thick fragrant soup into her bowl.

He demanded to hear all about the stabbing. Sigrid skimmed over the high spots, then asked, "Did you move my car?"

"Anne drove it over when she came for your clothes early this morning. She left it double-parked, but I drove it down to your garage. This place was a *madhouse* this morning. First Anne, then Oscar—I see he did deliver your clothes. I thought you two were coming straight back here. I waited till almost eleven and then I simply had to *fly*."

"Sorry. We must have just missed you. Something came up," said Sigrid, blowing gently on her first spoonful of steaming soup.

Without asking if she wanted it, Roman fixed her a small bowl of torn endive, parsley, and Bibb lettuce and cut a thick slice of brown bread which he smeared liberally with cream cheese. By then Sigrid was eating with such obvious relish that he said, "It's early for dinner, but I may as well join you. I shall make my anised veal for our entrée and—"

"None for me, thanks," Sigrid said hastily. "Soup's all I want tonight."

"Perhaps tomorrow then," he said, leaving Sigrid to wonder if she could pretend to forget and send out for pizza or something. She had never acquired a taste for ánise except in black jellybeans. Certainly not in veal and sour cream.

"Oscar was quite exercised about the explosion at the Hotel Maintenon. Was that what delayed you?" Roman asked. "*Do* say you're working on that."

"Now, Roman," she warned.

It was getting harder to deflect his excessive interest in her work. He was so certain that one ingenious murder mystery would free him from the magazine articles and fillers with which he supplemented his small private income but so far as he knew, only the dull and routine had come her way since the spring and he had begun to despair of the unimaginative ways by which so many New Yorkers dispatched one another.

"I hoped you might be able to tell me something—off the record, of course," he said wistfully. "Surely there's more than was in the paper? A multimillionaire killed, your colleague wounded, the glamorous Lucienne Ronay hovering in the wings! Is she really as beautiful as her pictures?"

"More," said Sigrid, happy that she could share that much at least. "I'm told she gave another dazzling performance last night. Jill Gill was there, by the way. She's one of the cribbage contestants."

"Jolly good," beamed Roman, whose cultured midwestern accent was overlaid by an Oxbridge accent that sounded suspiciously like too many old Peter Lawford movies to Sigrid. *"She'll* be able to describe all those delicious little details of dress and jewels that pass right over your practical head."

Roman Tramegra was the soul of tact and Sigrid knew he would never intentionally insult her. Yet, she found his blithe assumption that she was totally oblivious to all feminine artifice somewhat wounding. Just because she seldom wore makeup herself, just because she felt gawky shopping for clothes and didn't fuss with her hair every ten minutes, didn't mean that she was *never* interested in how other women achieved their glamorous effects.

"I noticed," she told him sharply. "Lucienne Ronay had on a very expensive, very attractive off-white dress this afternoon, long gold-and-pearl earrings, and several chunky gold bracelets. Her shoes were the same color as her dress, her hair was down about her face, and she wore a perfume that smelled like some sort of flowers."

Roman's spoon dropped back into the bowl with a surprised clunk.

"Very *good,* my dear Watson. The flowers are mignonettes."

"Mignonettes?"

"Her husband commissioned a perfume company in the Mediterranean to blend a special fragrance just for her."

Sometimes Sigrid wondered if her friend possessed a photographic memory. He claimed not to, yet he seemed a walking storehouse of trivia, with tidbits on almost every aspect of twentieth century pop culture. Sigrid recalled having once read about Lucienne Ronay's husband herself but details eluded her.

"He was something of a Svengali, wasn't he?"

"I think you mean Pygmalion," Roman corrected. "Svengali was an evil hypnotist; Pygmalion was a sculptor who created his perfect mate. G. B. Shaw, of course. And *My Fair Lady,* only that came later. That was Maurice Ronay though—Pygmalion and Professor Henry Higgins with the *tiniest* touch of Howard Hughes. A bit of a recluse with an eccentric sense of humor. He was a wealthy real estate investor, *years* older than she, and she was a little *nobody,* a peasant girl he found sleeping on the beach at Cannes, so the story goes. He brought her home with him, scrubbed off the dirt and found her so beautiful that he taught her how to walk and talk and carry herself, bought her clothes and jewels, and finally *married* her.

"They say everything that man touched turned into gold and his little peasant was no exception. He married her because she was beautiful and sexy, he said, and then she turned out to have brains, too."

"I remember that," said Sigrid. She went around to the stove and clumsily helped herself to more soup. "Didn't her husband put together some sort of real estate deal here in Manhattan about eight or nine years ago and those three hotels were part of the package he didn't want?"

"Quite right," he agreed, holding out his own bowl for more. "They were like three nice old dowagers: still respectable, but drab and a bit tatty around the edges."

"My great-aunts used to stay at the La Vallière when it was the Carstairs," Sigrid remembered.

"Everyone's great-aunt stayed at the Carstairs," said Roman. "Monsieur Ronay was going to dump it, along with what are now the Montespan and the Maintenon, when his charming wife announced that she was tired of being a plaything and wanted to work. So he gave her the three hotels for a Christmas present and she became something of a Pygmalion herself: cleaned them up, gave them elegant new dresses, and transformed them into three perfect jewels."

"Nice what you can do with money," Sigrid observed, savoring the warm buttery mushrooms in her soup.

"It always takes money to make it," Roman agreed. "But why not? They say she paid back his loan before he died."

"She does seem to have a flair for running hotels," Sigrid acknowledged. "Everything was under control today. No sign of any explosion except in the immediate vicinity of the bomb itself."

"Everyone says she's *so* pragmatic, that she's a termagant and a slave-driver, and perhaps she is. But underneath, she must have a romantic nature."

"Because she's so beautiful?"

"Outward beauty is only a manifestation of inner loveliness," he intoned in his solemn bass voice. "The *names* she chose for her hotels reveal everything."

"Do they?" Sigrid was weak on French history.

"Maintenon, Montespan, and La Vallière, my dear, were the mistresses of the Sun King, Louis XIV. I wrote an article on them when the hotels were rechristened. Sold it as a sidebar to *Newsday*, I think. Let me see now . . . Louise de La Vallière came first. She's the one they named the lavaliere necklace for. She was supplanted by Françoise de Montespan, who was three years older; Montespan in turn was replaced by Françoise de Maintenon, who was six years older still. She was almost fifty when she and the king were secretly married. She had beauty and intellect and held the king's heart until his death.

"If you think of it, Lucienne Ronay is much like de Maintenon herself. She was no infant when she married Maurice Ronay and—"

The telephone on the nearby wall interrupted his discourse. This phone and the one in Sigrid's bedroom were in her name. Roman had a separate line in his quarters. Sigrid lifted the receiver to her ear. "Hello?"

"Val says you haven't been by to question her yet," said Oscar Nauman.

"No, I thought I wouldn't bother her until tomorrow."

"She won't be there tomorrow," he told her. "She and the children are flying home with John's body tomorrow morning and they won't be back till after the funeral. I thought you'd want to know."

"I do." Sigrid weighed her weariness against the need to interview Val Sutton while the night's horrors were still fresh in the new widow's mind. "Perhaps I'd better call her and arrange a time."

"I told her to expect us at nine if she didn't hear from me. She's beat."

"Me, too," Sigrid confessed.

"So take a nap," Nauman said sensibly. "That's what Val's doing. I'll pick you up at eight–forty-five. Okay?"

"Okay." It might be a little unorthodox, but if Val Sutton

were given to hysterics, Sigrid wanted someone like Nauman there to help.

She looked at the clock.

Five past six.

"If I'm not up by eight-thirty, please call me," she told Roman and headed back down the hall for bed.

CHAPTER XIV

The Sutton apartment was less than ten minutes away from Sigrid's, a block off Bleecker Street. Most of the mourners had gone by the time she and Oscar Nauman arrived shortly after nine o'clock, although four or five of John Sutton's graduate students still conversed in low tones around the dining room table and an emaciated young woman with a chalk-white complexion and gold-enameled fingernails—one of Val Sutton's colleagues from the Feldheimer, Nauman told Sigrid—sat on the couch reading a bedtime story to the Suttons' young son and daughter.

Both children had solemn dark eyes and straight black hair and they leaned sleepily against the woman's almost anorexic body. The smaller child, a little girl, had detached a wooden hippopotamus from the woman's chunky necklace and was dreamily walking it back and forth across the flowers printed on her nightgown.

"She's waiting for you in his study," said the student who had admitted them.

Oscar Nauman led the way down the narrow hall, tapped at a door, and opened it without waiting.

The outer rooms of the apartment were furnished in what Sigrid privately tagged bohemian artsy—nubbly handwoven fabrics, earthtone ceramic jugs and bowls, and statuettes cast in bronze and iron. On the walls, abstract oils and stylized photographs were interspersed with batik hangings and South American Indian artifacts.

John Sutton's study was more traditionally academic. A

heavy oak desk faced the door and several comfortable chairs were placed before two walls lined with bookshelves in which leather-covered volumes were jammed beside paperbacks and scholarly journals. There was a Peruvian rug on the floor, though, and framed political posters on the third wall supported the presidential campaigns of Eugene McCarthy, Robert Kennedy, and Dick Gregory, among others. A floor-to-ceiling corkboard filled the wall behind the desk, displaying a thumbtacked collage of snapshots, newspaper clippings, political cartoons, and protest buttons for the last twenty years.

Val Sutton sat curled on a leather chair that had been pulled up before the black tiled fireplace. A coal fire blazed in the small grate. She looked up as they entered and Sigrid immediately recognized whose genes the two children had inherited. As Nauman had said earlier, Val Sutton could not be considered conventionally beautiful; yet there was an intense, exotic vibrancy about her: high cheekbones and alert brown eyes in a triangular face, thick black hair clipped level with her chin line, a lithe and sensuous body.

The widow greeted Nauman in a husky voice, but her eyes were for the woman behind him. Even in her grief she could be curious about this police officer whom Oscar had described as a cross between Sherlock Holmes and Wonder Woman. She half remembered that when Riley Quinn was poisoned at Vanderlyn College back in the spring, John had come home amused that Oscar seemed smitten by a police lieutenant. Knowing the caliber of women the artist was usually attracted to, Val expected someone not only intelligent, but physically striking as well.

What she saw was a woman in her early thirties, almost as tall as Oscar, with a spinsterish angularity beneath nondescript clothes, a long neck, and a mouth too generous for her thin face. On the other hand, her wide eyes were an interesting smoky gray and they held a quiet watchfulness which made Val think that perhaps Oscar hadn't exaggerated after all.

"Come sit by the fire," she invited. "I know it's too early in the season, but I just can't seem to get warm tonight."

Nauman pulled a third chair closer for himself and, with the familiarity of an old friend, concentrated on lighting an intricately carved meerschaum pipe.

"Oscar told me you were injured last night, too," Val Sutton said. "Does it bother you much?"

The husky voice suited her. Nauman had said she was musical

and Sigrid could imagine how effective a ballad might be in that timbre.

"The sling makes it look worse than it feels, thanks," she replied.

Interviewing a murder victim's next-of-kin usually meant an awkward beginning, but here in this bookish lamplit room, with a fire on the hearth and the comforting aroma of Nauman's mellow pipe, it seemed quite natural to lean forward in the brown leather chair and say, "I'm very sorry about your husband's death."

"Oscar says you don't know if John was the intended victim."

Sigrid looked at the catlike face closely. "Do you?"

"He'd damn well better be!" There was passionate intensity in Val Sutton's low voice and her dark eyes flamed.

"Why do you say that?"

"Because it can't have been for nothing! I couldn't stand that. I'd rather it be someone who hated him, who felt threatened by him, who wanted something he had—a *reason*. I don't care how insane and stupid the reason is, but I don't think I can bear it if John is dead just because he happened to be there at that damn table."

Tears glittered in the firelight and she brushed them away impatiently. "If it's John they were after, there will be something we can *do*."

"Did someone hate him?" asked Sigrid.

"John was the kindest, funniest, most thoughtful—" The vibrant voice broke, then steadied. "Before last night, I would have said he didn't have an enemy in this world. But he's dead now, isn't he? So there must have been at least one enemy. And you'll find him for me."

"Mrs. Sutton—"

"Please. Call me Val and let me call you Sigrid. Oscar's talked so much about you last night and today, I feel we're already friends."

"Val then. I don't know what Nauman's told you, but the New York Police Department's not the Northwest Mounted Police. We don't always get our man."

"You will this time," Val Sutton predicted firmly. "We'll take John's life apart—his friends, his students, his parents— everyone who ever knew him will help. Somewhere, somebody will remember something."

"Let's begin with you then," said Sigrid. "Nauman and your

husband were at the Maintenon on Wednesday. Did he tell you about it?''

Val shook her head and her lustrous hair swung like heavy silk. ''No, he didn't really have a chance. I was at a conference up in Boston. Left Tuesday and didn't get back until yesterday morning. We talked on the phone Thursday night, but that was mostly about the children and what time my train was due in.''

''Nauman says your husband briefly met Ted Flythe on Wednesday. He had the impression that Professor Sutton kept glancing at Flythe as if he might have known him.''

''Or was at least reminded of someone,'' Nauman clarified.

Again Val shook her head. ''That's what you said this afternoon, Oscar, and I keep thinking about Mr. Flythe and how he looked last night and he's no one *I* ever remember seeing. I'll ask around tomorrow, though.'' Her voice was steely. ''Most of John's old friends from our McClellan days will be at the funeral.''

Her eyes narrowed thoughtfully. ''What you just said, Oscar —that Flythe might have reminded John of someone. There was a guy in SDS. Not at McClellan, but from Syracuse or Cornell. *He* had a pointed beard like Flythe's. Maybe that's what Sam meant?''

She jumped to her feet and crossed swiftly to the large oak desk.

''Sam?'' Nauman was puzzled.

''Sam Naismith. When I phoned him this afternoon to ask if he'd be one of the pallbearers, he was so shocked; he said he'd just been talking to John one night this week; that they were mulling over the old days.''

She had seated herself behind the desk and pulled the phone close while flipping rapidly through a roller-card index.

''I wasn't paying attention,'' she muttered as her fingers punched out an area code.

There was a brief pause, then she said, ''Sam? This is Val again. Hang on a minute, will you?''

She placed the receiver in an amplifying device that acted like a two-way speaker and allowed Sigrid and Nauman to follow the conversation.

''Sam, a police officer is here looking into John's death. We need to ask you some questions.''

''Sure, honey,'' rumbled a solicitous male voice. ''Fire away.''

''You said you and John talked this week. When?''

''Wednesday night.''

Sigrid stood and approached the speaker. ''Mr. Naismith, this is Lieutenant Harald of the New York Police Department. Did you call Professor Sutton or—"

"He called me, Lieutenant. Said he was getting together some lectures about the protest movement and wanted to refresh his memory. We were in SDS at McClellan together a million years ago."

"Sam," said Val Sutton, "do you remember a guy who used to visit on campus from one of the upstate New York schools—Syracuse or Cornell? He had long hair and a beard."

"Who didn't?" chuckled Naismith.

"No, but his beard was cut to a sharp point. And his hair was always in a pony tail. I think his name was Chris or Crist—"

"Tris," Naismith said flatly. "Tristan Yorke."

"That's the name! Tristan Yorke. Did John ask about him?"

"Not really. I was the one who brought him up, Val, not John."

"In what connection, Mr. Naismith?" asked Sigrid.

"John said he'd gotten up to the point in his research where the Weathermen splintered off of SDS and went underground. We knew some who went that route. I don't know if you've ever heard of a group called Red Snow?"

"I've heard."

"Well, you probably know that their leader, Fred Hamilton, was from McClellan. They blew themselves up in a camp on Lake Cayuga the summer of 1970, but rumor had it that a couple of them got out alive. Some people said Fred was the one who got away, along with his girlfriend. Others said Fred was blown into a zillion bits of fish food and it was a pair of converts from California. John asked me who I thought might know for sure and we hit on Tris Yorke. He was in the Cayuga area and he used to help some of the conscientious objectors who wanted to go to Canada to evade the draft, you know, put 'em up for a night or two and then drive them over the border. If anybody knew who really survived the Red Snow blast, it'd probably be Tris."

"Could any former Red Snow members have a grudge against Professor Sutton?" asked Sigrid. She was watching Val Sutton's grim face.

"There were some hard feelings at the time," Naismith said reluctantly. "They got ticked off because SDS wasn't as confrontational as they thought it ought to be, but I never heard of them killing each other because of it. Besides, there can't be more than two former Red Snow members, remember? Frankly, I've always believed that those other two who're supposed to have jumped from

a balcony probably drowned just like the Xavier girl did. Otherwise
we'd have heard something by now. Like I told John, nobody stays
underground this long."

"Did he agree with you?"

"Oh, you know John—well, no," Naismith caught himself
abruptly, "I guess you didn't. Anyhow, he'd yes you to death and
then go merrily on his own damn way. Nobody's mentioned Tris in
years, but John made me promise I'd throw out a few lines and see
if I could locate him."

"You'll keep trying, won't you?" Val's voice rasped.

"If you want me to, honey."

"I do."

They went back over the conversation the two men had
exchanged Wednesday night, but nothing else suggested itself. John
Sutton had not mentioned cribbage, the Maintenon, or Ted Flythe.
So far as Naismith knew, Sutton's call had been motivated purely
by his desire to nail down all elements of the Red Snow episode for
his lectures. Naismith promised to keep trying.

"See you tomorrow," he told Val.

"Tomorrow," Val said huskily.

She lifted the telephone receiver from the amplifier and had
just replaced it on the cradle when the door opened and her thin,
pale-skinned friend said, "Can you come for a few minutes, Val?
They want you to tuck them in."

"I'll be right there." She paused in the doorway of the study.
"John's last notes are there on the tape recorder, Lieuten— Sigrid.
You might want to listen to them. Feel free to poke around in his
desk, too. Maybe you'll see something I've missed. Oscar, don't
you want something to eat or drink? People brought so much food.
And wine. I won't have to buy any rosé or Chablis for a year," she
said wanly. "Or there's coffee."

"Go kiss your kids good night," ordered Nauman gently.
"We can fend for ourselves."

When she had gone, he asked Sigrid if she wanted anything.
"Coffee would be good," she said and circled the desk to push the
tape recorder's play button.

John Sutton had possessed a pleasant baritone voice and an
easy style of delivery that helped explain why he'd been such a
popular teacher. On this tape he'd been enthusiastic, factual, and
confidential all at once, with touches of humor or self-deprecation
to lighten the heavy spots. Although older and presumably wiser,
he didn't belittle the idealism of the late sixties and early seventies.
He could acknowledge its weaknesses, but he had also been superb

at communicating the excitement of the times, the almost tribal closeness and heady optimism of kids who believed they could change things for the better, could make a difference, *could* replace guns with flowers and politicians with statesmen.

As the tape unwound, Sigrid studied the collage behind John Sutton's desk. It was like a multilayered scrapbook. Among the things that caught her eye were several old Doonesbury cartoons, a copy of the famous Kent State photograph, a banner headline *NIXON RESIGNS!*, and, over on the edge, a simple white button inscribed *Imagine . . . 1940–1980*.

Sigrid turned from the collage feeling depressed. Her arm hurt, she was tired, and she wished that the year wasn't heading into winter. Just then Nauman came through the door bearing a tray with cups of steaming coffee and wedges of warm apple pie beneath melted cheddar. "Room service," he smiled at her.

On the tape, John Sutton orally reminded himself, "Check with Sam and Letty. Find out if anybody ever really saw Fred Hamilton or the Farr girl after Red Snow blew themselves up."

CHAPTER XV

"Fred Hamilton and the Farr girl?" Sigrid asked.

"Brooks Ann Farr," said Val Sutton, who had returned from settling her children for the night and now nursed a hot cup of milky tea. Sigrid sat with her note pad balanced on the arm of the deep leather chair across from Val's.

"Her family was supposed to be quite wealthy," said Val. "I remember hearing that Brooks Ann went to a prep school in Switzerland and that she'd been accepted at Vassar and Wellesley both, but she'd fought with her parents and decided to go to McClellan to spite them."

"What was she like?"

"A nebbish." Val shrugged. "Bright enough, I suppose, but mostly average: average height, a little on the heavy side, mousy brown hair, round face that usually had a sour look on it. She was always finding fault with everything and everybody.

"Except Fred. Fred Hamilton walked on water. She was an absolute doormat for that man. Half the things Fred got credit for, Brooks Ann did. He'd be mouthing off, throwing out all these theories about what SDS should be doing, and the next day she'd have mimeographed a stack of position papers based on what he'd spouted the night before.

"I doubt Fred gave a damn about her, but he was a user and he certainly used her. John said she used to cash the monthly allowance check her parents sent and give it all to Fred. I was in a drugstore once and saw her steal a box of tampons because she didn't have enough money to buy them. John used to spend time with her. I think he felt sorry for her because she was so crazy about Fred and Fred was always quoting Ben Franklin behind her back."

"*Reasons for Preferring an Elderly Mistress?*" asked Oscar.

"Only John said that Fred changed it to homely mistress or doggy mistress."

"'Eighth and lastly, they are so grateful,'" Nauman quoted for Sigrid's enlightenment.

There was a pensive silence. A lump of coal slipped through the grate and fell upon the hearth in a shower of glowing sparks.

"Poor Brooks Ann," Val sighed. "She probably *was* grateful. Fred *was* a leader. He could stir kids up, make them ready to storm the barricades. And he certainly was sexy."

She watched Sigrid jot a few words on her pad. "Most of this is second hand," she warned. "I barely knew either of them except for what John told me over the years. I never went to any SDS meetings and I'd only been seeing John a month or two before Fred went underground. Brooks Ann was just one of several girls hanging around him. The others were prettier, more verbal—Brooks Ann sort of faded into the woodwork."

She spoke with the unconscious condescension of one who had never faded into any background. Anne Harald would probably enjoy photographing the dramatic angles of her catlike face, Sigrid thought, or those eyes, deepened into dark pools by the skillful application of mascara. Val's beauty lay in the way she held her head, in the way she moved, in the innate knowledge of her sexuality. As a child she must have been as odd-looking as I was, Sigrid thought despairingly, so how did she end up with so much assurance?

She drew a heavy line across the width of her note pad and carefully printed Fred Hamilton's name beneath.

"I get the impression that Hamilton was a little older?"

"He was," Val nodded, her heavy dark hair swinging forward. "Older than most of us anyhow. He was a senior, but more like twenty-four or twenty-five because he'd dropped out years before to join the Peace Corps. I think his father was an executive in chemicals or defense contracts and Fred couldn't get along with him, so he wouldn't ask his parents for money when he came back."

"He took his girlfriend's money instead," Sigrid observed.

"Put like that, it does sound hypocritical," Val admitted, "but nobody twisted Brooks Ann's arm. And remember, it seemed like poetic justice back then to let the Establishment support the protesters, too."

She stood and moved to the tray on the desk to pour herself another cup of tea. Her slender body was stooped with fatigue.

"It all gets so confused," she said, adding milk and sugar to the blue porcelain cup. "Sometimes I think I must be getting old. They say the older you get, the more conservative you become. I remember when the first bombs went off in a Brooklyn draft board. I wasn't particularly radical, but I thought, Hey, right on! Let *them* get a taste of warfare. But today, when abortion clinics get bombed, I'm outraged."

"Because you condone abortion and you didn't condone the draft?" Sigrid suggested.

"Or because they're on the Right and we were on the Left?" Val mused, turning to face her. "I don't think so. We were trying to stop the killing."

"Pro-lifers say the same," Oscar observed mildly.

"Oh God, Oscar, you're not going to equate abortion with the draft? Young men were *forced* to go to Vietnam. Women aren't forced to have abortions. It's not the same."

"I didn't say it was," he protested. "I happen to think women have a right to their bodies."

"So do I," Sigrid said slowly. "Even so, I can't quite reconcile some parts of it. I don't believe abortion's murder; yet if someone assaults a pregnant woman and kills her unborn child, I do think that's manslaughter. I guess I don't have a good definition of when life begins. Not like the right-to-lifers."

"I hate that term!" Val said passionately. "When villages full of babies were carpet-bombed in Vietnam, where were the right-to-lifers? When babies starve all over Africa, when babies go hungry right here in our own rat-infested slums, where are these so-called life-lovers? They care nothing about the quality of life once a baby's born, just that it gets born. They're so *sure* God's on their side!''

"Val—" said Nauman.

"No, Oscar, don't. I have to work this out, because that's what bothers me. We were just as positive our views were moral, that we were working for something *good* even if the *way* we worked . . .'' She looked at them, her face ravaged. ''Did we set precedents?''

"You're afraid you created an atmosphere that made violence an acceptable part of civil disobedience?'' Sigrid asked.

"Yes!'' Val said gratefully. ''And not just public protest, but private, too. Has it gone full circle?''

Her dark eyes filled with tears again. ''Is that what killed John?'' she asked hoarsely.

"Of course not,'' said Oscar. He crossed the Peruvian rug to put his arms around Val and hold her tightly while she wept softly against his chest.

Sigrid picked up the poker and punched at the fire. Carefully she raked the fiery chunks into a neat pile, then leveled them again into a glowing bed. Only the week before, she had flown down to North Carolina for the funeral of a close cousin and Val's grief rekindled her own so abruptly that she could not turn around and watch.

Presently the sobs behind her subsided. Val blew her nose and came back to her chair by the hearth.

"Sorry, guys,'' she said shakily. ''I keep thinking I'm cried out and then something sets me off again.''

Nauman shoved his chair closer to hers and held out her forgotten cup of tea.

She took a deep swallow. ''Don't you want more coffee, Sigrid? I'm sure they've probably made a fresh pot by now.''

"No, thank you. Describe Fred Hamilton, please.'' Her words were blunt and businesslike.

"Yes, of course. Let's see . . . about six feet tall, dark hair that he wore shoulder-length, muscular build. The sexiest eyes I've ever seen. I was teasing John about that—was it just last night? God! It seems so long ago.''

Again her eyes pooled and Sigrid felt such a rush of compassion that she was almost paralyzed. ''You and your husband discussed Hamilton last night? Who brought him up? You or he?''

"He did,'' Val replied, puzzled by her harsh tone. ''He asked if I remembered Fred and I said yes, he was a smoldering sexpot. We were kidding about it; you know how it is.''

Only as an outside observer did Sigrid know that teasing intimacy between wife and husband. She nodded stiffly.

"We were on our way out to the Maintenon while we were talking and I asked John if he thought Fred and Brooks Ann would ever turn themselves in—so many have over the years, you know—and John . . .''

She frowned as she remembered. "He said that it was odd I should ask or something like that and then a cab stopped for us and we wound up talking about other things.''

"But the way he said it?'' Sigrid probed.

Val nodded her sleek brown head. "The way he said it was as if he'd heard something about Fred recently.''

Sigrid leaned back in the deep leather chair. "Val, I asked you before but I want you to think again very carefully. Did you converse with Ted Flythe last night?''

"No, why?''

Sigrid made a noncommittal gesture and Val looked to Nauman for enlightenment.

He shrugged. "I suppose she wants to know if he reminded you of anybody besides that Tris Yorke.''

"Reminded? You think Ted Flythe is Fred Hamilton?'' They could almost see her mind sorting and comparing. "They're both the same height and coloring,'' she mused. "Flythe has a beard and Fred was always clean-shaven with much longer hair.''

"You said Hamilton had sexy eyes,'' said Sigrid. "One of my officers said the same about Flythe's.''

"They're similar,'' Val admitted, "but I don't think he's Fred.''

"He'd be the right age,'' said Nauman, playing devil's advocate. "Early forties, I'd put him.''

"No,'' Val said, with conviction. "I know it's been ages, but even if Flythe is Fred, why would he come back and kill John after all this time? They had an ideological split, not a blood feud.''

"Hamilton is still wanted by the FBI,'' Sigrid told her. "The amnesty program covered draft evaders, not murderers. Even if the deaths of those children were unpremeditated, it's still manslaughter. There's no statute of limitations to run out. Your husband might be one of the few who could definitely identify him.''

"But I knew Fred, too. Why wasn't I killed?''

"You said you were never in SDS. You weren't close to

anyone in the group except your husband," Sigrid said. "He might not remember you."

"People change in sixteen or seventeen years, Val," said Nauman.

Sigrid flipped through her earlier notes. "Flythe told me he graduated from a now defunct college in Michigan. Carlyle Union. Does that ring any bells?"

"No."

"He also said that he's guided several tour groups around Europe. Did you and Professor Sutton ever travel overseas?"

"Sure, but not with any tour group. We always rented a car and poked around on our own."

"What about some of the others who were supposed to have been killed in that Red Snow explosion? Could Flythe be any of them?"

"That I can't help with at all." Val shook her head. "Fred and Brooks Ann were the only two from McClellan as far as we ever heard. There was a black girl from the Panthers whom we'd met at one of the rallies, but I think her body was definitely identified. Oh, and there was a kid—what was his name? Victor? Victor Earle! He was with Red Snow near the end, but he wasn't in the lake house when the rest were killed. We heard he was in Canada or Sweden."

"What happened to him?"

"They couldn't prove he'd taken part in the bombing of that day-care center and draft board in Chicago, but when he came back to the States in the mid-Seventies, they hit him with drug smuggling and possession of illegal arms or something. I'm pretty sure he stood trial and drew a sentence, though he must be out by now." She shrugged helplessly. "I'm sorry. I just can't remember. It was so long ago. Anyhow, Victor couldn't be Flythe. He was much shorter and already starting to lose his hair on top."

Nevertheless, Sigrid added Victor Earle's name below Tristan Yorke's on her short list. It wouldn't hurt to learn Earle's whereabouts. The odds weren't favorable that he was involved; still, he might recognize Flythe or be reminded of someone who looked like Flythe. And it wouldn't hurt to ask for Fred Hamilton's prints either. They had to start somewhere. Sooner or later, surely something would connect if Sutton were the intended target.

They discussed the possibilities a few minutes more and might have talked even longer except that the door opened abruptly and a sobbing little boy hurled himself across the room and flung himself onto Val's lap. His face was swollen with sleep and his hair was as rumpled as his striped pajamas.

"I want Daddy to come home," he cried. "I don't want him to be dead. I want Daddy to come home!"

"So do I, Jacky," his mother murmured brokenly, smoothing his dark hair, so like hers. "So do I."

The rain had subsided to a cool, fragrant mist when Nauman finally parked on the deserted street outside Sigrid's walled garden. Her bandaged arm made getting out of the low car awkward, so he held the door and offered a strong hand up.

The streetlight down the block glistened on the wet leaves plastered along the sidewalk and haloed Nauman's silver hair as he unlocked her gate and handed back the key.

Moved by an inexplicable need, Sigrid touched his face with her fingertips and lifted her lips to his for a long intense moment.

Nauman held her thin body as lightly as if she were a woodland creature that might suddenly turn and flee and looked down into her troubled gray eyes. In the six months that he had known her, it was the first time that she had initiated an embrace.

"Hello?" he said, pleased and yet puzzled.

"I— It's— Oh damn it all, Nauman!" she murmured with her face against his shoulder.

"That's okay, love, I know," he soothed. His fingers tangled in her fine soft hair. "Come home with me, Siga?"

He felt the negative movement of her head. "Want me to stay with you?"

"No," she said regretfully, and pushed away from him and opened the wooden door with a deep breath. "I don't know what's the matter with me. I'm being totally unprofessional."

"You're being human," he said gently. "It's allowed."

"Yes. Well." Her voice was wry as she moved through the gate.

The moment had passed. Oscar turned to go. At the curb, he glanced back. The door remained open and he could still see her shadowed form silhouetted against the lights of her apartment.

"Sure you won't change your mind?"

"No."

Her low clear voice was again as cool as the damp October night and the garden door clicked shut between them.

CHAPTER XVI

The wind shifted in the night, pushing the rain clouds out to sea, and dawn brought crystalline blue skies and dryer air. As the sun came up, a clean autumnal freshness blew through the city's glass and stone forests.

Exhausted physically and emotionally, Sigrid had gone straight to bed the night before, but she slept badly, coming awake between uneasy dreams. Each waking took her longer to slide back under and the bedclothes twisted and tangled around her restless body. She almost never rose early by choice, yet by the time the odor of coffee drifted down the hall to her room, she had been lying wide-eyed and tense for more than an hour and she wearily kicked back the covers to join Roman over the Sunday *Times*.

Since moving in together, their Sunday mornings were usually quiet and companionable with the radio tuned to a classical music station and the luxurious sense of lazy hours stretching ahead free of all responsibilities.

Armed with coffee, juice, and a plate of jelly doughnuts, Roman would attack the thick newspaper from the end and munch steadily through to the front, pausing occasionally to dab away some powdered sugar and to read aloud a columnist or a comment that annoyed or amused him. He kept notecards beside his plate so he could jot down any stray sentence or quirky fact that struck him as the basis for a magazine article.

For her part, Sigrid usually bit into a French cruller and began at page one, moved on to the News of the Week in Review, zigged with the book reviews while Roman zagged with the magazine, then skimmed the other sections before diving happily into the puzzle page.

One could almost chart how long each had been awake by their respective places in the paper and by the number of pastries still in the bakery box on the table.

Today, however, Sigrid could not concentrate. A dull headache at the base of her skull echoed the faint ache in her arm and she felt thick-tongued and clumsy. She phoned the hospital and learned that Tillie was to be moved out of intensive care that afternoon. It was too early for any of the day shift to be at headquarters yet, so she returned restlessly to the newspaper.

Diagramless crosswords were her favorite puzzles, but even finding a pair of them at the back of the magazine section couldn't divert her this morning.

What she really wanted, what she truly needed, was a long session in the nearest swimming pool. Since childhood, swimming had been her principal exercise. She was not a team player, jogging bored her, and sweating heavily in a workout class had never appealed; but slicing through water, pushing herself physically until an almost mindless euphoria enfolded her, never failed to release all tensions and leave her mentally refreshed.

The knife wounds in her arm and hand placed pools off-limits, though, and just knowing she could not swim for several weeks knotted the muscles in her neck even tighter.

On the radio, the anxious drive of a Bach harpsichord concerto was starting to affect her like fingernails scraped across a blackboard.

Abruptly, she shoved the paper aside and went and changed into jeans and a bulky blue sweater.

"I'm going to walk along the river," she told Roman. "If anyone calls, tell them I should be back around noon."

"If you pass a deli, pick up some water biscuits," Roman said, without looking up from a fascinating article on a recently published Sumerian dictionary which could probably be understood by less than three hundred scholars worldwide. As the Bach concerto tinkled to an end, he began a reminder to himself on a notecard—"Where have all the Sumerians gone?"—and hesitated, his cluttered mind puzzled. Now what made him want to add "long time passing" to that question?

The city of New York began as a seaport and it remains an important gateway to the country, but at one time the Hudson was as clogged with traffic as Fifth Avenue at lunchtime. Tugs, ferries, fireboats, garbage scows, excursion boats, police launches, yachts, and barges jostled beneath the bows of huge freighters and sleek-lined passenger ships like the *Nieuw Amsterdam*, the *Liberté*, the *Michelangelo*, the *Queen Mary*, or the *Independence*. Weekly listings of arrivals and departures once filled many column inches of newsprint.

In those days, champagne corks popped while streamers, balloons, and brilliant confetti swirled down from railings to piers. Whistles blew, gangplanks lifted, and the great ships moved majestically out into the channel past flags from every seagoing nation in the world. A hundred busy piers had lined the West Side of Manhattan Island from the Battery up to West Fifty-ninth Street.

Now those piers which remained lay rotting and abandoned, fenced off with warning signs. The glamour and excitement of travel had shifted to LaGuardia and Kennedy. Instead of days on the *Queen Mary,* the rich and clever crisscrossed the Atlantic in hours on the *Concorde.*

Sigrid's street led straight down to the river and was lined with commercial buildings whose declining fortunes matched those of the docks. Until recently the elevated West Side Highway had stood here, speeding cars above the trucks that serviced the piers and jammed the intersections of West Street below. Time had taken a toll on it, too. Declared unsafe for vehicular traffic, huge sections of the highway had been pulled down and hauled away, opening up a wide, if not exactly lovely, vista of the docks and terminals of Hoboken and Jersey City across the river.

City planners had hoped to create Westway here eventually, a massive four-mile landfill with an underground highway and a riverfront esplanade of parks and high-priced residential and commercial buildings. But the project had bogged down in the courts and at present, the area was surprisingly deserted.

A young black artist sat with watercolors and sketchpad on one of the pilings, and an elderly man stood with a dog leash in his hand while his beautiful Labrador frisked along the edge of the pier. Otherwise, except for a handful of joggers and Sunday strollers, Sigrid had the place to herself.

The wind still blew from the north-northeast and the cool pungent air held a tang of salt mixed with creosote. Taking deep breaths, Sigrid headed upriver into the wind.

A hundred blocks north, Pernell Johnson finished his early morning cereal, quietly rinsed his bowl and spoon, and left them in the dishrack to dry as his aunt had taught him. He folded his blanket and sheet and closed up the couch he slept on. It folded with a loud screech of hinged springs and he glanced at the closed door apprehensively. There was still no sound from the bedroom where his aunt slept.

It would be another hour before Quincy Johnson rose for

church. As an assistant housekeeper at the Maintenon, she no longer had to work Sundays except in short-handed emergencies. Pernell hoped to be gone before she was awake enough to make him promise he'd get home in time for Sunday-night services.

God'd been mighty good to him lately, he thought, as he eased the front door open and hurried down the dark hall to the elevator, but God knew a man needed a little fun, too, and there was that foxy little gal that took her break the same time he did. A couple of years older and going to college full time, but the way she'd been looking at him all week, he just knew she'd say yes if he asked her to the movies tonight. Movies were all he could afford right now, but soon, very soon, there was going to be a lot more jingle in his jeans, he thought, happily pushing through the outer doors and into the sunlit Harlem street.

Wrapped in daydreams of innocent lust and avarice, Pernell Johnson loped toward the nearest subway station, unconsciously whistling jazzed-up snatches of the one tune that always bubbled up through layers of rock, soul, and rap whenever life seemed particularly blissful—"Can you tell me how to get, how to get to Sesame Street?"

In her penthouse atop the Maintenon, Lucienne Ronay sipped the last of her breakfast tisane and placed the fragile porcelain cup back on her bed tray. As if on cue, the maid returned from the pink marble bathroom where she'd filled the tub and sprinkled special bath beads over the warm water.

With a ritual "Will that be all, ma'am?" she lifted the breakfast tray from Madame Ronay's lap and silently exited.

Lucienne Ronay stretched luxuriously between the pale silken sheets, then threw back the down-filled comforter and drifted over to the windows that looked out over a breathtaking array of midtown skyscrapers. It was a view of which she never tired and one of the reasons she'd coaxed her husband into letting her take over these hotels he hadn't wanted to bother with.

Maurice! She still missed his strong presence.

Since his death, other men had wanted to spoil her, adore her, use her. Occasionally she even let them. How unimportant they were, though. How infantile. Maurice Ronay had bullied her with his power, laughed at her tantrums, then taken her breath away with grand romantic gestures. Yet they both knew he had not loved her as much as she loved him.

She found herself thinking about Leona Helmsley, a rival

hotelier with whom she was often, to their mutual displeasure, compared. Leona was wealthier. Was she also more fortunate in her marriage?

Madame sighed and resolutely put away the self-indulgent *tristesse* that Maurice's memory always evoked. She was Lucienne Ronay now, La Reine, with a kingdom to guard and administer.

That explosion Friday night could have been a disaster, she knew. Fortunately, there was no structural damage and once the mess was finally cleared away today, they would know better what would need doing. Perhaps it was time the d'Aubigné Room were completely refurbished anyhow?

Allowing a cribbage tournament had been a lapse of judgment she would never repeat, but order would soon be restored and thank heavens the public had short memories of where disasters occurred.

She loosened the ribbons of her negligee, felt the lacy folds slip along her ripe body to the floor, and walked naked to her bath.

Her complacency would have been shattered had she but known what the day held in store for the Maintenon.

Eighteen floors below the penthouse, in the suite Graphic Games had booked for the use of tournament personnel this weekend, Ted Flythe knotted his tie, then leaned across the bed to smack the bare rump that protruded from the tumbled covers.

"Up and at 'em, sunshine!" he said briskly.

"What time is it?" came the sleepy mumble.

"Time to haul ass."

She rolled over and struggled to look cute and pouty and seductive all at the same time. "Come back to bed, Teddy."

Flythe repressed a sigh. Why did these stupid cows always act as if one night changed all the guidelines?

He slipped on his jacket and said, "Rule one: Don't call me Teddy. Rule two: No fraternization during business hours. Rule three: When I say haul ass, I expect it to be hauled. *Subito!*"

The girl's brown eyes widened and for a moment, Ted Flythe thought she was going to go sulky on him. Instead, she gracefully rolled onto the floor, sashayed across the room to gather up her clothes, and with a hip-swinging, exaggerated shuffle toward the bathroom, said, "Yessuh, Mr. Bossman! Coming right up! I'se haulin' jest as fast as I kin haul. Yessuh!"

As her sassy little round bottom disappeared behind the door, Flythe grinned appreciatively. He might just have to add her name and number to his rotary file. Let's see now, was she Marcie or Trish?

The windows of Vassily Ivanovich's efficiency apartment overlooked the United Nations complex. With the sashes thrown wide, the big Russian was puffing through his daily exercise routine, a variation of the Royal Canadian Air Force plan with a dozen deep knee bends thrown in for good measure. Not bad for an old man, he thought, as he duck-walked back and forth in the cool morning air.

On the dresser was a long message from his son back in Moscow. Ivanovich accepted philosophically the evidence that his friendship with an American naval officer was under scrutiny and the subject of communiqués back and forth, but he did think his son would have more understanding of what he'd intended this trip to be. Alexei's message was almost schizoid in its effort to admonish and exhort without giving anyone any ammunition to use against either of them.

Ah well, thought Ivanovich. The boy is yet young.

He closed the windows but lingered for a moment to contemplate the gleaming buildings of the UN, buildings that hadn't even existed when he and his old friend roared into port near the end of the war. Already there were those who said it should be torn down, moved to another country, that nothing good had come from the millions of words spoken there these forty years.

The year was beginning to turn. Perhaps even now snow was falling on the Valdai Hills above his village. Perhaps it was time to go home.

But first there was one thing more to be done.

The efficient Miss Vaughan had left several sheets of messages neatly stacked on Zachary Wolferman's gleaming desk in the study. Breakfast over—despite Emily's coaxing, he'd only wanted tea and a few bites of toast—Haines Froelick turned the pages slowly, mechanically noting each name. Many of them recalled fleeting memories of times past; of weekends, dinners, long-ago parties or committee meetings.

A longish message from Zachary's lawyer caught his eye. It would appear that at some time in the past, his cousin had prepared detailed instructions for his own funeral. Mr. Froelick read them carefully. As far as he could tell, the arrangements he'd begun yesterday were in accordance with Zachary's wishes: the correct church, the desired undertaker, even the pallbearers. Entombment would, of course, be in the family vault in Greenwood. As a final request, Zachary had asked that two small objects of sentimental value be entombed with him. One was a gold locket containing the picture of a girl who died of influenza in 1939; the other was an Austrian schilling that he'd carried as a good luck piece.

Emily and Miss Vaughan had located the locket, and Mr. Froelick opened it to look at the sweet young face inside. Zachary always said Maria's death robbed him of the only girl he could ever marry, but Mr. Froelick privately believed that even had Maria lived, she could not have gotten him to the altar.

The schilling, however, was another matter. He and Zachary were mischievous lads climbing upon an equestrian statue in Graz one rainy summer day when Zachary found the coin tucked beneath a massive hoof. As soon as he touched it, the sun came out and Zachary declared it was an omen. After that, he carried the schilling all the time.

Zachary was not exactly superstitious, Haines had decided, but certainly that schilling had taken on certain quasi-mythical proportions over the years.

It had given him the confidence to do his best on school examinations and turning it between his fingers seemed to help him focus on the right decisions at work; so it was only fitting that Zachary should face the next world with his schilling in his pocket, thought Mr. Froelick.

According to Miss Vaughan's tidy memo, the housekeeper had been unable to locate it, so Miss Vaughan had spoken by telephone to a police sergeant in charge of personal property and learned that while the police were holding Mr. Wolferman's wallet, wristwatch, rings, and other small items found upon his person Friday night, they had no schilling.

She had then taken it upon herself to call the undertaker, who disavowed any knowledge of the coin's existence. Her call to the Hotel Maintenon had been equally unsuccessful, she wrote. Could Mr. Froelick suggest further places to look?

Mr. Froelick could not. Unless perhaps it had been flung under a table Friday night and lay hidden among the debris? Possibly it was still in that room. He seemed to recall that premises were often sealed by the police in cases like this. But surely not for very long when they were part of a public hotel? Even now, the Maintenon's personnel might be sweeping or vacuuming or whatever they did. He could telephone, but messages relayed through a third party would not convey the urgency of the situation.

Surely he owed this much to Zachary?

Sighing, he touched an intercom button on the desk and spoke to the kitchen. "Emily? Would you ask Willis to bring the car around, please?"

With her three-inch heels tucked inside an attaché case and scuffed sneakers on her feet, Molly Baldwin dashed for her bus as the driver eased off the brake.

The Sunday morning was still too fresh and sunny to have eroded the driver's temper, so he kept the door open and let her hop on instead of grinding away from the curb as he might have on a busier or rainy weekday.

"That was awfully nice of you," Molly smiled, dropping her coins into the meter. She always exaggerated her disappearing Florida drawl for busdrivers and cabbies. It usually made them more helpful, she'd found. She hated to be snarled at, though goodness knows she'd had to learn to take it since coming to New York.

Not that Madame Ronay snarled, she thought, taking a seat near the middle of the lurching bus; but she certainly could make life miserable when she was displeased about anything. If she knew about Teejy—

Molly shut her mind to that avenue of thought. Madame Ronay *didn't* know. And neither did Ted Flythe. And all she had to do was keep a firm grip on herself and remember that this cribbage tournament would end tonight and, with it, all her problems.

CHAPTER XVII

By the time Sigrid had walked up to West Twenty-third Street and back down again, her headache was gone and color had returned to her thin cheeks. She even slipped her arm out of the sling and went to look over the shoulder of the artist who sat on the rotting pier at the foot of her street. The artist looked up, gave her a friendly smile, and kept sketching.

A horn tooted along West Street. Sigrid paid no attention until it tooted again and someone called, "Lieutenant? Lieutenant Harald!"

She turned and saw Alan Knight loping across the traffic lanes to join her. His driver, the same bewildered yeoman, pulled gratefully alongside the empty curb and cut the engine.

"I've been all the way down to Battery Park looking for you," Knight called as he neared her. "Your friend said you were walking along the water but he didn't know what direction."

"Up," Sigrid gestured.

"Down's right nice, too," he drawled, matching her long strides. "They've got a real pretty park there."

Sigrid observed the crisp crease in the trouser legs of his dark blue uniform. "Are you on duty today or has something come up?"

"Both. I had a report waiting on my desk first thing this morning." There was an embarrassed look on his face.

"And?"

"You know those pictures Vassily Ivanovich showed us of his sons yesterday? Remember that nice boy who pulled a few strings so his sweet old papa could enjoy a vacation in America?"

Sigrid nodded.

"KGB," Knight said bitterly.

"Well, he did tell us his son was something in the Party," Sigrid recalled.

"Go on and say it."

"Say what?"

"I told you so."

"I never said Ivanovich was connected with the KGB."

"No, but you said he might not be as innocuous as he looks."

"Yes," Sigrid admitted.

"You were right. We've just learned that Ivanovich was the Russian equivalent of an EOD during the war."

"What's that?"

"Explosive Ordnance Demolition."

"Someone who dismantles bombs?"

Lieutenant Knight nodded. "Among other things."

"Then he'd know how to put one together."

"I don't see how we missed it. Or how Commander Dixon ever got a security clearance with what amounts to a Russian godfather in her background."

"Maybe she didn't know," Sigrid suggested reasonably as she paused to let three joggers pass. "Her father died over twenty-five years ago and if the two men hadn't corresponded since forty-eight or forty-nine—well, she was just a child then. She didn't try to keep him secret when he contacted her last spring, did she?"

"No." Lieutenant Knight glanced at her with disappointment. "I thought you'd be excited to hear that Vassily might be our bomber."

"I'm interested," Sigrid agreed, resuming her pace, "but it may not pertain. John Sutton seems the more logical target to me."

"The professor? Why?"

"It's beginning to look as if he recognized a Red Snow survivor."

"A who?"

Belatedly Sigrid recalled that Knight had not joined them at headquarters yesterday until after the discussion about the radical group that blew themselves up in the summer of 1970, so she summarized for him the facts and speculations they had about Fred Hamilton and Red Snow and how John Sutton had been so deeply involved in the war protest movement out at McClellan State that he could probably have recognized anyone from those days.

"Like Ted Flythe?" Knight suggested shrewdly.

"Mrs. Sutton didn't think so when I raised the possibility last night."

"How's she handling it?" Alan Knight's handsome face was immediately sympathetic.

"She's handling it," Sigrid said bluntly. Her voice remained cool and matter-of-fact, betraying no hint of how grief-wrenched she'd felt watching Val Sutton and her small son last night. She carefully confined her narrative to the pertinent facts. "And even though she doesn't think he's Hamilton, we'll get his fingerprints from FBI files and compare them with Flythe's."

A pair of sailboats slipped by them, headed downriver. Their pristine white sails ballooned in the steady breeze. A clatter of rotors passed overhead, and Knight shaded his eyes to follow the helicopter's flight until it dropped down out of sight at the heliport many blocks north.

"In a way, I hope you're wrong," he said, tugging at the brim of his hat. "I hope it turns out to be Ivanovich."

"For Commander Dixon's sake?" asked Sigrid, recalling how determined Val Sutton had been that her husband be the intended victim.

"Yeah." He walked along beside her in silence, then stopped to face her, his chiseled features bleak. "They had to take her arm off."

"When?"

"Last night. They tried to graft in new blood veins, but it didn't work."

Sigrid listened mutely, then strode on without comment. She had not met Commander T. J. Dixon, had not even seen a photograph, unless one counted the snapshot Vassily Ivanovich carried of her as a baby. Yet everyone commented on her prettiness; a feminine woman who enjoyed her beauty and used it to keep at least four men interested. How could she adapt to such a monstrous loss? Would she accept it philosophically, or would she withdraw into isolation, feeling mutilated and hideously disfigured?

Lieutenant Knight trailed along beside her and her silence began to fuel his youthful indignation. The naval officer possessed the Southern charm that remains a birthright of all young adults— male and female—reared by mothers to whom manners are almost more important than morals and who instill both in their children with equal vigor. He was by nature friendly and easygoing and willing to meet anyone more than halfway, but he couldn't see that Lieutenant Harald had budged an inch beyond the first five minutes of their introduction yesterday.

If anything, she was becoming steadily more distant.

He remembered his young yeoman clerk this morning. Her tender blue eyes had pooled with tears when she relayed the hospital report, repeating how dreadful it was and how sorry she felt for Commander Dixon until he'd finally seized on the information about Ivanovich to clear out of the office for a few hours.

So it certainly wasn't that he wanted Lieutenant Harald to burst into tears, he told himself. But not to say a word? To keep walking like T. J. Dixon's arm was nothing more than a piece of meat to be thrown in the river?

He'd worked with some hard-nosed senior women officers in his five years with the Navy, but he'd found that if he was friendly and properly respectful of their rank, they soon climbed down and opened up, while this one—

Oblivious to his growing resentment, Sigrid moved through the sunlit morning almost blindly as she thought how devastated the commander would be when she recovered enough to realize that she'd lost her arm by a fluke, a bad coincidence of time and place. She thought of how bothersome her own arm was, yet it was only wounded and would soon heal.

She turned to Lieutenant Knight abruptly. "How much of her arm did they amputate?"

"How much does it take, Lieutenant?"

His hostility took her by surprise.

"I guess police officers get like doctors after a while," he said.

"What—?"

"Cold. Detached. *Objective!*" His soft Southern drawl heaped scorn on the word. "Doctors can tell you about watching a baby die like I'd tell you about the Mets losing to St. Louis. They say it's 'cause they can't let themselves feel; that they'd burn out if they grieved over every patient. After a while, they don't have to worry. They've got no feelings left." His bitterness was scalding. "Is that what happened to you, Lieutenant Sigrid Harald of the New York Police Department?"

"I don't know what you're talking about," she said icily, without stopping.

"Is that how you quit being a woman with a woman's softness and a woman's tender heart?"

Goaded now, Sigrid turned on him, her gray eyes blazing. "I'm a professional investigator, Lieutenant. It's my job to stay detached and objective. Will grieving replace Dixon's arm or bring Val Sutton's husband back to life? Will crying keep whoever did this obscene thing from doing it again? I don't think so, Lieutenant. And what's more, if I had a sick child, I'd rather have a doctor cold enough to keep fighting against death than one too choked up to work, so you can take your tender little chauvinistic heart and go to hell!"

She jerked away from him, striding across the dilapidated pier, to the very edge, where she stood staring down into the murky water that lapped against the rotting pilings. She wished the water was cleaner, the day warmer, and that she could just dive in and swim toward the sun until all the churning inside her was washed away.

Her arm throbbed viciously and she slipped it back into the sling and pressed it with her free hand to ease the pounding.

Knight had followed her and he sat down on one of the nearby pilings. "I'm sorry," he said. "I guess I spoke out of line."

Sigrid shrugged and continued staring down into the river, grateful for once that her hair was loose and that the wind kept blowing it across her face and hid what she never willingly allowed anyone to see.

On the next pier over, an oriental man walked out almost to the end carrying a large bundle of red material. He was accompanied by a small girl in pigtails, who frolicked about him like a puppy. They were obviously father and daughter and he called warnings as she ran too near the edge, while her laughter bubbled out in lilting joy.

While Sigrid and Knight watched, the man placed his red bundle on the pier and began working on it. Curious gulls wheeled overhead.

Knight glanced over at Sigrid. "I'm sorry," he said again. "I keep forgetting that all women don't show—"

"*All* women don't do anything," Sigrid said between clenched teeth. "No more than *all* men."

"Hey, I'm no chauvinist," he protested. "I like women. Really."

Still unsettled and now annoyed at herself that she'd lost her temper, Sigrid brushed aside his protest. "Forget it. It's not important."

On the next pier, the long mass of red cloth grew a ferocious golden dragon's face and became first a limp red wind sock and then a swelling sinuous dragon with streamers that caught the wind as it clawed its way into the sky. The child clapped her hands gleefully as it dipped and soared against the blueness like a wild untamed beast straining against its leash. At one point, it toyed with disaster and skimmed the surface of the water, then a twitch of the line sent it climbing again.

It was innocent and graceful and without realizing it, Sigrid began to relax.

"I'm not really a chauvinist pig," Alan Knight said coaxingly. "Thick-headed at times maybe, but not sexist."

"No?" Sigrid gave him a jaundiced look, for he suddenly reminded her of some of her Lattimore cousins when they meant to wheedle her into trying something she didn't particularly want to do. Whenever the charm switched on, she'd learned to tread warily.

Sensing a slight softening in her manner, Knight smiled persuasively and held up three fingers, with his thumb and pinkie touching. "Scout's honor. I truly do like women."

Sigrid brushed her hair back behind her ears and looked down into his deep brown eyes.

"That must make your wife very happy," she said sardonically.

Beneath the brim of his hat, his handsome face became unexpectedly flushed. "Uh— Well, you see, I'm not exactly married."

She shot a telling glance at the gold band on his left hand.

"I've never been married," said Knight.

"Then why—?"

"The ring? I bought it in a pawnshop and started wearing it in college."

"Why?"

"Well, look at me."

Bewildered, she looked him over completely and saw nothing to alter yesterday's original impression. Lieutenant Alan Knight was a remarkably attractive specimen of American malehood.

She said as much.

"Yeah, *now,*" he said without vanity. "Up until my sophomore year in college, I was an Alfred E. Neumann lookalike: my ears stuck out like jug handles, my front teeth made Bugs Bunny's look good, I was as tall as I am right now, but weighed a hundred and ten sopping wet, and I had cowlicks fore and aft—goofiest looking face outside a comic strip."

Sigrid lowered herself to the dock and leaned back against the next piling with her left knee drawn up and her right leg dangling over the edge.

"What happened your sophomore year?"

"I worked on my uncle's tobacco farm, ate my aunt's cooking all summer, and put on twenty-five pounds. It seemed to make everything fit together. Then before I went back to college, my sisters hauled me down to their beauty shop and they found a way to cut my hair so it didn't look like a haystack in a hurricane. All of a sudden, I looked pretty much like I do now."

"And that was bad?"

"Scared the living bejesus out of me," he replied earnestly. "I told you I like women and I do. I grew up in a household with six sisters, a terrific mom, and more aunts than I can count, but I never had a sweetheart. Girls at school used to tell me all their problems 'cause they knew I'd understand. They never wanted to go out with me, though. As far as they were concerned, I was just good old dumb-looking Alan. They kept telling me I was almost like a brother to them, only no girl wanted to date her brother."

Across the way, the pigtailed child had her hand on the thick cord that bound the majestic dragon to the earth, and they could hear her lilting tones as she cajoled her father to let her fly it solo.

Alan Knight leaned down to scoop up a handful of loose gravel scattered along the pier and began plinking it into the water.

"When I got back to college that fall, I didn't know what hit me. I sort of liked it, having girls like me—who wouldn't? But I also didn't know how to handle it. Most guys, the guys that girls go after, have time to get used to how to act. From kindergarten, most of them; and certainly by junior high; and there *I* was, all the way in college, for God's sake."

Sigrid smiled.

"Yeah," he said self-mockingly. "Funny as hell, right? And the worst thing about it was that after a while I missed having girl friends. I don't mean lovers, but friends who are girls. Sorry, I guess I should say women."

"I'm not hung up on semantics," Sigrid said mildly.

"No? Anyhow, every time I'd try to be friends with a female, she'd either slap me down or expect us to go to bed together. It got to be such a hassle that I bought the ring and told everybody it was a secret marriage and that she'd promised her parents to finish school out west somewhere first. That took a lot of pressure off right away."

"I shouldn't have thought a ring had that much power anymore."

"You'd be surprised."

"What happens when you're attracted to someone?" she asked curiously.

"I take it off. Or I tell her my wife and I are separated at the moment."

"So you have your cake and eat it, too."

"At least I'm not trying to pretend the cake doesn't exist," he said; then added boldly, "Why are you?"

"In case you hadn't noticed," she answered flatly, "I'm not a college sophomore. I did all the growing up and filling out I'm ever going to do and, unlike you, I didn't turn into a swan."

"But women are different," he said. "There's so much you can do to help the swanning along."

"Oh Lord, don't start on the hair-makeup-sexy clothes bit."

She pulled both knees up sharply and rested her strong chin on them.

"Why not? What are you afraid of?"

"I'm not afraid of anything, and frankly, Lieutenant, I can't see that it's any of your business."

"The guy you're living with— Is he the one trying to get you to nibble some of the cake?"

"Oh for God's sake," Sigrid groaned and swung herself up to leave.

"That's what my sisters always used to say when I got uncomfortably near the truth," he called, striding after her.

"I'm surprised they didn't smother you in your crib," she muttered as he caught up with her.

"They tried. Mother wouldn't let them." He smiled at her persuasively.

She did not smile back.

"Look, I'm sorry if I've insulted you. You're right. It's none of my business if you don't like cake. Truce?"

Her suspicious gray eyes probed his. The mischief that had lurked there a few minutes ago was gone now and he seemed serious again.

"I think it might be better if you worked with someone else in the department," she said doubtfully.

"I don't. Besides, your partner's still out and your captain mentioned you were short-handed. Why don't we head on up to the Maintenon," he suggested craftily, "and get Flythe's finger-prints?"

Sigrid glanced at her watch. Roman usually served Sunday's main meal in the middle of the day. If she stretched it out a little, she could probably miss his anised veal completely.

"First we'll drop in on Molly Baldwin," she told him.

Behind them, the crimson dragon with the golden face stalked sea gulls far out over the water.

CHAPTER XVIII

During the week, Manhattan lives up to the image set forth in a thousand books, movies, songs, and sermons. It is indeed a money-grubbing, smart-talking, elbow-shoving, glitzy, rude, so-phisticated, dirty, elegant, international metropolis. But on Sunday mornings, it becomes an astonishingly small town. Except for the

Times Square area which never completely shuts down, the rest of the island grows hushed and lazy. Wall Street is a ghost canyon, footsteps echo through Grand Central Station, families stroll leisurely to church along empty sidewalks, and best of all, if you happened to be a nervous young sailor who learned to drive on a dirt road in rural New Hampshire, the streets unclog on Sunday mornings and become wide boulevards.

He and Lieutenant Knight had dropped the skinny lady police officer off at a green door in a high brick wall, then gone searching through the food stores along Hudson Street.

"Water biscuits?" he'd asked.

"Big round crackers," explained Lieutenant Knight, and gave him a brief history of what food used to be like on clipper ships.

By the time they returned with her crackers, the lady officer had changed from jeans into gray slacks and a navy blue jacket. Soon they were zipping along up Tenth Avenue, catching green lights all the way.

Now this was more like it, thought the yeoman.

Tenth Avenue became Amsterdam Avenue as they sped north paralleling the park. Upon approaching the West Nineties, he slowed down and eventually turned left to pull up before the address Lieutenant Harald gave him.

"We shouldn't be long," said Lieutenant Knight as the two officers got out of the car.

In fact, they were back in less than three minutes, the time it took to lean on the intercom button in the lobby until they roused one of Molly Baldwin's late-partying roommates and were told that Miss Baldwin herself had left for work at least two hours ago.

"Never mind," said Alan Knight when Sigrid started to apologize for taking them out of the way. "It was a good idea to try to catch her off guard. To the hotel?"

"To the hotel," she agreed.

"To the hotel!" echoed their neophyte driver. With renewed confidence, he boldly cut across Central Park, cruised down Lexington Avenue, and swerved in at the hotel's curb with style and panache.

It was exactly three minutes past eleven.

They found the Bontemps Room much as they had left it yesterday, although some of the older players beneath the glittering chandeliers were beginning to look a bit weary around the edges. They had been split into two groups after the mid-morning break at ten-thirty. The smaller section competed for the main prize, now reduced to seven thousand dollars; the others were playing for small but numerous consolation pots.

Sigrid saw that Jill Gill was still in the running for the main prize. The entomologist gave her a distracted wave, but her attention was all on the cards.

"They have to keep at it if we're going to finish by five," Ted Flythe told them. "The breaks are supposed to last fifteen minutes, but it takes almost a half hour to get them settled down again."

As they spoke, Sigrid tried to visualize him without a beard, as he might have looked fifteen years ago without bags under his hooded eyes, his dark hair longer and without the beginning traces of gray. One thing about his habit of smoothing his beard into a sharp point: his fingers would leave nice clear prints.

If he were Fred Hamilton, the main thing was not to alert him of her suspicions. Let him continue in this role of laid-back aging roué.

After a few desultory remarks, she took out a fresh white index card and, casually holding it by the edges, said, "Would you mind jotting down your address and telephone number, Mr. Flythe, in case we should need to contact you after the tournament's over?"

"Sure, Lieutenant, but let me give you my card."

He pulled a thin leather case from an inner pocket of his jacket and extracted a card with a Graphic Games logo and his business address on the front. He turned it over and scribbled down a number in the East Nineties.

"I'm on the go a lot, all up and down the East Coast," he warned, handing Sigrid the card, "but the office usually knows how to reach me."

Sigrid thanked him and carefully stowed his card between the pages of her note pad. Before leaving the house earlier, she had called headquarters and set in motion a rush request for Fred Hamilton's fingerprints. With even minimal efficiency, they should be able to do a rough comparison by tomorrow morning.

The ranks of cardplayers seemed to have thinned slightly. Flythe told them that several of the losers had opted to drop out after elimination rather than play for the consolation prizes. Sigrid spotted Vassily Ivanovich among the also-rans, as well as several others she had helped interview the day before.

"We were looking for Miss Baldwin," said Alan Knight. "Is she here?"

"Yeah, she's been in and out all morning." Flythe looked

around vaguely. "Talking to the busboys and things. I haven't seen her since the break, though."

"Did you remember to bring those copies of the first pairings?" asked Sigrid.

Flythe nodded. "As a matter of fact, I gave them to Miss Baldwin. I didn't realize you people were going to be back today, so I thought she could pass them along to you."

There was no sign of Molly Baldwin in the room and when they inquired among the green-jacketed busboys standing around the hospitality table, they met with shrugs and blank expressions.

In the large serving pantry beyond the service door, they found the room steward somewhat testy because a fresh tray of coffee cups had not arrived from below. A cribbage tournament might not draw the Maintenon's usual class of patrons, but Mr. George scrupulously preserved the standards. Not even for cribbage players would he allow Styrofoam cups to sully the Bontemps Room. Coffee at the Maintenon was dispensed from silverplated urns into china cups.

"So where are the clean cups?" shrilled Mr. George. "And where are Johnson and LeMays?"

His question was partially answered as the rumble of a service cart and the tinkling of china heralded the arrival of cups through the doors of the serving pantry. The cart was pushed by a single busboy.

Mr. George's patience was frayed. "Where's Johnson?"

"He wasn't with me," the youth shrugged. "I ain't seen him since break."

"I'm sorry, Lieutenant," said the distracted steward when Sigrid persisted with her questions about Molly Baldwin. "I've got my hands full here and I really can't say where Ms. Baldwin is right now."

He looked around sharply. "LeMays, I need two dozen of those cups lined up beside the urn. Ruiz, you and Pacabelli can start with the ashtrays again. You know Madame Ronay's rules: no more than three butts before you give them a clean one. What if she comes back and sees that mess out there? Hop to it!"

Threatened with La Reine's displeasure, the busboys hopped.

Sigrid and Alan Knight followed them back into the Bontemps Room. Sigrid was struck again by the disparity between the room's eighteenth-century regality and its decidedly twentieth-century proletarian clientele.

As they entered from the rear, one of the tall, gold-tipped doors at the front opened and revealed their quarry.

"There she is!" said Alan Knight.

The two officers started across the wide floor. At the sight of their purposeful advance, the color drained from Molly Baldwin's face.

"Ms. Baldwin," called Sigrid.

They were passing one of the consolation tables and Vassily Ivanovich's grizzled head came up from his cards and swung in the direction they were headed. "What you say? That is little Molly?"

"Hey, where're you going?" cried his opponent as the big Russian joined the charge.

"I quit! You are winner this time," Ivanovich flung back over his shoulder. Beyond the tall lieutenant's head, he saw a slender brown-haired girl in the doorway and roared, *"You!* You are T.J.'s Molly?"

It was too much. Molly Baldwin turned and fled.

There was a brief traffic jam at the doorway as Sigrid, Knight, and Ivanovich each tried to get through.

At the end of the hall, where the main staircase created a wide landing, Molly was waylaid by an elderly gentleman in a dark suit.

"Excuse me, miss, but are you with the hotel? I need someone on the housekeeping staff to—"

At that precise moment, the elevator across the landing chimed and Madame Ronay stepped off, followed by three frightened-looking maids.

"Ah, there you are, Miss Baldwin," said the Maintenon's owner in a steel bladed tone that could have ripped through solid teak. "May I ask why I've had to—"

Abruptly she became aware of the others and the steel was instantly sheathed in French velvet.

"Lieutenant Harald, Lieutenant Knight? But what has happened here? You have changed your mind?"

The maids were edging away toward the opposite hall that led to the d'Aubigné Room.

"Moment!" ordered Lucienne Ronay.

"Changed my mind?" asked Sigrid.

"Did you not say yesterday that you were finished here and that my people may restore order today to my poor d'Aubigné Room? Have you different thoughts now? And is this why," she asked with a pointed look at the wretched Molly Baldwin, "work has not yet begun there?"

"No, we've finished," said Sigrid.

"Alors!" said Madame Ronay and the maids scuttled down the hallway and disappeared into the wrecked ballroom.

"I— If you'll excuse me," Molly Baldwin said hopelessly, "I'll just get them started."

Before anyone could object, the dark-suited gentleman said, "May I come with you? I'm Haines Froelick and—"

"Monsieur Froelick!" exclaimed Lucienne Ronay, now transformed into a solicitous and totally sympathetic hostess. *"Je suis très desolée.* Your poor cousin! I grieve with you. That such a dreadful thing should happen *here* . . ."

Mr. Froelick thanked her gravely and explained his errand concerning the missing schilling. "I know it seems silly to care about such a small thing when so much has happened, but if your staff could watch for it, it would mean so much."

"Certainement. Miss Baldwin will— *Mais, non!"* Madame interrupted herself meaningfully. "To make certain my wishes are carried out, I myself will instruct them. Come, *M'sieur.* Molly?"

"I'm sorry, Madame Ronay," said Sigrid, "but we've a few more questions we need to ask Ms. Baldwin at the moment."

"So?" The shrewd hazel eyes compared Sigrid's calm demeanor with Molly Baldwin's apprehension. "So," she nodded. "When you have finished, Molly, I too have questions for you."

"Yes, Madame," the girl said unhappily.

As her employer escorted Mr. Froelick across the landing, Miss Baldwin faced them in resignation. "There's a small room down there where we can talk."

"Is true?" rumbled Vassily Ivanovich, looming up behind them. "You are T.J.'s cousin?"

The girl looked into his glowering face and burst into tears.

Sigrid was appalled, Ivanovich flustered, but Alan Knight was only clinically interested. With six sisters, he was long inured to the sight of bawling females.

Which was the only way to describe Molly Baldwin at that moment. This was no momentary misting of the eyes, no delicate sniffles hidden away behind a dainty handkerchief, no sun shower that would disappear as suddenly as it had come. This was an all-out storm.

"Batten down the hatches," murmured the naval officer, and flourishing his large white handkerchief like a hurricane warning flag, he strode forward, put his arm around her and said, "There, there, honeybunch, it's gonna be all right. Here, blow."

Still sobbing, poor Molly blew.

"Atta girl! Blow again."

Gradually, the sobs diminished, abating into snuffly hiccups.

The fiery red blotches began to fade from her cheeks, leaving just her eyes and the tip of her snub nose a glowing pink.

"Okay now?" asked Alan Knight.

She nodded like an embarrassed child and started to speak, when one of the maids burst from the d'Aubigné Room and darted toward them.

"Lieutenant! Lieutenant!" she cried breathlessly. "Come quick. There's been another murder!"

CHAPTER XIX

At first glance, Sigrid could almost believe the still form had been lying there since Friday night, overlooked in the chaos of the explosion. It was well under one of the back tables near the fatal Table 5, hidden by a heap of water-stained linen.

The maid, pale but excited, described how she had been stripping the tables of the long white tablecloths and throwing them onto the pile already begun. When her co-worker trundled the laundry cart down the aisle, she had tried to gather up the heap, realized something heavy was tangled in the linen, gave a mighty jerk and out rolled the body of a slender young black man dressed in the short green jacket and black trousers of a Hotel Maintenon employee.

He looked familiar to Sigrid, but she couldn't remember which busboy he'd been among the several on duty during the cribbage tournament. Besides, he seemed to have been strangled with his own tie and his face was not a very pretty sight.

There was no pulse, of course, and his skin was cool to the touch.

Sigrid straightened up. "Who is he?"

Molly Baldwin had stopped weeping and now looked as if she were going to be sick. "I don't know," she whispered.

"Madame Ronay?"

"Forgive me, Lieutenant. There are so many and he is—" She also seemed queasy and smiled gratefully when Haines Froelick took her arm and drew her aside.

"Could be Quincy Johnson's nephew," offered one of the maids with trepidation.

Madame Ronay forced herself to look again. *"Ah, pauvre petit. C'est possible."*

Sigrid herded everyone to a front table, handed Alan Knight her note pad, and curtly ordered: "I'm going to phone headquarters. Please take their names and addresses and don't let anyone leave or enter this room until I get back."

Lucienne Ronay began to expostulate about the need to call her public relations agent and channel the flood of bad publicity this second death was sure to undam.

There would be plenty of opportunity for that later, Sigrid told her crisply. "If you and your people cooperate, perhaps we can keep a lid on most of the sensationalism."

"But of course we will cooperate," said Madame Ronay, drawing up at the very suggestion that she and her staff would do otherwise.

Sigrid left them, remembered which alcove held a telephone booth, and summoned help from headquarters. Afterward, she went back to the Bontemps Room and plucked Mr. George from the midst of his duties. He tried to object but Sigrid knew the magic words. "Madame Ronay," she murmured and Mr. George trotted along like a little lamb.

Outside the d'Aubigné Room, she paused. "A little earlier, I heard you ask where Johnson was. Is that one of the busboys?"

"Sure, why?"

"When did you last see him?"

The little steward frowned. "I don't know. About break time, I guess. 'Bout an hour ago? He and Ms. Baldwin were talking in the passageway outside the service door. Why? What's he done?"

"What makes you think he's done something?"

"You asking questions. La Reine wanting to see me. It's about Johnson, isn't it?"

"Yes. A body's been found. One of the maids thinks it might be your missing busboy. I'd like for you to look and tell me if it's Johnson."

The steward opened his mouth to protest, but nothing emerged.

Wordlessly he followed her past the table where his employer sat, her two hands folded on the tabletop, a large sapphire ring glowing on her right hand. Sigrid pointed to the body and said, "Is that Johnson?"

"Oh my God!" the steward moaned. "Who's gonna tell Miss Quincy?"

"Come here, George," ordered Madame Ronay from the front of the room. "Do you say this is Quincy Johnson's nephew? Pernell, *est-ce qui?*"

"Yes, Madame," the steward answered faintly. "She was so proud of how good he's been doing. I was going to speak to you about him tomorrow, recommend a bonus for the kid."

"Bonus?" Madame Ronay asked sharply. "*Pourquoi?*"

"Because of the way he kept his head Friday night. After the explosion, he's the one who grabbed that extinguisher and rushed over and put out the fire before it could spread. A few minutes more and you'd have had to replace not just the carpet, but part of the paneling, too."

"You should have told me this before." Lucienne Ronay's graceful blonde head drooped sadly. "*Hélas!* Now it is too late forever for me to reward him."

She drew a deep breath and began to function like an executive again. "Someone must be sent to tell Miss Johnson. Who, George?" Her ring flashed blue fire as she pointed to him. "You?"

"Not me," said the steward even before Sigrid could voice her own objection to letting him leave the hotel just yet.

"Hester Yates is downstairs. She and Miss Quincy are real good friends. You want me to send her?"

Both looked at Sigrid.

"This is permitted, Lieutenant?" asked Madame Ronay.

"In a moment," said Sigrid. "First, I'd like to hear everything you can remember about Pernell Johnson's movements today. What he did, who he talked to. If you would be patient a few minutes longer, Madame?"

Lucienne Ronay nodded graciously, turning the sapphire ring with her restless fingers.

Haines Froelick cleared his throat. "What about me, Lieutenant? Is it all right if I look around for my cousin's schilling?" He gestured hesitantly toward the back of the large room, to the corner where Zachary Wolferman had died.

"I'm afraid not," she replied. "Nothing can be disturbed till after our crime scene crew has had a chance to examine things. I'll tell them to keep an eye out for it."

"Then perhaps I should leave now," he said and Sigrid thought she detected relief in his face, as if she'd saved him an unpleasant task by her denial of his request.

"I'm sorry, Mr. Froelick, but I'll want your statement as well as the others."

"*My* statement. Oh my dear young lady, I've no statement, I assure you."

"What we need will only take a few minutes," Sigrid said. "After we've talked to Mr. George. Perhaps you and Madame Ronay—?"

Lucienne Ronay took the hint and wafted Froelick across the room to a loveseat upholstered in peach-colored silk beneath a large gilt-framed painting that easily fell within Nauman's Cool Whip parameters.

"All our paintings here are originals, Mr. Froelick," Sigrid heard the Frenchwoman murmur. "One of the finest *ateliers* in Europe is under contract with us."

Molly Baldwin sat wrapped in mute misery at one end of a long table while Vassily Ivanovich glowered at her from the other end. At a nearby table, just out of earshot, Sigrid and Alan Knight listened as Mr. George informed them that Pernell Johnson had come on duty at eight o'clock, as prompt and efficient in his work as always.

The steward was a small black man of ramrod posture, receding gray hair and a penchant for fussy details. Sigrid soon learned that he had approved of Johnson and had interested himself in the youth's progress at the hotel. "That boy had a real future here, Lieutenant. He was a hard worker like his aunt. I know he might have gotten in a little trouble down in Florida, but up here he was one of the good ones. Never messed with liquor or dope or none of that stuff far as I ever heard."

"Florida?" asked Alan Knight.

"Trouble?" asked Sigrid.

"Miss Quincy told Hester Yates and Hester Yates told me and now I'm telling you, but nobody else. And certainly not Madame." He removed a crumb of cigarette tobacco from the table. "Not many boys that don't have a brush with the law 'fore they get grown. You know that. He and another kid stole some hubcaps or something down there and his grandmother, Miss Quincy's mother, shipped him up here to get him away from that stuff."

Sigrid remembered now: the thin youth with the soft drawl who'd brought her a glass of water the day before. A helpful person, eager to please, and, according to Mr. George, a "noticing" worker.

"Some of 'em can't see a thing that needs doing till you tell 'em. Johnson did, always. Dirty glasses and ashtrays didn't pile up around his stations. Somebody look around for a glass of water, cup of coffee, Johnson was right there.''

A noticing kid.

Had he noticed something Friday night, Sigrid wondered, and been incautious enough to let the wrong person know?

If so, Mr. George seemed unaware of it. According to him, Pernell Johnson had been as puzzled as everyone else as to how the cribbage board was rigged and planted.

Yes, he said, Pernell had been one of his helpers when the long tables were covered with snowy linens on Friday afternoon. After supper, Pernell was among the busboys who came in when the service door was unlocked at seven o'clock and he had been in and out while the Graphic Games people put the finishing touches on the tables and Ms. Baldwin and Madame Ronay made a final check of the room.

Madame had approved everything except the ashtrays. Instead of the heavy cut glass, she called for the lighter pressed glass which were easier to clean and, admitted Mr. George, less expensive to replace if any of the contestants had sticky fingers; so there had been a scurrying five minutes to change the ashtrays and then the doors were opened at seven-thirty and if Pernell Johnson had noticed anything suspicious after the room began to fill with five hundred cribbage players, Mr. George hadn't heard of it.

"Who changed the ashtrays at Table 5?" she asked.

The steward's brow furrowed. "I think it was Johnson."

Except for that, Mr. George's testimony was virtually a repeat of what he'd told them yesterday. It confirmed what each of the busboys had said as well. If Pernell Johnson had held anything back, no one had picked up on it. They would have to question the staff again, of course.

Sigrid returned to this morning.

Mr. George and his crew had stocked the hospitality table with urns of hot coffee and trays of light pastries at eight–fifteen. Play began at eight–forty-five. Almost nothing distinguished this morning from yesterday. Coffee and pastries again this morning, to be followed again by coffee, soft drinks, mixed nuts, and crudités in the afternoon. Pernell had performed as efficiently as ever, with nothing to make his movements remarkable.

There was a break for the cardplayers at ten-thirty.

"No matter how we try to corral them, they wander all over the hotel during the breaks," said Mr. George. "The service doors are clearly marked for staff only, but there're always a few that duck out that way. It's a little shorter to the restrooms. Johnson could have been around during the break, but I don't remember seeing him.'' He turned in his chair and his voice carried to the next table. ''Like I said before, the last time I definitely remember seeing him was about ten–twenty-five, talking to Ms. Baldwin here.''

Molly Baldwin looked startled. ''Was that Pernell Johnson? I didn't know. I was warning him about the ash stands in the lobby.''

Sigrid held up a forestalling hand. ''Please, Ms. Baldwin, hold your comments for now until we can take your statement.''

But Mr. George had nothing more to add. Ten–twenty-five was the last time he had seen Pernell Johnson.

Alan Knight had been quietly taking notes throughout the interview and he detained Mr. George with one question: ''Where in Florida did Johnson live before he came north?''

''Miami, I believe,'' said the steward.

Ivanovich gave an interrogative rumble.

They released Mr. George with the request that he tell no one about Johnson's death except Hester Yates. Madame Ronay told him to send Yates up to Harlem in one of the hotel's cars and to instruct the driver to put himself at Miss Johnson's disposal for the rest of the day.

As he left, several crime scene technicians entered with satchels and cameras. They looked around the opulent ballroom with quizzical eyes. ''Lieutenant Harald? We heard you've got a body for us.''

Sigrid conferred with them briefly and as they began their professional routine, she returned to question Haines Froelick. The elderly club man continued to doubt if he could help them. He had arrived at the hotel about ten–forty-five that morning and came upstairs as the tournament break was ending.

Seeing the players stream back and forth from the left hall off the landing, he had become confused and thought at first that they were still using the room in which the explosion had occurred. He had even entered the Bontemps Room and almost walked its full mauve and purple length before he realized his mistake. As he left by the rear door, Mr. Flythe was calling for order. He had wandered through the back halls thoroughly muddled for several minutes—making a brief stop at one of the men's rooms, he added, with a faint air of courtly embarrassment, avoiding Sigrid's eyes, and eventually wound up back at the main landing again. It was there that he remembered how he and his cousin had turned right at the top of the grand staircase on Friday night, not left.

He finally reached the red and gilt d'Aubigné Room at perhaps ten past eleven, he told them. No, there was no one inside.

"Were the lights on?" asked Sigrid.

"Why, yes. Not as many as now but enough to see that the room was empty. I began to walk back and forth across the floor, working my way toward the rear, when it occurred to me that perhaps I should not be here without permission, so I went back out to the landing to see if I could find someone who could tell me if the schilling had been found or if anyone minded my looking."

"And all this time, you saw no one?"

"Not in here. There were a few people passing back and forth at the foot of the stairs down in the main lobby—guests, of course—but I wanted a member of the staff and I couldn't seem to find one until I crossed the landing and recognized this young lady from Friday night. I had only begun to inquire of her when you joined us."

Sigrid glanced across at Alan Knight. He had entered a list of times on her note pad and was now doodling clock faces across the bottom of the sheet.

"Have you any questions, Lieutenant Knight?"

"Thank you, Lieutenant Harald," he replied gravely. "Mr. Froelick, when you first opened the door to this room and looked in, was the service door back there open or closed?"

"Closed," Mr. Froelick answered without hesitation.

"You didn't see the body under the table?"

"I didn't get that far."

"And no one was over on this side of the landing either time you came along the hall?"

"Quite deserted, I assure you."

Knight returned to his doodling. "No more questions from me."

Sigrid thanked Mr. Froelick and said he might leave, adding that they would appreciate his discretion for the time being.

"You won't forget about Zachary's schilling, will you?" he asked anxiously. "The funeral is tomorrow."

Sigrid promised they would not and Froelick made his adieux to Lucienne Ronay as if he were leaving a garden party that had unfortunately been rained out. Sigrid watched him thoughtfully. Was the courtly Mr. Froelick, she wondered, truly as color-blind as his account would appear to make him?

CHAPTER XX

While the forensic technicians photographed and made a minute examination of the body and its immediate surroundings, Sigrid and Alan Knight continued with their questions at the front of the room.

They tried to send Vassily Ivanovich back to the tournament but the big Russian refused to be dislodged. "First I am speaking to Molly," he growled stubbornly. It was obvious to all that a *tête-à-tête* with Ivanovich was the last thing Molly Baldwin wanted. Or perhaps the next to last thing. She did not appear anxious to converse with her employer either and was patently relieved when Ivanovich was exiled to the loveseat and Madame Ronay was summoned for her testimony.

The volatile Frenchwoman moved lightly to the table and smiled up at Lieutenant Knight as he held her chair, but it was an automatic gesture. Her heart didn't seem to be in it. Her lovely face had begun to show signs of strain and was pinched around the mouth and eyes.

"What is happening here?" she asked them sadly. "*Cette bombe* Friday night. At first I can think this is a crank. Someone who hates my poor Maintenon or who wants to make some big statement about the politics in his country, but this! *Ce petit* Johnson? *Non!*"

"No," Sigrid agreed. She rested her elbows on the tabletop with her fingers tented together and watched Knight's pen poised over the note pad as she gathered her thoughts. "Tell us please, Madame, of your movements this morning. When did you arrive on this floor? What did you see or hear?"

"When did I arrive? The first time it is perhaps ten or fifteen minutes past ten. On Sundays I am very lazy, you understand. I sleep late and I do not rush straight to my office below. It is a good day to poke around, to look in supply closets, to check the kitchens, to make certain all is as it should be, *comprenez-vous?*"

They nodded. Interviews with the staff yesterday had given

them both a clear idea of La Reine's ways. Not a reign of terror exactly, but something more akin to *l'ancien régime* intimidation, surprise inspections and unexpected appearances at the most awkward moment.

"So, I enter through there," she said, indicating the service door. Her right hand flashed with diamonds almost as large as the sapphire on her left finger.

Knight had sketched a rough floor plan of the area and he showed it to them now.

The grand staircase rose to a wide landing, at the rear of which were a bank of three elevators and the two wide halls leading off in either direction. On one side of the elevators was an inconspicuous door marked "No admittance," which opened onto another spacious landing with two more elevators, a large one for freight and another for staff, that used the same shaft as the passenger elevators out front.

A maze of corridors led to various storerooms, pantries and the service entrances of both the d'Aubigné and Bontemps rooms.

"How very clever you are," Lucienne Ronay told him. With a pink-enameled fingertip, she traced her route this morning.

"First, I come down on the staff elevator here, then I go through the halls here. I see no one on this side."

"Were the lights on?" asked Sigrid.

"No, and this makes me *très agitée*. I turn on lights as I come and when I push open that door *là*, I see all is as before. You have said we may begin to repair the damage and yet no beginning has been made! I look at all that must be done and then I come out the front door—"

"Was it locked?"

"*Oui*. I must turn the knob and push the buttons so. And before you ask, I will tell you that I left the door unlocked."

Again her polished fingernail touched Knight's sketch and her rings glittered.

"I come along the corridor here, and go down the stairs to Miss Baldwin's office, but she is not there. Someone says she is upstairs at this card tournament, so back I come."

"Immediately?" asked Sigrid. "About ten-thirty?"

"Perhaps. People are coming from the Bontemps Room as I ascend the stairs. I look all through the room, but no Miss Baldwin. I speak to Mr. George about a doughnut I see on the floor and then I give up and go to my office and try to concentrate on letters my secretary has left for me to sign, but my mind will not."

She shrugged her slender shoulders and made a charmingly

rueful face. "Never can I be *tranquille* when things are left undone. At last, I go and find some maids who are not very busy and I come myself to show them what must be done. The elevator stops, we get off, and there is Miss Baldwin with you and M'sieur Froelick. We speak and you know the rest, *non?*"

By now, more police officers had trickled into the room. Sigrid saw that the medical examiner had finished with the boy's body and was waiting to speak to her. Elaine Albee and Jim Lowry had arrived together and Sigrid motioned them over as she finished with Lucienne Ronay.

"We'll try to be as unobtrusive as possible," she promised. "The body can go down in the freight elevator and out the back if one of your people will show them the way. Again, you'll have to wait to begin clean-up on this room and we'll want to talk to everyone who worked this floor today."

"I am resigned, Lieutenant," said Madame Ronay with a fatalistic sigh. As she stood, her eyes fell on Molly Baldwin and her face was stern. But the sight of so much misery seemed to soften her. "Poor Molly! Do not look so fearful, *chérie*. This time I forgive all your faults."

"Thank you, Madame," murmured Molly, but she seemed only partially relieved as Lucienne Ronay left the room almost as if she expected the police to have harder questions. From the way Molly braced herself apprehensively, Sigrid knew that the waiting must be getting to the girl, but there was no help for it. Joined by Lowry and Albee, she and Knight walked back toward the body to hear what the assistant M.E. had to tell them.

"Not much for now," said Cohen in his usual breezy manner. "The kid bought it between, oh, say ten and eleven, give or take a little. He was probably unconscious when the tie cut off his air supply."

"Hit over the head first?" asked Sigrid.

"Now, Lieutenant, it's too soon to tell. No obvious blow to the head, but no scratches around the throat as would've been if he was awake and fighting it. I'll let you know more tomorrow, okay?" He unwrapped a stick of gum and cheerfully turned his back on them.

The ambulance attendants had already lifted the slight body onto the gurney and strapped a covering over it, and a hotel employee appeared to escort them out through the basement garage.

"Sorry to keep you waiting, Ms. Baldwin," Sigrid said as they passed the young assistant manager. "It won't be much longer now."

She assigned a uniformed officer to keep an eye on the girl and motioned for Vassily Ivanovich to accompany them to the Bontemps Room.

"No, I wish to stay here," said the gray-haired Russian, who had seldom taken his eyes off Molly since entering the room.

"You can speak to Ms. Baldwin later," Sigrid told him firmly. "Right now, I want all the players back at their tables."

Reluctantly, the big man followed.

Three reporters were waiting outside in the hall. Sigrid made a brief statement and continued toward the Bontemps Room. The lunch break was scheduled for twelve-thirty and already a few early finishers were pushing through the doors.

Albee and Lowry had been joined by three other officers, who herded the players back inside while Sigrid and Alan Knight briefly apprised Ted Flythe of the current situation. The hotel grapevine had reached him a moment or two before, however, so they were deprived of his initial reaction. At the moment, he seemed totally exasperated.

"That does it! There's no way we can finish now. You're going to question everybody again, aren't you? Get 'em all stirred up—"

Alan Knight began to bristle, and to stop him from alerting Flythe of their suspicions, Sigrid interrupted coldly. "I realize this tournament is important to you, Mr. Flythe, but we are investigating three murders here."

Flythe immediately backed down and tried to repair the damage. "It's just that there're so many people and so much money involved, Lieutenant. Makes it complicated. But that's not your problem, of course. Don't worry. We'll work something out."

"I'm sure you will," Sigrid said flatly. "Lowry, Albee, ask the staff to come in, please."

The players listened in shocked silence as Sigrid spoke into the microphone and told them of the young busboy's death. "We know you've had a long morning and that you'll want lunch now. As you leave the room, please show some identification to the officers at the door. They'll check you off the list and we'll be talking to each of you after lunch."

In an attempt to help the cardplayers remember, she asked the remaining busboys to come forward while she gave a brief description of the dead youth and then introduced Detectives Albee and Lowry, to whom most had already spoken.

"If any of you recall seeing Pernell Johnson during the break or if you spoke to him then, please tell one of these officers before you leave for lunch. Thank you."

A dismayed babble of comments and exclamations arose from the crowd and Ted Flythe took over the mike to promise that he would have a statement for them at two o'clock, after lunch. He stepped down from the podium and called, "Lieutenant?"

He was too late. Sigrid had disappeared into the crowd to join Alan Knight and Mr. George with the busboys, who were having trouble believing that one of their own was so abruptly gone.

"Man, he was right here!" one protested incredulously. "We were jiving him about Terri Pratt."

To Knight's questions, they all shook their heads. As with Mr. George earlier, they were ready to swear that Pernell had seen nothing Friday night.

"We were tight, man," said another. He held up crossed fingers. "Like that. No way he wouldn't have told me. All he could talk about was how things were breaking right, how once Mr. George gave him a good report about putting out the fire, maybe he was gonna get to work the Emeraude Room like he'd been wanting ever since he got here."

A different busboy said he'd seen Johnson enter the Bontemps Room after speaking with Miss Baldwin. That was immediately before the ten-thirty break, he thought. Once the break began and people were milling about, no one noticed Johnson again.

"What about Ted Flythe?" Sigrid asked. "Where was he during the break?"

More shrugs, this time punctuated with an undercurrent of knowing snickers.

"Mr. George?"

"Probably upstairs with one of his girls. Graphic Games has a suite on eighteen and the maids say he's been keeping the sheets hot, if you'll pardon the expression, Miss."

"I thought Miss Baldwin was his current interest," said Knight.

"The man's a Baskin-Robbins freak," quipped one of the busboys.

"Ice cream?" asked Sigrid as they moved away.

"Thirty-one different flavors," Knight told her.

"Oh."

To avoid the crush of people and reporters, they slipped out the rear service exit and walked along the deserted back corridors.

"Any suggestions?" Sigrid asked Knight.

"Nope. You seem to be covering all the bases. Want me to locate the girlfriends?"

"Flythe's?"

"And Johnson's."

"Later. I'd rather you sat in on the interview with Molly Baldwin, if you don't mind. You can be the good cop and keep your handkerchief handy. If all else fails," she added dryly, "I'll even tell her you aren't married."

"She looks too scared to care," he grinned, pleased with this first sign of her letting down barriers. "I guess you got that about Miami?"

"With you and our Russian friend practically waving flags, how could I not?"

Inside the d'Aubigné Room, Sigrid paused by one of the technicians who was dusting the table where the body had been found, looking for usable prints. She gave him Flythe's card, explained what she wanted, and received his promise to develop any fingerprints on the card for comparison with Fred Hamilton's when the FBI passed them on.

A photographer was dispatched to the Bontemps Room.

"Make it look as if you're merely following the usual routine," Sigrid told her, "but try to get a clear profile and full frontal of Flythe without letting him know it."

"Gotcha," the girl grinned.

"I mean it," Sigrid said seriously. "If he's who I think he is, he made J. Edgar Hoover's list fifteen years ago. I don't want him scared into bolting."

"He won't feel a thing," the photographer promised. "Trust me, ma'am."

While Sigrid heard progress reports and detailed an officer to locate Pernell Johnson's girlfriend among the maids, Alan Knight had gone on ahead, ostensibly to put Miss Baldwin at ease.

Molly tried to return the smile the naval officer gave her as he put his hat down on the table, smoothed his straw-colored hair, and opened the note pad. He was very friendly looking, she thought, and abruptly found herself wishing he was a police officer and not a Navy lieutenant, one of her cousin's colleagues.

By now she knew that he hadn't known Teejy, but he couldn't have missed hearing that awful Russian bellowing about being T. J. Dixon's cousin; so the mere fact that he was in the Navy made things even more unsettling.

"Do you want coffee or something?" he asked solicitously. "I could probably send for it, if you like."

"No, nothing," she said. He seemed so nice. Maybe this wouldn't be too bad, after all. "Will it be much longer, do you think? There's so much—"

"I'm sure it won't be. Lieutenant Harald's very thorough, but you don't have to worry. You just tell her what you did this morning and that'll be that. They say she can be pretty rough at times, but as long as you're telling the truth, you'll be fine. Okay?"

Molly's heart sank. "Okay," she murmured faintly.

Her small hands clenched into involuntary fists in her lap as she watched Lieutenant Harald's approach. The tall policewoman seated herself across the table. Her wide gray eyes were unsmiling and her voice was professionally cool as she said, "Now then, Ms. Baldwin."

CHAPTER XXI

Earlier that day, Sigrid had spoken to Alan Knight of professionalism and objectivity, yet it was not objectivity but the experienced value of thoroughness that now made her question Molly Baldwin as carefully as any of the others. At this point, she truly believed that John Sutton was the intended target of Friday night's explosion; therefore she saw no point in shilly-shallying over minor points.

"Why did you lie about your relationship with Commander Dixon?" she asked the girl baldly.

"I didn't! I really *wasn't* sure at first it was her and then when

I knew . . ." Her voice died away under Sigrid's openly skeptical gaze.

"I—It's not what you think," Molly stammered.

Alan Knight gave her an encouraging smile. "We're sure it's not, Miss Baldwin, but you have to admit it's a little odd."

Molly turned to him gratefully. "You see, Teejy—that's what I've always called her—we had this awful fight last summer. I was really having trouble finding a decent job after college and she got really uptight and cut off my allowance just like that! It wasn't fair. So *I* got mad and we hadn't written or anything since. It was a totally unreal summer. I was so broke. Then I landed a job at one of the resort hotels and that led to this. My training probation's up next month. Everything was going pretty good and I thought Madame Ronay would probably offer me a permanent position but I didn't want to tell Teejy until I knew for sure."

"So on Friday night you were still angry with Commander Dixon?" asked Sigrid.

"Oh, that's not why I didn't say we were cousins."

"Then why, Ms. Baldwin?"

"Because of the tournament," she said, as if it were obvious. "When I saw her name on the pairings chart, I freaked. I didn't know what to do. She's crazy about cards and the tournament's not supposed to be open to family members of the staff and Teejy's my family, see?"

Clearly they did not.

"Well, I couldn't pop up two days before the tournament started when it was too late for her to get her entry fee back and all and say 'Here I am and you can't play because I work here,' now could I?"

Was the girl as naive as she appeared? wondered Sigrid. Did she really think the term "immediate family" covered a cousin she hadn't spoken to in over a year?

"I was petrified that Madame or Mr. Flythe would find out."

Evidently she was that naive.

"Ms. Baldwin—"

"Oh, I *know* it was wrong of me, but what else could I do? I left a message on Teejy's answering machine to pretend not to know me if we met unexpectedly and she *did*. And then when the bomb went off— It's been so horrible for me! I haven't known *what* to do."

Her pretty blue eyes began to resemble rain-drenched forget-me-nots again.

Sigrid glanced at Alan Knight. There was a faint expression of distaste on his face and she gave him a nudge under the table. Immediately, he made soothing noises and proffered his handkerchief.

"Please, you won't tell them, will you?" she asked, dabbing at her eyes.

"Only if it becomes unavoidable," Sigrid assured her expressionlessly.

"The hospital won't give me any details over the telephone," moaned Molly. "I guess I could have gone down, but if she was unconscious, that wouldn't do her any good, would it? And I was afraid you'd have someone there, you see, and then you'd *know*."

She looked at Alan Knight timidly. "She's going to be okay, isn't she? I mean, she's not going to die or anything?"

"No," Knight said tightly. "They expect her to live."

"Oh great!" she said with an exaggerated sigh of relief.

Hastily, Sigrid asked, "Lieutenant Knight, would you ask somebody to get us something to drink? I'd like coffee. Black. Ms. Baldwin?"

"Ginger ale, please."

Wordlessly, Knight went himself.

So much for good cop/bad cop, thought Sigrid.

By the time he returned, with their beverages on a tray and his distaste on hold, she had led Molly back over Friday night again. The girl still insisted that she hadn't particularly noticed Pernell Johnson's movements. She did, however, remember Ted Flythe's.

"He rushed around and helped change the ashtrays with the rest of us. The cut-glass ones are so much prettier, but harder to clean and with cardplayers— Mr. George has to put out fresh ones every three hours. Those people smoke like chimneys."

Alan Knight glanced at Sigrid, who acknowledged with a slight nod how easy Flythe might have found it to switch one cribbage board while everyone else was switching hundreds of ashtrays.

"Let's move on to today," said Sigrid. "Several people say you spoke to Pernell Johnson at the service door shortly before the ten-thirty break."

"That's right. I didn't know his name though. I was asking him to keep an eye on the ash stands on the landing. Madame Ronay has a thing about dirty sand. People can be so messy. They drop chewing gum off there, or leave candy wrappers. So I asked him to tend them during the break."

"And did he?"

"I guess I forgot to look."

"Madame Ronay stopped in at the Bontemps Room during the break to look for you. She says you weren't there then."

"No, I'd gone down to my office."

"But she'd just come from there and didn't find you."

"We must have just missed each other. Mr. Flythe had given me the copies you wanted of the pairings and after I spoke to the busboy, I went on down the back way. I put the sheets in a folder for you, took care of some things on my desk, and then returned by the grand staircase about forty-five minutes later."

Knight had been following her story on his sketched floor plan. "It could have happened like that," he said. "As many exits and elevators and halls as this place has, you could play ring-around-the-rosy all day."

"Madame Ronay spent some time in her office, too," said Sigrid. "Is that near yours?"

Molly gave a feminine hoot. "*My* office is in that warren back of the main desk. La R—I mean, Madame Ronay's is up on thirty, next to the boardroom. On thirty, even the broom closets are bigger than my office."

"So from approximately ten-thirty till eleven-thirty, you were at your desk alone?"

Molly Baldwin nodded her curly brown head.

"Did you see anyone, speak to anyone along the way?"

"Gee, I don't know. You know how it is: you just nod or wave; you don't stop to talk every time. There was the desk clerk, of course, and the bell captain. There're always people coming or going."

"In your office, too?"

"Well, no. Clerical staff don't have to work on Sundays. Just a skeleton crew down in the secretarial pool in case of emergencies. They mostly goof off or read or knit 'cause nothing ever happens on Sunday."

"Now, Ms. Baldwin, you've told us that you did not know Pernell Johnson except by sight and only as a staff member employed here at the hotel. Is that correct?"

As Sigrid's voice became more official, Molly tensed again. "That's right," she said anxiously.

"We've heard that he recently moved here from Miami. That's where you're from, too, isn't it?"

"But I didn't know him," Molly protested. "Miami's huge.

That's like saying I ought to know you because we both live in New York.''

"So, in fact, he gave no indication that he'd ever seen you around Miami either?''

Molly Baldwin shook her head.

"Very well, Ms. Baldwin,'' Sigrid concluded. "If you'll bring me those pairings sheets, I think that'll be all for now.''

The girl looked at Alan Knight entreatingly. "Would you tell them about me at the hospital?'' she asked. "My name, I mean, and that I'm Commander Dixon's cousin so they won't give me a hard time about letting me see her?''

"Certainly, Ms. Baldwin,'' he said formally.

"Oh, thank you,'' she breathed, and slipped away to fetch the papers.

"Aren't you going to tell her?'' Sigrid asked.

"Let her find it out at the hospital,'' said Knight. "Did I apologize for thinking *you* were callous about Commander Dixon? And Dixon's her only relative, for God's sake.''

One of the uniformed officers whom Sigrid had instructed earlier came over with a slender young black girl in tow.

"Lieutenant Harald, this is Miss Terri Pratt, the victim's friend.''

She was a winsome child, not pretty exactly, but with a sunny intelligent charm that shone through her shock over Johnson's death. They soon learned that she was a part-time employee at the hotel and a full-time student at Hunter College. She hadn't actually dated Johnson yet, "But we were working at it. We'd taken a couple of breaks at the same time. He was a little younger than me, but pretty sharp. Had his act together. I liked that.''

They had snatched a few minutes in passing since Friday night, she told them; had even planned to meet for lunch today; but if Pernell had known anything important about the explosion, he'd given her no indication of it.

"And he would have,'' Terri Pratt assured them. "At least I think he would. He talked about everything else that happened that night.''

At the end, Sigrid thanked her and added, "We're very sorry about your loss, Miss Pratt.''

The girl shook her head. "We weren't that far yet. Things were just starting between us and there was so much else we needed to do first: school, work. Pernell wanted to start a chain of small resort hotels in Florida. He'd have done it, too. He could've done anything.'' Her face drooped as she spoke of what would now never be. "He was so—oh, I don't know. Innocent? And very, very sweet."

Her voice shook as the finality of his death sank in.

In the lull after Molly Baldwin brought them the pairings sheets and went back to her work, Alan Knight suggested that they might as well grab a bite to eat while they waited for the cribbage players to regroup after their own lunch break. The hotel's coffee shop was jammed, so he and Sigrid went to the tavern across the street, where Sigrid let herself be persuaded that a large mug of rich dark ale could substitute for the pain tablets she'd forgotten to bring with her.

Sandwiches there were pricey but generous. The corned beef was sliced thinly and laid on an inch thick, the mustard was dark and spicy, the dill pickles crisp and tender.

As they ate, Alan regaled her with exaggerated tales of his upbringing in a Southern household tucked in amongst six sisters. He seemed to have decided on a big sister–kid brother scenario for their temporary partnership and Sigrid could feel herself being drawn in. His knack for instant friendship was seductive to someone who found getting past the initial barriers difficult.

Kinship was a whole different matter though, even this artificial kinship. Her mother possessed rafts of uncles, aunts, and cousins and so had her father, which meant Sigrid had grown up accustomed to having strangers suddenly introduced as Uncle this or Great-aunt that, people who by blood were entitled to speak to her familiarly, chaff her on her shyness, or ask personal questions that would be a gross impertinence in someone unrelated. Brothers she had never known, but Alan Knight was not unlike some of her Lattimore or Harald cousins and unconsciously she found herself reacting to him in the same manner; so that when he asked her why she had joined the police force, instead of replying that it was none of his business, she answered him honestly.

"Probably a combination of genes and aptitude. My father was a policeman killed in the line of duty when I was a child. I barely remember him, but I guess I grew up thinking it was an honorable profession. And I've always liked puzzles—word games, jigsaws, solitaire, any kind of logic problems."

"The Norwegian with a dog lives next door to the man who smokes Parliaments?" smiled Knight.

"So who owns the zebra?" She nodded. "And when I was a child, I used to tangle a ball of twine deliberately and then spend hours undoing the knots. Bringing a little corner of the world back to order, I suppose. Who knows? I've never analyzed it much."

She sipped the last of her ale. "Why did you join the Navy? To get away from women?"

He laughed. "You sure don't find many on shipboard yet."

"Are you making it a career?"

"I didn't plan to, although I'm working on my second tour of duty right now. With seven kids, we all had to scrape around for tuition. If you sign up for ROTC, they give you four years of college for four years service. I'm being ordered to Naples in December. Join the Navy, see the world. It's not a bad life."

"Commander Dixon seemed to like it," Sigrid said. "What will happen to her now, do you suppose?"

"The Navy will take care of her. Military hospitals must know everything there is about prosthetics and therapy. She may have a choice between full disability or retraining."

It sounded awful to Sigrid.

Better than the alternative, he reminded her.

Back at the hotel, the crime scene technicians were packing up their equipment, having collected all the physical bits of evidence they could find. It wasn't much. Or rather, it was too much. Too many people had used the room since its last cleaning. Trying to sort out what might be pertinent from the mass of fingerprints, fibers, and cigarette butts would be almost impossible.

Nevertheless, they would go through the motions.

"Oh, and we did find this," said one, and handed over Zachary Wolferman's schilling to Detective Eberstadt, a heavyset officer entering middle age. He sucked in his stomach and slipped the coin into his watch pocket for safekeeping.

Down in the Bontemps Room, Ted Flythe called the players to order. A telephone conference with his superior at Graphic Games had left the ball in his court and now he bounced it on to them. "We have two options," he told them. "There are sixty-four players still in contention and you sixty-four have the vote. You can draw lots and have a winner-take-all playoff, or you can call it quits and split the prize money. It comes to just over a hundred and fifty each."

There was hasty consultation among the weary and beleaguered players. The vote went overwhelmingly in favor of calling it quits before anyone else got killed.

Graphic Games' Second Annual New York City Cribbage Tournament was officially over.

CHAPTER XXII

The tournament may have been over, but questioning the cardplayers dragged on into midafternoon. It could have been worse. Of the three hundred or so players, less than twenty were positive that they had seen Pernell Johnson after the break began.

Jill Gill was the player to pinpoint his last movements. Others had seen the young busboy policing the ash stands out on the landing—"I felt so guilty," confessed one woman. "He'd just picked three butts out of the sand and here I came with another!" —but only Dr. Gill could tell Elaine Albce, "It was exactly 10:41. I looked at my watch because our break was supposed to last fifteen minutes. Almost nobody'd started back inside though, so I thought I'd still have time to duck into the ladies'.

"You know how you'll look around for the nearest inconspicuous door? Well, I saw the busboy pass through a door next to the elevators and I started to follow and then I saw 'No admittance,' so I went elsewhere."

If anyone else had seen young Johnson after 10:41, they weren't saying.

The service landing beyond that door was not visible from the service door at the rear of the Bontemps Room; but LeMays, the busboy who'd used the corridor and freight elevator to fetch more cups from the kitchen, swore the area was deserted when he went down at eleven o'clock.

He and two others agreed that Ted Flythe left by the rear hall shortly after the break began. They didn't think he had returned that way. Nor could any of the Graphic Games people alibi Flythe. It was generally agreed that he did not return to the Bontemps Room and call for order until 10:55.

Fourteen minutes between the last glimpse of Pernell Johnson and the next view of Ted Flythe.

"You could go anywhere in this building and back again in fourteen minutes." Alan Knight frowned. "Aren't you going to question him?"

"Not yet," said Sigrid, touching her hair in absent-minded uneasiness. Roman had used a gentler hand than hers when helping to pin up her hair earlier that morning and she didn't trust the dark mass not to come sliding down. "If he's Fred Hamilton, it's taken more than good luck to stay out of prison all these years."

"ESP?"

"Or the science of body language or whatever else you want to call it," she said patiently. "No, he can't read minds, but he's probably good at picking up unconscious signals like voice tones or eye tension. We'll know for sure when the prints come in tomorrow, and then we'll arrest him and do our questioning where there's no chance of his disappearing for another fifteen years, okay?"

"You're the expert."

"And you're not?"

Knight shrugged. "Look, they gave me a sailor suit, a cram course at Newport, and told me to go read a couple of books. I'm pretty intelligent but whether that qualifies me for Intelligence, I couldn't say. I probably shouldn't tell you this, but you're my first real field operation."

"Somehow that doesn't surprise me," she said.

By then, it was nearly four, most of the players had gone, and the Graphic Games crew were packing up the last of their boards and dismantling the display cases out in the hall.

Feeling somewhat guilty because she'd avoided his Sunday dinner, Sigrid phoned Roman Tramegra to ask if he'd like something from the deli for supper.

"Don't bother, my dear. I've held the veal."

Her heart sank.

"Is the tournament over?" he asked. "Why don't you ask Dr. Gill to join us? There's enough."

Fortunately, Jill Gill had not yet departed. "He probably wants me to vet his cockroach article," she said cheerfully when Sigrid relayed the invitation. "I told him I would."

"Cockroaches?" asked Alan Knight curiously.

"Five hundred spine-chilling words on an insect that can and does live anywhere man can. I believe he hopes to sell it to *The National Enquirer*. Can't you see the headline now? 'Biological Time Bomb Already in Place.'" She smiled at Sigrid through her rhinestone-and-turquoise glasses. "I'll be happy to come."

"It's anised veal," Sigrid warned.

"I can eat anything the roaches eat."

"Me, too," said Alan Knight, with a hopeful expression on his handsome face.

Sigrid was taken off guard.

"Oh, let him come," laughed Jill, pulling on a bright red sweater. "He'll balance the table and anyhow, Roman will love him. He's never done an article about the Navy, has he?"

It was true that Roman would like having fresh brains to pick. But more importantly, thought Sigrid, four people sharing a meal originally planned for two should certainly ensure no leftovers.

In the end, five sat down to dine on Roman's creation. Nauman turned up unexpectedly with a bottle of wine and some tapes and chapter notes which he thought might interest Sigrid from John Sutton's office at Vanderlyn College. To help Val, he had volunteered to clean out her husband's desk and pack up his books and personal effects. Nauman had also brought along some snapshots he found of the Suttons' McClellan days, including one fuzzy group pose.

"There's John," he said, "and I think that's Fred Hamilton."

"He doesn't look much like Ted Flythe," said Knight, peering over Sigrid's shoulder at the faded photograph.

"Ted Flythe?" asked Dr. Gill from the kitchen sink where she was peeling avocados for Roman. She wiped her hands on a dishtowel and leaned across the breakfast counter where they were clustered in order to see, too. "Why would Professor Sutton have a picture of Ted Flythe?"

"There's a possibility that he was once part of a terrorist underground organization that began out at McClellan State." Sigrid explained the Red Snow connection as she turned the picture so that Jill Gill could get a good look and tapped the figure in the foreground. "What do you think?"

The entomologist adjusted her harlequin-shaped glasses and examined it closely. "The eyes are similar," she agreed.

"Cut the hair, add a beard and fifteen years," Sigrid said.

"Insufficient data," Jill replied and went back to peeling avocados. "Don't you have fingerprints or something?"

"They should be coming tomorrow."

"Then tomorrow you'll know for sure, won't you?" Jill observed sensibly.

Unperturbed by three extra mouths to feed, Roman was doing a loaves-and-fishes act with salad greens, avocados, and mushrooms. He flourished two large Vidalia onions and in his deep bass voice queried, "Who's unalterably opposed to onions?"

Alan Knight flashed an insouciant grin in Sigrid's direction. "Anybody planning to do some kissing later?" he drawled.

"Where did you find Huck Finn?" asked Nauman, draping his long body onto the couch.

"Does he strike you as Huck Finn?" Sigrid asked absently. "I've been thinking he's more barefoot boy with cheek."

They had repaired to the living room alone after dinner with John Sutton's tapes and notes, and Sigrid was distracted with extension cords for her portable tape cassette player.

From the direction of the kitchen came the rumble of Roman's voice interspersed with Jill and Alan's lighter tones. Roman was reading aloud from his cockroach article while the two guests cleaned the kitchen and made ribald observations on the mating habits of *Blatella germanica*.

Dinner had been a cheerful and slightly rowdy meal, not unusual when people are meeting for the first time and talking over and around each other in layered degrees of familiarity. Oscar and Jill had known each other for years, Sigrid first met all three last spring, and she and Roman had become accidental roommates back in the summer; yet this was the first time the four had dined together. And, of course, this was Nauman and Tramegra's first meeting with Alan Knight.

Conversation had ranged from insects to Lucienne Ronay, from nouvelle cuisine to art nouveau, from naval maneuvers to marine zoology—whereupon Alan Knight suggested to Roman that he might get a good article out of crawdads.

Nauman's salad fork paused in midair. "What the hell's a crawdad?"

"You don't know what a crawdad is?" grinned Knight, who'd been a bit awed earlier to realize who Nauman was.

"No, I don't know what a crawdad is."

Somehow this clash of cultures so delighted Sigrid that she burst into infectious laughter.

Roman chose that moment to bring on his entrée. "Here we are: *veau d'anise avec étables verts*," he announced in his mangled French.

"What?" asked Nauman. "No chitlins or harmony grits?"

During dinner they had finished Oscar's bottle of wine, opened a second, and Sigrid had now brought the remains of a third to the living room with them.

"Should you be drinking this much with your medication?" Oscar asked when she spread John Sutton's notes next to the tape player on the low table before them and held out her glass.

"Nope," she said happily. "But I haven't taken a pill since morning, so more wine, *garçon.*"

"I've never seen you tipsy before."

"I'm not tipsy." She took a slow sip of the amber wine and reconsidered. "Relaxed, perhaps, but definitely not tipsy."

She turned on the tape player, slipped off her shoes, and leaned back lightly against his shoulder with her feet tucked under her.

Pleasantly surprised by her unaccustomed initiative, Oscar shifted slightly so that she fit more comfortably into the curve of his arm while John Sutton's voice filled the room.

CHAPTER XXIII

Monday began brightly enough, although the kitchen radio was predicting rain by the afternoon.

Sigrid was in good spirits as she poured herself a glass of juice. She'd slept well and for the first time since Friday night's incident, her arm barely ached. With her hair tightly braided and pinned into a secure knot at the nape of her neck, she felt more like herself than at any time since the knifing.

Roman had again helped with her hair, but he was a mixed blessing this morning, surprised that she felt so cheerful, and unconvinced that she wasn't hiding a headache or a hangover.

"I did *not* have too much to drink last night and I did *not* pass out," she told him firmly. "I barely slept Saturday night and then worked all day yesterday. That's the only reason I fell asleep on the couch."

Roman sniffed.

Sigrid supposed she deserved his skepticism. True, it had been a little disconcerting to wake up sometime in the middle of the night in the living room with the apartment dark and silent and a blanket tucked around her, but she'd been too drowsy to care. She'd simply stumbled sleepily to her room, shed her clothes, and crawled into bed where she promptly zonked out again.

"What time did everyone leave?" she asked Roman.

"Around ten. I wanted to wake you, but Oscar wouldn't let me. He said he had an early meeting this morning and Jill was yawning, too, so he took her home then."

The street gate buzzed and Roman went over to push an electric button that released the latch. "That'll be young Horatio Hornblower. He told me he'd pick you up this morning."

But the figure who opened the gate was neither Alan Knight nor the yeoman driver. This sailor was dark and wiry, the sleeve of his navy-blue jumper had a couple of extra hash marks, and his eyes squinted across the courtyard as if he were staring through the briny spray from a fo'c'sle deck, whatever that was. Sigrid was weak on Navy terminology.

She opened the door.

"Lieutenant Knight sent me, ma'am," he said in as flat a North Jersey accent as Sigrid had ever heard. "He said you'd be expecting him."

"I'll be right out," said Sigrid and hurried down the hall to put on her gun and load the pockets of her jacket with wallet, ID, and other necessities for the day. In passing, she snagged a thin zippered leather folder that held her notes on the bombing and was out the door before Roman could remind her to carry an umbrella.

As she pulled the gate shut, the driver jumped out of the gray station wagon and held the door next to the curb for her to enter. Alan Knight was in the far corner with a suspiciously pasty look on his face.

"You look awful," Sigrid said by way of greeting. "Are you all right?"

"It's going," he answered, popping another digestive mint into his mouth. "I always thought I could eat anything, but for some reason, I keep tasting licorice this morning."

He looked at her closely. "You don't seem the worse for wear. I thought you'd look like I feel."

"I don't know why everyone seems to assume I had too much wine last night," Sigrid said stiffly.

She would have said more, but their driver swerved abruptly with a sharp blast of his horn at a cab that had encroached on his lane. Monday morning rush hour traffic clearly held no terrors for him.

"Petty Officer Schmitt's my regular driver," said Knight unnecessarily.

The driver's eyes met Sigrid's in the mirror. "Ma'am."

Sigrid gravely returned his nod.

At headquarters, her first order of business was to call the hospital. Tillie's condition continued to improve, they told her.

Her office was too small to hold everyone working on the Maintenon bombing, so at 9:06 they carried their coffee cups and doughnuts into one of the conference rooms.

At 9:07, a fingerprint technician licked powdered sugar from his fingers and said, "I'm afraid I have bad news, Lieutenant. The FBI sent us the prints we requested and Ted Flythe's are nowhere close to Frederick Hamilton's."

"Dead end," sighed Lowry.

Sigrid was dismayed. "You're certain?"

"Yes, ma'am. See for yourself."

She studied the photographic enlargements of both sets of prints. Small arrows had been superimposed on distinguishing loops and whorls. Sigrid was no expert in this area, but even she could see that none of the comparison points matched.

"That's not all," said the fingerprint technician. "I requested the prints of all known Red Snow members and Flythe's don't match any of them. Sorry, ma'am."

It was a bitter disappointment.

Sigrid's assumption of a Red Snow link between John Sutton and Ted Flythe had infected them all. Consciously or unconsciously, they'd let similar assumptions affect the diligence with which they'd looked at other possible suspects that weekend.

Because Haines Froelick seemed a harmless dilettante, Peters and Eberstadt had only gone through the motions in checking his background; Elaine Albee shared Sigrid's instinctive rejection of Val Sutton as a killer—"Besides, she wasn't anywhere near the

Maintenon yesterday," said Albee—and those who'd heard of Molly Baldwin's lies about her relationship to Commander Dixon had marked the girl as an uncomplicated, self-centered airhead, much as Vassily Ivanovich was their idea of a comic Russian.

"There's nothing comic about an ex-demolition expert with a KGB son," said Sigrid, setting her blue mug on the table with a firm thunk. "Let's stop thinking in stereotypes and start at the beginning again. Comments? Suggestions?"

"Well, we know how much money Zachary Wolferman left Froelick," said Peters, "but what about Commander Dixon if the girl's her closest relative?"

"Nothing like six million," drawled Lieutenant Knight, "but I'd say not much under six hundred thousand."

"*What?*"

"Damned if I didn't join the wrong service!" Lowry whistled.

"We ran a check on her financial records," Knight said. "As a single officer with twenty-two years in service, she's been putting a right tidy sum in her credit union account every month. She seems to have inherited some rental property in Miami a few years back and there were some stock certificates. One way or another, I'd say at least a good half-million."

Sigrid looked at him suspiciously. "Did you check her financial records before or after you learned of Ivanovich's KGB connection?"

"After," he admitted, returning her gaze blandly. "Standard operating procedure, Lieutenant."

"Did you learn anything else you'd care to share with us?" she asked dryly.

"No, but I was going over my notes just now and if you remember, Ivanovich told us that Molly Baldwin began college as a chemistry major."

"That's interesting," said Jim Lowry. "Chemistry might give her the knowledge to cook up something explosive."

"*I* think it's right interesting how Ivanovich stuck it in his testimony," countered Knight. "Sort of spreads the wealth around a little."

"From each according to his ability?" Sigrid murmured. "Perhaps."

They continued to pool the scraps of information collected over the weekend, seeking a new pattern. The M.E. had sent the results of Pernell Johnson's autopsy and Sigrid skimmed the report, then passed it around the table.

"From the bruises on the body, Cohen thinks Johnson was first immobilized with something like a karate chop to his neck and diaphragm, then strangled with his tie."

"Could the girl have handled that?" Peters asked, ignoring Elaine Albee's glare.

"He wasn't very big, was he?" said Lowry, reading from the medical report. "Five-six, a hundred and twenty pounds, slender build. You could have taken him, Lainey."

"I could take *you*, hotshot, but I've had training. Has Baldwin?"

"Find out," said Sigrid. "From the top then: We know that Ted Flythe handed Molly Baldwin the pairings sheet with all the players listed sometime in midweek—"

"Tuesday morning," Knight reminded her.

"—So if Baldwin didn't read through the names and learn then that her cousin would be playing, she certainly knew by Thursday when the chart came back from the hotel's graphics studio and Flythe reprimanded her for leaving it in a public area for anyone to see."

"Which might have been deliberate on her part," said Detective Eberstadt, disappointed to find no more doughnuts in the box Albee had brought. "More of that spreading the wealth around."

Sigrid agreed and continued through her notes. "Now a cribbage board was taken from the unlocked display case—a case Baldwin conveniently forgot to lock—the same day. That gives her a day and a half to construct the bomb."

"Did she have a chance to switch boards?" asked Peters.

"Absolutely," Albee and Lowry chimed in unison. They paused to grin at each other, then Elaine Albee continued.

"She was in charge of all the arrangements for the d'Aubigné Room and she was the one who ordered the steward, Mr. George, to use the wrong ashtrays. He'd suggested the plainer ones, but she overrode him; and sure enough, as soon as Lucienne Ronay stepped into the room for a last-minute check, she ordered them changed."

"George said he tried to tell Baldwin that's what would happen," said Lowry, picking up the narrative, "but she wouldn't listen. You could make a good case for her planning it to happen that way."

"If she's it, she either switched the boards then," Eberstadt offered, "or counted on it looking like that's when it was done so that everyone had the opportunity."

"The busboy probably noticed, so he had to be killed, too," Lowry concluded.

"Maybe it wasn't just ash stands she spoke to him about," said Alan Knight, contributing his own scenario. "What if she told him to meet her in the d'Aubigné Room, perhaps on the pretext of getting started on clearing the room? She doesn't have a real alibi for that time period."

"That we know of," Sigrid cautioned. "Albee, Lowry, speak to the desk clerks who were on duty yesterday. See if they can confirm her story. Any further thoughts on Molly Baldwin?"

There were murmured negatives around the conference table.

"Moving on to Haines Froelick then. Peters, why don't you and Eberstadt give us what you have for him?"

"Like we said Saturday, he seems harmless enough," said Peters. "Used to living well at the Quill and Shutter Club off Park Avenue. Probably spends more on camera equipment than wine, women, or song, but that could be because he doesn't have as much money as he used to."

"Oh?"

"Yeah," said Matt Eberstadt, who had consumed three jelly doughnuts and was now virtuously sweetening his coffee with a packet of artificial sugar. "We haven't actually seen his bank statements, but we get the strong impression that money's been a little tight for Froelick these last couple of years—like his income wasn't keeping up with inflation."

"Whose is?" asked Peters, who had no idea how he and his wife were going to fit a third baby into their budget. "Anyhow, six million will buy a lot of cameras. You've seen Froelick. He's ordinary looking, well-dressed; hundreds like him go in and out of the Maintenon every day. There's nothing to say he'd be noticed if he wandered through the hall where they were coming and going, getting ready for the tournament. The seating chart was out in the hall by the display cases for anybody to stop and read, right? With the cases unlocked, it wouldn't take more than fifteen seconds to reach in and grab the cribbage board, stick it in his pocket and be on his way."

"Those boards are at least a foot long," Albee objected.

"Well, up his sleeve then," Peters said impatiently. "Or inside his newspaper." Young though he was, Peters wasn't entirely happy with female colleagues and sometimes his disapproval slipped out. "The point is, a man like Froelick is so ordinary, he's almost invisible."

"And what about that fishy story of his yesterday?" asked Jim

Lowry skeptically. "Wandering around the hotel looking for a dime to bury with his cousin? Sounds like a good excuse to get back in the d'Aubigné Room."

"It was a schilling," Albee corrected.

"The coin was found," Sigrid reminded them.

"Yeah," said Eberstadt, "and the housekeeper started crying when we took it over yesterday afternoon. Claims Wolferman always carried it."

"Just the same, Froelick could have put it there before he killed Johnson," said Elaine Albee. "Then if anyone came in before he'd lured the busboy there—hey! Maybe that's how he got Johnson there in the first place. Everybody says he was a helpful kid. If some old gentleman came up to him and spun out a story about a lost lucky coin, it would be just like Johnson to stop whatever he was doing and go help look for it."

"Nobody saw the kid go down the hall, so who's to say Froelick wasn't with him?" mused Peters, trying to compensate for his earlier shortness.

"We'll ask Dr. Gill if she noticed," said Albee. She knew she was smarter than Peters and seldom took offense at his latent chauvinism.

"Okay," said Sigrid, overlooking their byplay. "That gives us Froelick and Baldwin as possibilities. Each could have rigged a bomb in order to inherit a cousin's wealth and then killed Johnson yesterday because he saw—or they thought he saw—them do it. Now what about the Russian? Lieutenant Knight?"

He shrugged. "Obviously we haven't had a chance to talk to Commander Dixon yet, so all we have is Ivanovich's version of their friendship. It jibes, though, with what's been observed: he and Dixon's father did meet in the Second World War as he described, he does have a picture of Commander Dixon as a baby, and they've maintained frequent contact since he arrived in New York in July.

"As far as we can ascertain, Ivanovich is unofficially retired. His duties with the delegation are almost nonexistent and look like a polite fiction to justify what's essentially a nice long capitalistic vacation."

As Knight paused to drink from a foam coffee cup, Sigrid was inwardly amused to note his drawl almost disappeared when he spoke officially.

"He may look like a friendly Russian teddy bear," she said, "but without a Red Snow link for Flythe, Vassily Ivanovich is our only sure expert in handling high explosives. Could he have been sent here simply because he once was friendly with Dixon's father and could get close to her without arousing suspicion?''

"It's possible," said Knight.

"What about her work?" asked Elaine Albee. "Does Dixon work with secret documents or something? Is anything missing?"

Knight hesitated. "I can't go into a lot of detail. There's not a lot to go into, actually. Most of her work is in a supervisory capacity and deals with computer-generated—well, call it code work. So there aren't any documents per se."

"Floppy disks? Software?" asked Lowry.

"Her people have been working double shifts since Friday night trying to check. If anything's been compromised, they haven't found it. And just for the record, there's never been the slightest question of Commander Dixon's loyalty or integrity. Her people say that if Ivanovich had made the smallest overture, no matter how subtle, she'd have reported it immediately.

"On the other hand," he said with a wry grin, "that's what every spy's friends and co-workers have said."

"Makes security officers old before their years, I'm told," Sigrid said with such dryness that Jim Lowry began to wonder for the first time if maybe Tillie'd been right about the lieutenant having a sense of humor.

"The problem with Ivanovich, though," she continued, "is that he's at least six-three and doesn't look like Peters' invisible man. If Ivanovich had been lurking around the Maintenon's display cases Thursday, they certainly would have spotted him."

Elaine began riffling through her notes. "I can't find it right this minute, but someone—oh, here it is. One of the players was ticked off because Ivanovich got up and walked out on their match a few minutes after eleven o'clock."

"Yes, he followed us out into the hall," Sigrid said.

"What annoyed the man was that Ivanovich was late getting back after the break. If you're more than five minutes late, it's supposed to be an automatic forfeit; but the guy decided to be nice about it and then, two hands into their match, Ivanovich just split."

Alan Knight recalled the timetable. "Pernell Johnson was last seen at ten–forty-one. Flythe called for order around ten–fifty-five, so that makes it no earlier than eleven o'clock for Ivanovich to sit down to play." The drawl was back. "Looks like a few cribbage players'll have to be questioned again; see if any of 'em saw what Comrade Ivanovich was doing during that time."

Albee grinned and said she'd be plumb tickled to do that little old thing.

"Has anyone spoken to Johnson's aunt?" asked Sigrid sharply. There was no criticism in her tone but the others shifted uncomfortably as her slate-colored eyes swept around the table.

"I'll go," volunteered Jim Lowry, somewhat nettled with Elaine for flirting with Knight.

"That brings us back to Ted Flythe. Even without a Red Snow connection, he's still in the running. He was in the hotel Wednesday morning when the CUNY professors met to discuss their dinner, he had ample opportunity to steal a cribbage board from the display and switch it when the ashtrays were being changed, and so far as we know he doesn't have an alibi for those missing fourteen minutes when Johnson was killed. Somewhere we might find that his path *has* crossed Sutton's."

Matt Eberstadt cleared his throat. "Now that everything's up for grabs again, what about the possibility that the bomb was meant for Tillie?"

"I don't know," Sigrid said doubtfully. "We haven't seen any linkage. On the other hand, if the commander hadn't dropped a peg so that her chair was pushed away from the table and Tillie was actually under the table when the bomb went off, they probably would have been killed, too."

"It would certainly help if we knew who the real target was," Albee complained.

"The right jack," said Knight.

They looked at him curiously.

"It's a cribbage term," he explained. "When you're counting up points after the hand's been played, if a jack in your hand matches the suit of the turned card, you get an extra point. It's called the right jack."

"So all we have to do is find out what suit the turned card is?" Elaine Albee smiled.

"You got it, honeybunch."

CHAPTER XXIV

While Alan Knight used her typewriter to type up his notes from all their interviews that weekend, Sigrid went to Captain McKinnon's office to deliver a progress report. She had never felt entirely at ease with him and had tried in the past to cover it with strict professionalism. Knowing now that he and her father had once been partners, that he must have recognized her the moment she was assigned to him and yet had never spoken of it—all these combined to make her more distant than ever.

A gruff man who did not lightly suffer fools, McKinnon was usually accessible to his staff. "If my door's open," he was wont to say, "then walk in. If it's closed, stay out."

The door was open today and Sigrid paused on the threshold while her boss finished speaking to one of the clerks.

As the other man left, McKinnon beckoned for Sigrid to enter. "Close the door and have a seat."

She closed the door, but remained standing. "This will only take a moment. I wanted to post you on the status of the Maintenon homicides."

"I understand Detective Tildon's better," he said, sounding equally stiff. He was large and solid and he filled the battered leather chair behind the wide cluttered desk. His big hand absently shuffled papers.

"Yes, he was moved out of intensive care into a regular room yesterday. I plan to see him after lunch today."

"And that Navy commander. Too bad about her arm. How's your arm?" he asked, glancing at the loose sling.

"It feels much better. My doctor's going to take a look at it today."

"Not rushing things too much, are you?"

"No, sir."

The crisp monosyllables seemed to bring him back to the official nature of her visit. "Okay, what do you have?"

As she succinctly outlined the facts learned, people interviewed, alibies established, and theories they had formed, Mc-
Kinnon leaned back in his chair and listened with half his
attention, while the other half studied her face.

An odd combination of her parents, he thought. Leif's tall
slender build and Anne's coloring, although Anne's eyes were
more hazel than gray.

His thoughts flew back across the years. "She's such a serious
little thing," he remembered saying as he watched Leif and Anne's
baby daughter try to wind the musical toy he'd brought for a
Christmas present.

"It's her eyes," Anne had laughed. "They're too big for her
face right now. Our baby owlet. She'll grow into them."

Anne had knelt gracefully on the carpet to turn the blue knob.
As a nursery tune tinkled from the toy radio, the child's large gray
eyes caught the glow of the Christmas tree and her solemn little
face had beamed in delight.

"Will that be all, Captain?" Sigrid repeated, and a tinge of
color flushed her thin cheeks, as if she were aware of his scrutiny
and his memories.

"No, that's not all," he growled. "And sit down, dammit!"

She sat and gazed at him warily.

"I've been calling all weekend," he said bluntly. "Anne
doesn't answer the phone."

"No, she's on assignment in Peru."

"Peru?"

"An interview with El Diego, the poet."

"Oh."

McKinnon had picked up a pencil from the desk top and he
turned it in his big hands while the silence grew.

"She should be home this weekend," Sigrid said at last. "I'll
tell her you were—"

The pencil snapped.

"What did she say about me Friday night?" he asked, not
meeting her eyes.

"That you and my father were once partners."

"That's all?"

"And that you were with him when he was killed. She blames
you for Dad's death, doesn't she?"

"Is that what she said?" Suddenly he looked more tired than
she had ever seen him, and sad.

"No, but why else would she—?" Sigrid took a deep breath

and began again. "She's heard me speak your name, yet she never once asked if you were Dad's partner. And you! You've known all along who I was, haven't you?"

"Yes."

"Then why, Captain? Is Mother right? I always thought he was killed in the line of duty."

"He was." McKinnon looked up from the broken pencil ends he'd been fitting back together and his brown eyes met hers squarely. "Pull the report and read it yourself."

"Who wrote it?"

He gave a short bitter laugh. "Right."

Sigrid flushed. "If I'm wrong—"

"No, don't apologize for your instinct. Anyhow, you're right. I wrote most of it. But not all. And every word's the truth. Leif got careless. The guy that did it—a penny-ante small-timer messed up in something bigger than he could handle—he was holed up in a hotel room off Times Square and scared out of his skull. Your dad knew him. From the days when he was walking the beat. He figured he could just walk in the guy's room and waltz him down to the station. He laughed at me because I had my gun out."

His voice trailed off as he remembered. Sigrid waited quietly.

"He was a Viking. Do you remember him? Big and blond and so sure of himself." There was pain in his voice.

Sigrid shook her head. "Not very clearly. There are pictures, of course. And I remember standing at a high window once and waving good-bye to him down in the street. A few things like that. Not much more."

"You were so young." He looked at her and his smile was almost wistful. "I don't suppose you remember the trot-a-horse rides you took on my knee?"

"No. What happened to the man who shot him, your penny-ante small-timer?"

"I saved the state the cost of a trial," McKinnon answered flatly. "It's all in the report."

"If that's the way it happened, why did Mother react the way she did?"

"You'll have to ask her." He'd gone back to twisting the pencil ends. "Maybe she thought I should have shot sooner or maybe she thought I should have been the one to go into that room first. She wouldn't talk to me or see me after the funeral. I tried. God knows I tried. She called me a murderer and said she hoped to heaven she'd never see me again. I don't know. Maybe she was right. Maybe there *was* something I could have done. I couldn't bring Leif back, but I could get out of her life and I did.''

"Why didn't you tell me when I was first assigned to work here?''

He shrugged and threw the broken pencil aside. "What was the point? At first I thought you knew and chose not to speak of it. Later I realized you probably didn't know and then it seemed best not to rake up the past. You're a good officer. I didn't want you to transfer out.''

"I wouldn't do that! I fought for this job. It's all I ever wanted to do.''

"So maybe I should let you get out of here and do it,'' McKinnon growled, reverting to the gruff superior she'd always known.

She rose and crossed to the door.

"Keep me posted on these Maintenon killings,'' he said as she stepped through the doorway. "And, Harald?''

"Sir?''

"Would you let me know when Anne comes back?''

Returning to her office, Sigrid passed Peters and Eberstadt in the hallway, Peters knotting his tie as he hurried on short legs to keep up with his partner.

"We thought we'd catch the Wolferman funeral,'' said Eberstadt. "It's at eleven up at St. John's.''

That explained the somber suits, Sigrid realized. Usually the two men wore casual sports jackets and went tieless as much as possible.

She turned the corner and almost bumped into Elaine Albee.

They did those ridiculous mirror movements of two people trying to dodge each other until Sigrid grasped what was happening and stood still, a good strategy except that the other officer adopted it at the same moment and now they stood motionless, face to face.

Elaine Albee stared at her, embarrassed, and then began to giggle. "Sorry.''

As Sigrid stepped around her, Albee said, "Lieutenant?''

"Yes?''

"I was wondering. About Lieutenant Knight.''

"Yes?''

"He's married, isn't he? I mean, I'm sort of getting mixed signals. You know? And I don't waste time on married men.''

Sigrid looked at the younger officer. There was a gun strapped under her arm and she was a good cop, but at the same time her blonde curls were stylishly clipped, a bright blue cotton sweater echoed her eyes, and there were pretty gold studs in her ears. Albee was feminine, forthright, and unafraid of emotional entanglements; and for a moment Sigrid felt a pang of sympathy for Jim Lowry.

"There hasn't been a legal divorce," she said carefully, "but I don't think they're living together."

"Thanks, Lieutenant," said Albee and darted on.

Alan Knight was just typing a final paragraph as Sigrid entered her office. She took one of the side chairs and began to read through the notes, trying to make an orderly pattern in her mind. This was where she missed Tillie the most. Careful and methodical, he was excellent at spotting minute details that slipped past her. There were times when she could skim across mountain tops, but not without Tillie building careful bridges beneath her, shoring up intuition with concrete specifics.

But if the killer's identity were anywhere revealed in this sheaf of notes, Sigrid couldn't see it. She sighed and set the pages aside. "Who do you like for it?" she asked Knight.

"Seems to me that it's a toss-up between Baldwin and Flythe, with Baldwin winning on points."

"How?"

"Well, they both had opportunity, I think; but Baldwin's got the motive. She probably goofed and put the board at the wrong place. She's not the most efficient person I've ever met."

"No, but is she the most cold-blooded?"

"Why not? Look how she's more worried about losing her job than about her cousin losing her arm. Or so she'd have us believe. *I* think she's ashamed to look Dixon in the eye myself," he said indignantly, frowning down at the typewriter.

"That's just immaturity," Sigrid argued. "Think about it, Alan. Whoever booby-trapped that cribbage board had to know he would be killing at least two people. He *knew* there would be even more wounded, seriously wounded—eyes, limbs—and he didn't care. To kill one person, he was willing to kill or maim a dozen others. We're not talking about schoolgirl self-centeredness. This is a complete disregard for human life."

"Like Red Snow when they bombed that draft board in Chicago?"

"And didn't notice—or care—that there were children on the other side of that partition." Sigrid nodded. "There has to be a link. Flythe has to be connected somehow."

She handed back the sheaf of notes. "There's a Xerox machine at the end of the hall. Would you copy these? And where's that sketch you made of the Maintenon's floor plan? We'll need a duplicate of that, too."

"What are you going to do?" Knight asked, smoothing out his crumpled drawing.

"When I called the hospital this morning, they said Tillie was conscious and able to talk and watch television. If he can watch television, he can read. Maybe he'll see something we've missed. After all, he was there Friday night."

CHAPTER XXV

Tillie's hospital room was painted a cheerful melon, several vases of flowers sat on the dresser, get-well cards were taped to the wall beside his bed, and a cluster of silvery helium balloons bobbled near the ceiling with colorful ribbons streaming down.

There were bruises on his round face and he was extensively taped and bandaged, but he was able to press the controls that lowered and raised his bed, to manipulate the channel selector for the television on the opposite wall, and, with slightly more difficulty, to answer the telephone on his bed table.

Eyes are the windows of the soul, someone once said, but Sigrid had never recognized the truth of that remark until she saw the friendly intelligence shining in Tillie's gaze and remembered the blank stare she'd seen there Saturday.

"Marian told me you'd been hurt, too," he said when greetings were over and Alan Knight had been introduced.

"It's healing properly," Sigrid said. She'd stopped by the doctor's on their way over and he'd put on fresh dressings. "What about you?"

"You know what they say—it only hurts when I laugh. As

long as I'm still, it's okay. Everything feels tight. And I keep falling asleep. That's the concussion, I guess.''

"Do you remember much about Friday night?"

"Everything. The doctor says some people don't with a concussion, but I do.''

Methodically, Tillie reconstructed the whole evening, beginning with the lamb chops he'd had for dinner after Sigrid dropped him off at the Maintenon Friday night and ending with groping under the table to find the peg Commander Dixon had dropped.

"How is she?" he asked. "The paper said she was in critical condition, too.''

"We'll probably go over when we leave here," Alan Knight said. "She wasn't quite as lucky as you, Detective Tildon. They had to amputate her right arm.''

"Oh, Jesus!" Tillie said, shocked. "She was so nice. Beautiful, too. That red dress. When I read her name on the seating chart, I thought she'd be a man, of course. Commander T. J. Dixon. And she laughed and asked did I expect someone with tattoos up and down his arms.''

His voice wavered and his eyes became watery. "Her arms were so white and smooth.''

Sigrid knew how close to the surface lay the emotions of someone seriously ill or wounded. "Tillie—" she said helplessly.

"We've brought you all the notes of our interviews," Knight interposed smoothly. "Lieutenant Harald said you'll spot whatever we might be missing.''

Tillie was diverted. "Did she?"

He listened quietly while they went through the notes, explained to him the diagrams and photographs, and discussed who had alibis and who didn't. He agreed with Sigrid that a Red Snow connection seemed more likely than a KGB plot or a girlish attempt to speed up an inheritance, and discounted the possibility that the bomb had been meant for him or Commander Dixon, "After going to that much trouble, they wouldn't put the rigged board at the wrong place.''

A nurse came in as he spoke and asked if they would mind waiting outside in the hall.

"We've finished," Sigrid said, thinking that Tillie looked too tired to continue anyhow. She got to her feet. "Don't try to do too much, Tillie. Just get better.''

"Don't worry, Lieutenant," he said, leaning back into the pillows. "I'll be out of here soon.''

They went down a modern hallway painted turquoise and

white, but the smells were old-fashioned regulation hospital, a
blend of disinfectants, antiseptics, and floor wax.

"I hate these places," said Knight.

"Morgues are worse," Sigrid told him.

Commander Dixon's hospital lay across town and while Petty
Officer Schmitt made child's play out of mid-day traffic, Alan
Knight fretted about arriving empty-handed.

"We ought to take her something," he said for the third time.
"What about magazines?"

"Hospital volunteers provide them. What about flowers?"

"Flowers are a cliché."

"Clichés don't become clichés unless a lot of people like
them," Sigrid observed calmly.

"You were just in the hospital. What did you miss most?"

"I wasn't in long enough to miss anything, but I was laid up at
school once with a broken leg and someone brought me a back
scratcher. You know, one of those little hands carved out of a long
piece of rattan or bamboo? It was the most practical thing they gave
me. I could even slide it down inside the cast."

Knight leaned forward. "There's a Japanese place off Fifth
Avenue," he told Schmitt. "Two more blocks and hang a left."

"Yes, sir."

While Alan Knight rattled around at the rear of the store for a
back scratcher, Sigrid discovered a shelf of snow domes, those
crystal balls usually filled with flecks of white that children love to
shake, then watch as the flecks settle over a wintry scene like falling
snow. These were like none she'd ever seen. Instead of a fir tree or
a snowman, the glass ball held a miniature cherry tree in full
bloom; and when she shook it, tiny flecks of pink swirled like
drifting blossoms.

Charmed, Sigrid bought one, thinking it might amuse Commander Dixon. As she paid, Knight emerged triumphantly from
the rear of the store with a small plastic hand fastened to quite a
long bamboo stick and a kaleidoscope.

"I always liked these," he confessed, looking more like five
than twenty-five and making Sigrid smile.

As it was now nearly two o'clock, Schmitt was encouraged to

double-park at the corner of Eighth and West Fiftieth and hop out for a round of frankfurters from a pushcart.

"Sauerkraut or onions, ma'am?" he asked.

"Sauerkraut, please."

"Onions for me, Schmitty," said Knight, "and get yourself a couple, too."

Sabrett frankfurters are the smell of New York and their redolence filled the car as Alan Knight waxed nostalgic about Southern hot dogs, the buns stuffed with chili, cole slaw, and finely chopped raw onions. "Took me a long time to get used to pickled cabbage on my franks."

"I've eaten what the South calls a frankfurter," Sigrid said. "Fire-engine red, limp and mushy, no snap to the casing. Give me these any day."

An amiable argument about the merits of regional foods lasted almost to the hospital. It served as well as anything else to distract them from the interview that lay ahead, but both had fallen silent by the time Petty Officer Schmitt pulled up to the entrance of a grim, soot-stained building erected in the twenties.

Alan Knight lagged behind as Sigrid approached the main desk to ask directions.

"I'll be back in a minute," he said.

It was more than a minute and Sigrid was becoming impatient when he returned from the gift shop with a small, prettily wrapped box.

"Perfume," he said as they rode up in the elevator. "Just in case she needs to be reminded that she's still a beautiful woman."

And she was. Even with the cuts and bruises and the deep black circles under her eyes, the slender woman who lay sleeping on the steel-framed hospital bed possessed a more than average beauty. There was strength in the small pointed chin, intelligence in the sweep of her brow. She was said to have had short white hair that curled all over her head—"A nest of stork feathers," was the way Vassily Ivanovich had put it—but smooth bandages now encased her head, reminding Sigrid of the white linen bands that nuns used to wear under their black veils to hide their hair.

She wore a bleached and faded hospital gown and the sight of it made a slow anger against Molly Baldwin begin to burn. Somehow Sigrid sensed how much Commander Dixon would hate that gown. Lacy lingerie and pretty negligées were Sigrid's secret self-indulgence, so surely a woman as feminine as Ivanovich and Tillie had described would have dozens of frilly gowns and bed jackets. Someone should have brought her her own things instead of sentencing her to this ugly cotton shift.

Damn that girl!

The gown had wide short sleeves and the bandaged stub could be clearly seen. Commander Dixon's arm ended halfway between her elbow and shoulder.

No elbow joint, Sigrid thought numbly. She had hoped the surgeons had saved it. Without the elbow, any prosthetic device would probably be clumsier and bulkier.

She glanced at Alan. He was white-faced. "Maybe we ought not to wake her," he whispered.

Sigrid would have liked to run away, too, but she steeled herself and approached the bed. "Commander Dixon?"

A frown furrowed the woman's smooth features. Her eyes opened, blankly at first, then awareness filled them as if she were coming back from a long distance. She looked at Sigrid without curiosity.

"Doctor?" she murmured.

"No, Commander. I'm Lieutenant Harald, New York City Police."

"Police?" Her gaze fell on Alan Knight's blue uniform with its two gold stripes on the sleeve. "Lieutenant?"

"Alan Knight, ma'am. ONI."

"Yes . . . of course." She tried to push herself more erect on the pillows and grimaced with the pain of the effort.

"Shall I crank you up?" Knight asked anxiously, bending for the handle at the foot of the narrow bed.

"Just a little, please," she whispered. Her eyes went to her bandaged arm and a low moan escaped her lips.

"Every time I wake up, I keep hoping it's been a bad dream."

Anguish hung in the room like an almost palpable miasma and Sigrid could feel herself stiffening. "If you'd rather, Commander, we can come back another time."

"No. I'm all right."

"Can you talk about Friday night?"

"Friday." The frown reappeared. "What's today?"

"Monday."

"That's right. The nurse told me that at—breakfast? Lunch? I'm sorry. Everything keeps getting muddled."

She spoke with some effort and her voice was low, but there was a musical undertone that was very appealing and it reminded

Sigrid that Haines Froelick said that he and Zachary Wolferman had been equally enchanted by the commander's voice.

"Commander, do you remember the cribbage tournament?" Sigrid asked.

"Yes . . . Vassily and I . . . the Hotel Maintenon. We had drinks and there was a nice old gentleman and his cousin. We talked and then—"

Her voice broke off and she looked at them in mute appeal.

"Was anyone else badly hurt?" she whispered. "They said two men were killed and the man I was playing against—a policeman—was seriously hurt but they didn't mention any women."

"Your cousin is fine," Sigrid said bluntly, guessing what lay behind her question. "She was at the far side of the room and wasn't hurt at all."

"You know about Molly?"

Her head sank deeper into the pillows and tears seeped out around her closed lids. "I've been so worried," she whispered. "And I couldn't ask. She said not to and I didn't know if she was in trouble . . . or what. You're sure she's all right?"

"We're sure," Knight said.

She opened her eyes and looked at them gratefully. "Then why hasn't she come?"

"I'm sure she has," Sigrid lied impulsively. "You were probably too groggy to remember."

"Yes, that's it. That must be it."

"Commander," said Alan Knight, "you mentioned Vassily Ivanovich. Could you describe your relationship with him?"

Commander Dixon turned her head on the pillow and smiled faintly at him. "Isn't he a love? He and my dad were friends once. He remembers so much about Dad that I had forgotten. Hell-raisers, both of them."

"There's been some suggestion that perhaps Ivanovich's visit here isn't quite as innocent as it appears," said Knight.

Her eyes widened. *"Who* suggested?"

"After all, ma'am, with your job and security clearance—"

"I forgot you were Intelligence," she said and her bell-toned voice held the first hint of amusement. "Always looking for spies under the bed. Forget it, Lieutenant. I don't talk about my job to anybody, not even to long-lost friends of my father. Anyhow, Vassily's never asked. I don't think he would. Even if they told him to. I know it's hard to understand, but he really does love

Americans. My father pulled him out of the water himself. He'd never do anything to hurt my father's child.''

The words had tired her, but she seemed compelled to make him understand. "Some things go beyond ideology, Lieutenant."

"But, ma'am—"

"No buts, Lieutenant," she said softly.

He let it drop for the moment and helped Sigrid lead her through what she had observed Friday night. It added nothing to what they already knew. No, she had noticed no one hovering around Table 5 before they were asked to take their places; no, she hadn't paid any attention to the cribbage board at the next place. It was the first time that she'd realized that Zachary Wolferman was one of the dead men and her eyes misted.

"What about his cousin? Mr.—Froman?"

"Froelick," Sigrid told her. "He wasn't hurt."

"That's good."

Her attention drifted toward the packages they had placed on her bed table. "Are those for me?"

The things they had chosen somehow seemed frivolous and incongruous now.

"We didn't know—" Knight began awkwardly, then glanced at Sigrid for help.

"Are there any books you'd like?" asked Sigrid. "Can we bring you anything from your apartment?"

"Thank you both, but I'm sure Molly will do it."

She smiled at the back scratcher and kaleidoscope and seemed charmed by Sigrid's cherry tree inside the glass dome. "I was stationed in Japan for two springs," she told them, mesmerized by the tiny pink petals that swirled around the tree. "Washington, too, of course."

But the gift wrap and tape on the small box defeated her. "I can't," she said wretchedly. "It takes two hands."

She lifted her left hand. "I can't write with this."

Her eyes focused on her slender fingers, at the chipped red enamel; and she gave a strangled sob. "I can't even take off my own nail polish."

Afterward, Alan Knight was to insist that somebody must have rubbed a magic lantern and that the girl who suddenly appeared in the doorway with a small valise and an enormous bouquet of asters and fall chrysanthemums must have been a genie.

"Commander Dixon?" she chirped. "Hi! A Mr. Haines Froelick sent me. I'm from Elizabeth Arden. Mr. Froelick thought a nice facial might cheer you up. I can do your nails, too, if you want.''

"Now there's a man who clearly knows a thing or two about hospital presents," said Knight, as he and Sigrid waited for the elevator to take them down.

CHAPTER XXVI

As they hurtled downtown in the gray Navy station wagon assigned to Lieutenant Knight, Sigrid found herself increasingly exasperated. "That's hardly a logical decision," she told him.

"I don't care," Knight replied. "Anyhow, it may not be logical, but it's certainly reasonable."

He peered out at a passing street sign. "Weren't we supposed to turn there, Schmitty?"

"No, sir," said their patient helmsman as he navigated the tricky waters of Greenwich Village.

"You can't dismiss Froelick as a suspect simply because he did something nice for Commander Dixon," Sigrid said.

"The hell I can't! If you can take Molly Baldwin off your list because she's too immature, I can take Haines Froelick off mine because he's thoughtful. Somebody empathic enough to send over a beautician is too damn decent to bomb a roomful of people." Pleased with his circuitous logic, Knight grinned at her.

Unconvinced, Sigrid leaned back, shaking her head. "How long did you say you've been doing intelligence work?"

"This the right place, ma'am?" asked Petty Officer Schmitt, drawing up before the gracious Greenwich Village brownstone that housed the Sutton apartment.

"This is it."

Before leaving the hospital, Sigrid had checked in with headquarters and learned that Nauman had left a message that Val Sutton was back and wanted to see her.

When Sigrid rang the doorbell on the second floor, Nauman himself answered.

"That was quick." His welcoming smile dimmed as Alan Knight loomed up behind her.

"Sir," said Knight, touching his hat in a half salute.

"I see you're still babysitting," Nauman muttered in Sigrid's ear.

A bearded graduate student with a giggling Sutton tot on each shoulder passed them in the hall headed for the kitchen. The children had become somewhat jaded by the presence of so many people in the last few days and paid no attention to the new arrivals.

In the study, Val Sutton was leafing through a stack of sympathy cards. She wore a loose black sweater dress belted with a gold chain, and a pot of vivid yellow chrysanthemums brightened the cold hearth.

"I don't mind 'Our thoughts are with you' or 'In your time of sorrow,' but I'll be damned if I'll look at 'God has a purpose!'" she said, kiting the offensive message toward the fireplace. "How can they drivel that disgusting pap? Laying John's murder on God!"

A pudgy rumpled man in baggy corduroy pants and even baggier rust-colored sweater rescued the cards from the sooty hearth. "A little more charity, Val," he admonished mildly. "They mean well."

"When the world has reduced itself to a polluted ball of rubble, the last man will probably erect a stone that reads 'They meant well,'" she replied; yet the shadow of a sardonic smile softened the bitter words and her smile widened as Nauman appeared in the doorway with Sigrid and Alan Knight.

She greeted Sigrid warmly and was introduced to Knight, but Sigrid immediately noticed how tired she looked. Something about her face had hardened. She was still exotic, still resembled a sleek expensive cat, but something was gone, thought Sigrid. Youth? No, not youth exactly, nor confidence either . . . Vulnerability, she decided. Val Sutton was in the process of growing a chip-proof shell and unless something intervened, it would slowly harden around her like the chrysalis of one of Jill Gill's butterflies, smooth and beautiful and utterly impervious to rain or sun.

And the man knew it, she thought, extending her hand to the one Val was introducing as Sam Naismith.

"We met by phone Saturday night," Sigrid reminded them.

"Sam's going to act as John's literary executor," said Val. "Finish John's book."

"Won't that be rather difficult?"

"Val's rounding up all his notes for me," said Naismith, with a gentle smile. "And don't forget that John and I roomed together at McClellan, so we shared a lot of the same experiences."

"Sam spent the weekend phoning all over the country to locate Tris Yorke," said Val, motioning them to take chairs.

"I'm sorry you went to that trouble," said Sigrid. "We learned this morning that Ted Flythe's definitely not Fred Hamilton. The fingerprints are completely different."

"But Hamilton's really alive!" said Naismith. "I finally tracked Tris down at a wilderness camp he's running for terminally ill kids near Niagara Falls. Back in 1970, when he was working at a country hospital as a C.O.—"

"C.O.?" asked Alan Knight, wondering how a war protester became a hospital's commanding officer.

"Conscientious objector," explained Naismith. As a college professor, he had grown inured to the realization that his recent history was *terra incognita* to a younger generation. "Those who could prove that they objected to the war on long-held conscientious grounds were allowed to perform alternate service. Tris worked as an orderly in a little hospital in upstate New York."

Resuming the main thread of his story, he said, "Two days after the explosion at Cayuga Lake, Fred Hamilton and the Farr girl showed up at his place looking like a couple of singed chickens. Tris said at first he didn't want to help them because of the draft board bomb that killed the kids, but Fred talked him around. Told Tris it wasn't his fault, that it was all a miscalculation on someone else's part. Tris finally bought it. He got them clothes and papers and drove them up to Montreal himself."

"Montreal?"

"Yeah. Fred spoke fluent French—he'd worked in French Guiana with the Peace Corps—and he figured he could blend in there. That was Tris Yorke's last sight of Fred."

Sigrid leaned back in the leather armchair, her fingertips lightly touching across her lap. "It's interesting, but I'm afraid it doesn't really get us any closer to who booby-trapped that cribbage board. Flythe's fingerprints were compared with all known Red Snow members and there's no match. We brought pictures—"

Alan Knight extracted them from his briefcase. The police photographer had done an excellent job. Her black-and-white eight-by-tens showed Ted Flythe both full-faced and in profile; his hooded eyes, sensuous lips, and pointed beard were sharply detailed.

"Red Snow aside, have you seen this man elsewhere?" Sigrid

asked. "We're running a background check, but nothing's come in yet. Remember, Val? He said he graduated from a small college in Michigan. Carlyle Union. He says he's done a little of everything, including guiding European tours."

Val studied the prints minutely, but finally frowned and shook her head. Naismith was no more successful.

"I can see why he reminded you of Tris, though," he told Val, covering the lower half of the photo with his broad hand. "Same sort of eyes."

He handed the pictures back to Alan Knight. "If you've ruled out Red Snow, I guess you aren't interested in Victor Earle."

"Who?" asked Sigrid.

"Victor Earle. He's the guy I mentioned on Saturday who was out of the country when Red Snow self-destructed. Served a couple of years for drugs and illegal arms. Tris saw him when he first came back to the States; said he'd run into Fred in Europe. Tris did some calling, too. Earle's out on Long Island now. Mantausic."

"This Victor Earle was an active member of Red Snow? He'd know everyone on sight?"

"He should."

Naismith took a handful of paper scraps from his pocket and dug through them till he found one with a Mantausic address scrawled on it.

"Why don't you show him your pictures?"

"Thanks," said Sigrid. "Perhaps we will."

Nauman followed them from the apartment. As Knight went on down the steps to find Petty Officer Schmitt, Oscar and Sigrid lingered at the top in the thin sunlight. There was a damp feel to the air. It would rain before nightfall. Brown and gold leaves fell from the few trees which stood in little circles of dirt encased by concrete. Across the street, a well-dressed matron swept leaves from her steps with jerky stabs of the broom, watched by a tiny poodle.

"Sleep well last night?" Nauman inquired mildly, leaning back against the wall to light his meerschaum pipe. The sweet smoke smelled vaguely autumnal.

"Sorry about that. I hope you don't think it's because of the wine?"

"Never crossed my mind," he teased.

"Or that I was bored?"

"Nope. I decided it was because you felt at ease with me. Unthreatened." He checked his watch. "It's early and I have to see some students at six, but why don't you send Ralph Rackstraw home and let's go have a drink."

"I'm a working woman," she said. "With miles to go before I drink. But I haven't forgotten that Piers Leyden opening tomorrow night."

Alan Knight had collected Schmitt, and the car was now parked in front of the apartment with the motor running.

"I have to go," Sigrid said, starting down the steps.

"How much longer are you going to keep this naval escort?" Nauman asked irritably.

"You'd prefer the army?" She smiled back up at him from street level.

"I'd prefer somebody who didn't look like a young David and make me feel like old King Saul," muttered Nauman.

But Sigrid was already crossing the sidewalk and if she heard, she didn't respond.

CHAPTER XXVII

It had taken several phone calls the previous afternoon to locate Victor Earle. Or rather, to locate someone who knew him, since he did not seem to own a telephone. The landlady at his boarding-house sounded reliable and she had promised Sigrid to tell Earle to expect her the next morning, Tuesday, around ten.

"You don't have to come," she'd told Alan Knight, but he pointed out that she could hardly drive herself the length of Long Island with one arm in a sling and besides, he wanted to see this thing to the end.

Mantausic, on South Oyster Bay, was a scruffy little sea town, the kind that could be found all up and down the Atlantic coast. Unlike the towns that serviced Fire Island a little further east, Mantausic had never drawn a white-wine-and-brie crowd, and it did not pull down the shades or roll up its waterfront after Labor Day. Mantausic was home port to a small fleet of charter boats and

October had always been a good month for blues, weakfish and flounder.

Dedicated sportsmen from all over Brooklyn, Queens or Nassau would arise before daylight and drive through the dawn hours to be at the dock by sailing time at six A.M., tackle boxes and coolers in hand.

It was a little past ten and all the boat slips were empty as a car from the Navy's motor pool drove slowly along Front Street looking for the repair shop where Victor Earle was said to work.

Petty Officer Schmitt had been left in the city and Sigrid sat on the front seat beside Alan Knight and peered through the windshield.

"There it is," she said, pointing to a tin-sided garage with a sign over the open sliding doors that read "Kryschevski's Marine Repairs—Diesel Engines Our Specialty."

"Sorry," said Mr. Kryschevski, straightening up to wipe his hands on a grease-smeared rag, when they inquired for Earle. "'Fraid you've got a little wait. The *Margie Q* was short-handed this morning so Vic went out with her."

"Out where?" asked Sigrid. "Maybe we could—"

"Out on the water," said the mechanic. "Don't you worry though. The *Margie Q*'s only a half-day charter. They don't go all the way out. Just do a little bottom fishing off the point. They'll be back around twelve-thirty, one o'clock."

"We thought he worked here," said Knight.

"Does. But when things are slow like they are right now, Vic picks up a day now and then on the water."

"Has he worked for you long?"

"'Bout a year now, off and on." Kryschevski walked over to a drink dispenser, pushed in some coins, and popped the top of a diet cola. He took a long swallow, eyeing them carefully all the time. "Vic in trouble again?"

"What makes you ask that? Has he been in trouble before?"

"No, no." Kryschevski took another swallow. "Not really. There was that business with the *Peconic Pearl*. You're Navy though, aren't you? Not Coast Guard."

With prodding, Kryschevski described a little scrape the *Peconic Pearl* had gotten herself mixed up in late one night back in the summer. The Coast Guard accused her of rendezvousing with a Colombian freighter a few miles off shore and perhaps taking on a few bales of drugs. By the time they overtook her and searched her, though, the *Peconic Pearl* seemed to be clean and there was no proof.

"Was Earle aboard the *Pearl* that night?"

"Yeah. The Coast Guard was around next day to talk to him."

"What about this past weekend?" asked Sigrid.

"This weekend?"

"Friday night or Sunday morning?"

"Well, Friday night he helped me work on the engine of the *Seabreeze II* till after midnight. Sunday? I don't know. Seems like he might've gone out on the *Pearl* Sunday. You'll have to ask him."

Kryschevski told them they were welcome to wait inside the garage, but Sigrid and Knight decided to poke around the small town instead.

It had rained during the night and heavy gray clouds overhead promised more, but they left the car parked near the berth of the *Margie Q* and walked up the main street, a tree-lined thoroughfare that led directly from the waterfront. They walked past two pharmacies, a bank, a grocery, and a tackle shop—the usual small town assortment—and paused before a window full of what would be antiques over in the Hamptons but were here unpretentiously labeled Frank's Used Furniture.

They had excellent coffee in the Chowder Bowl, browsed through the reduced book table at the Inglenook Book Shop, and read all the tombstones in the tiny graveyard surrounding the Mantausic Anglican Church at the end of First Street.

Beyond lay a marshy area that had been designated a wildlife refuge for sea birds. Knight was ready to explore it, but Sigrid became uneasy whenever her feet left concrete, so they turned back.

It was a little past eleven.

They crossed to the other side of the street and Knight paused in front of the Lobster Pot Café. "Want another coffee?"

"Not really."

"Too bad they don't have a movie or something."

"You didn't have to come," Sigrid reminded him.

"I wanted to come. I just didn't know we'd have to hang around doing nothing for three hours in the world's most boring town."

"Why don't you buy a paper and go read in the car?" she suggested, drifting on to the next shop.

It was a small beauty parlor with a dozen or more sun-faded

pictures in the windows of an eclectic range of hair styles, from rock punk to country club conservative.

"That cut would look good on you," said Alan, pointing to a multilayered style very short on the top and what looked like a rattail hanging down the back.

Mantausic on a gray Tuesday morning did not seem to have provided the fortyish woman inside the shop with any customers and she peered out at them with a hopeful air. Sigrid shook her head.

"What makes you so afraid of looking feminine?" Alan asked curiously. "Worried that you can't command if the troops find out you're a woman? Or that Oscar Nauman will wrestle you to the nearest bed?"

"Don't be an ass," she snapped and started past.

Possessed by a sudden spurt of mischief, he grabbed her free hand and brashly tugged her into the shop. "Good morning," he caroled before Sigrid could protest. "Do you have time to style my friend's hair?"

"I think I can work her in," the woman answered solemnly. "Let's see. Yes, I believe station three has just opened up."

To Knight's complete surprise, Sigrid strolled over to that chair and sat down without any argument.

"You'll really do it?" he asked, stunned.

Sigrid flashed a wicked smile at him through the mirror and spoke to the woman. "I haven't been able to shower with my arm bandaged like this. Could you give me a shampoo?"

"And a cut," said Alan Knight, refusing to give up.

"And a cut," Sigrid agreed serenely. "I usually take about an inch off every month, but that's something else I can't do with my arm out of commission."

The beautician began pulling pins from the braided bun at the nape of Sigrid's neck. "Did you break your arm?" she asked in a sympathetic tone.

"I meant a *real* cut," Alan protested. "Throw away your inhibitions."

"Go away, Alan," Sigrid said. "I'm not going to have you stand there and nag me for the next forty minutes. Go torpedo something in the bay."

"A real cut," Alan begged the beautician. "Something wild and completely different."

"I'll meet you back at the car," Sigrid said in a voice that brooked no further argument.

He went.

The beautician loosened the thick braid. "Your hair's as fine as baby silk. Doesn't hold much curl either, does it?"

She lifted the soft dark mass in her capable hands and looked at Sigrid in the mirror, considering the younger woman's thin face, high forehead, and wide gray eyes.

"Have you ever worn bangs?" she asked.

At 12:35, the car door opened and Sigrid got in beside him. Alan Knight lowered his newspaper and his jaw dropped.

"Don't say a word!" Sigrid said in a strangled voice. "Not a single word. I mean it, Alan."

A light misting rain had begun and Sigrid stared through the windshield, straight out at the steel gray water. One of the half-day charter boats had returned but it was not the *Margie Q.*

"Couldn't I please say just one word?"

"Well?"

"Wow!" he breathed.

She looked at him anxiously. "Honest? Do you like it?"

"It's terrific," he assured her. "God, it looks great! I can't believe you really did it."

Gone was the bun and the pulled-back severity. The silky dark hair was now feathered and full on top and very short on the sides and back. Wisps of bangs softened her high forehead. Freed of the heavy mass of hair, the newly defined shape of her head sat more elegantly on her long neck.

She ran the tips of her fingers through the ragged bangs experimentally. "It's going to be easier to take care of, I think. Ida showed me how to use a blow-dryer to give it more body."

"Ida?"

"The beautician. She was really rather nice."

"I bet she could sell Chryslers to the Japanese," said Alan, peering at her more closely. In the overcast daylight, it was hard to tell. "Are you wearing blusher?"

"What do you know about blusher?"

"My six sisters," he reminded her. "And is that eye shadow, too?"

Sigrid tilted the rearview mirror so she could examine her face. "It's not too much, is it? I've never felt comfortable with makeup before, but Ida took some of the mystery out of these things."

She opened the pink plastic bag she'd brought from the shop to show Knight an assortment of small bottles and tubes.

"I always thought you had to use a lot and I hated all that thick goop. It's the first time anybody's ever explained the theory to me," she confessed almost shyly. "Ida says there are books in the library."

He was touched by her delight in her new look yet he couldn't help laughing. "Trust you to approach the frivolity of makeup in a rational, systematic way."

"I don't have six sisters," she replied with some of her usual tartness.

Ahead of them out in the bay, the shape of a trim little fishing boat emerged from the foggy gray of sky and water.

The *Margie Q* was heading in.

Val Sutton had remembered Victor Earle as short and getting thin on top. Seventeen years later, Earle was completely bald. Even his eyebrows were scanty. All the hair on his head seemed to have repositioned itself around his mouth. His top lip supported a thick brown handlebar moustache that swirled out with exuberant panache on either side of his mouth. He had very pale blue eyes and a disconcerting stare.

After identifying themselves, they had led him to a table in the Lobster Pot Café and he had followed without protest, still wearing his rubber waders. His yellow slicker hung across the back of his chair. He gazed straight into the eyes of his questioners and long minutes seemed to pass before he blinked. The last time Sigrid had seen that sort of unblinking gaze was in the eyes of a man who had killed and then sodomized the bodies of three small boys.

There seemed to be a momentary pause between the end of each question and the beginning of his response, almost like the two-second delay when a question is bounced off a satellite to someone being televised halfway around the world. Earle answered them willingly enough, but that spacy stare and the hesitation before his response made Sigrid suspect he might be on drugs.

Earle expressed neither surprise nor resentment at being sought out by the police and only minimal curiosity that they should be interested in Red Snow.

"Hell of a way to die," he told them, his fingers tapping the rubber waders. "Messing around with C-4."

"Is that what it was?"

"That's what Fred said. I never messed with that stuff. M-4's and Uzis, even hand grenades, okay, but—"

"Fred? Fred Hamilton? When did he tell you that?"

Victor Earle turned his pale-eyed stare upon Sigrid. "In France. One of those resort towns on the Mediterranean."

"Where is Hamilton now? Still in Europe?"

Earle continued to gaze at her. "Yeah, he's still there."

His moustache twitched up and down and it took a moment to realize that he was laughing. There was no sound and no change in the expression in his eyes, just that jerk of brown handlebars and the flash of teeth beneath.

"He loaded his needle with the wrong stuff one night and woke up dead the next morning."

"When?"

"Seventy-one. April, I think it was."

"What about the girl that was with him?"

"Brooks Ann?" He shrugged. "Who knows? She split. She was walking the streets for rent money and one night she didn't come back. Probably went home with one of the Johns."

"Did you ever hear of any others getting out alive from that burning lodge?" asked Sigrid.

"Nah."

As the interview continued, they learned that Victor Earle did not watch television or read the papers, so he claimed to know nothing about the Maintenon bombing or John Sutton's death. In fact, he seemed not to know who Sutton was.

"McClellan? Nah. I was never at McClellan."

Alan Knight showed him the group photo taken of the McClellan SDS group and asked him whom he recognized. He picked out Fred Hamilton, a couple of the women, and Tris Yorke, but not Sutton. Even when they pointed to him, Earle shook his head.

Then they spread out the photographs taken at the hotel over the past weekend. Knight had remembered to bring along Sigrid's magnifying glass for studying the tiny faces in the background.

Absentmindedly rubbing his bald head, Earle moved the glass methodically across the pictures. A surprising number of cardplayers and hotel workers were to be seen in the background and the two officers pointed to those of main interest: Haines Froelick, Vassily Ivanovich, Molly Baldwin, and, of course, Ted Flythe. He admitted knowing none of them.

"Who are those geeks?" he asked, pointing to a view of the Bontemps Room Sunday afternoon.

The photographer had taken it in an attempt to get Flythe's profile without her target noticing, so Flythe was well to the right of the picture. On the left, Madame Ronay seemed to be instructing the remaining busboys and Mr. George, the head steward. Every face was in sharp detail.

Sigrid explained who they were.

Earle's pale blue eyes gazed vacantly into her face. "This George guy. He works for her?"

"They all do. It's her hotel," Knight said impatiently. "Do you recognize them? Have you seen this George before?"

Another pause.

"Nah."

Before they started the rainy drive back to town, Sigrid telephoned headquarters and left a message for Eberstadt or Peters to start checking Mr. George's background.

CHAPTER XXVIII

Sigrid had never before realized how many reflective surfaces she passed every day, nor how often she saw herself subliminally. Not just mirrors, but windows, glass partitions, doors, polished vinyl or metal. Each time came as a fresh shock. She rather liked her new haircut, the way it looked and felt, but those unexpected reminders of it were disconcerting. Even more, she wished her co-workers didn't feel compelled to stare and comment. It was bad enough feeling the silent looks that followed her through the halls when they returned to headquarters Tuesday afternoon. Things were no better in what should have been the sanctuary of her office.

Alan Knight was beginning to act as if he had cut her hair himself; and when Elaine Albee came in to report that Jill Gill thought no one had followed Pernell Johnson through the staff door Sunday, Sigrid cut through her startled compliments and crisply asked if anyone could alibi Ivanovich between ten-forty-five and eleven o'clock.

"Not yet, Lieutenant. Everybody went home Sunday night and I'm having trouble locating some of the witnesses."

"Wouldn't it be simplest to ask Ivanovich himself and go from there? Or is it too complicated?"

"You're better than those knives they sell on late-night television," Knight scolded when Albee escaped. "You can slice through steel easy as butter."

"Since you have all the data on Ivanovich, why don't you go help lighten her task?" Sigrid asked irritably.

"All she wanted to do was make nice about your hair."

"Then let me reciprocate," Sigrid said sardonically. "Albee asked me about your wife yesterday morning."

Alan Knight perked up. "She did? What did you tell her?"

"I said I thought you two were separated."

He got up and ambled toward the door. "Now that was real sisterly of you," he drawled.

Sigrid worked undisturbed for another half hour until Jim Lowry tapped on her open door. He'd spent the previous afternoon up in Harlem talking to Pernell Johnson's aunt, a tougher interview than usual. Quincy Johnson had been devastated.

"They're taking his body back to Florida today," said Lowry. "That's what the grandmother wants. You know, Lieutenant, every time a kid gets killed, his family will tell you what a Boy Scout he was; and then later his friends and neighbors will tell you what he was really like. This time it sounds true. Everybody says he was hard-working and clean—no drugs, not even beer or cigarettes—church on Sunday, respectful of his aunt. I'd stake my career that if Pernell Johnson knew something about that bomb, he didn't even *know* he knew it."

"So that he might have made an innocent remark that panicked the killer?"

"Something like that."

For a moment, Sigrid was silent, remembering the slender youth in his white linen pants and short green jacket. "I spoke to him, you know. On Saturday. He told me about putting out the fire and about his duties that night. I wish I'd pushed him more."

Sigrid glanced up and saw that Lowry was looking at her oddly. Quickly she said, "What did the desk clerk and bellman say about Baldwin's story? Can they confirm it?"

"Not really. They think she came downstairs sometime after Madame Ronay showed up looking for her and that she did go down the hall that leads to her office, but they don't know if she stayed there. No one noticed when she left again."

"Too bad."

"What about you? Anything new on Fred Hamilton?"

"According to Victor Earle, he OD'd in France in the spring of seventy-one."

"*Merde!*"

"My sentiments, too."

Lowry stood to go and there was indecision on his good-natured face. "Did you do something to your hair, Lieutenant? It looks different."

"I had it cut."

"Looks nice."

"Thanks. Was there something else, Lowry?"

"Well, I was wondering if you'd seen Albee. She's not at her desk and—"

"She's out checking on Ivanovich's movements Sunday morning," Sigrid answered guiltily, and was relieved when a uniformed officer from Communications stuck her head in the door and said, "Lieutenant Harald? This just came in for you."

Lowry started to leave; but as Sigrid scanned the telex, she called him back and handed it to him. According to the Michigan branch of a certain religious denomination which presently held all the records of Carlyle Union College from its founding in 1883 till its closing in 1979, the only Theodore Flythe ever to graduate from dear old CUC was an Alfred Theodore Flythe, Class of 1907.

"Funny, he doesn't look that old," said Lowry.

"Want to go talk to him about it?"

"Sure."

"And now that we know he's not Fred Hamilton, you might ask him where he was between 10:41 and 10:55 on Sunday morning. One thing more, Lowry. It doesn't look as if Flythe was one of the Red Snow terrorists; but just the same, take somebody with you. Eberstadt maybe. Or Peters. Whoever killed Pernell Johnson was quick with his hands."

"You don't suppose Albee's coming back soon?"

"I doubt it," Sigrid said, and hoped he wouldn't notice that Lieutenant Knight seemed to be missing as well.

Her wristwatch showed well past four now and she'd promised to meet Nauman at Piers Leyden's art exhibit before six. Normally she'd have gone straight from work, but today . . . Her hand touched the back of her neck and that strange lightness returned, almost as if the cutting of her hair had also cut away some of her inhibitions.

She thought of a certain claret-colored dress Anne had

brought her from London last fall. Nauman had never seen her in red.

She was halfway down the hall before she remembered and went back for the little pink plastic bag of cosmetics.

Daylight was fading as Sigrid stepped from the cab a few doors off Fifth Avenue. The small elevator that conveyed clients to the third-floor gallery was lined with smoky gold-threaded mirrors and she gave her reflection a final worried inspection.

The purplish-red dress was simply cut, with a softly flared skirt and long full sleeves that nicely concealed her bandaged arm. It was topped with a short paisley-embroidered tabard of rich jewel tones, and she'd found a small black patent leather shoulder bag with skinny straps to match her shoes.

There hadn't been time to do her nails, but she'd followed Ida's instructions exactly on the makeup and come away with a new respect for women like Madame Ronay and Commander Dixon. It had taken her four tries before she got the eyeliner on straight. Under the fluorescent light in her bathroom, it had looked a little exaggerated, but Ida was right: in this subdued lighting, her eyes did look deeper and more interesting.

The elevator came to a stop and a small empty spot of stage fright settled in Sigrid's diaphragm. As the doors opened, she took a deep breath and stepped out into a babble of voices.

"Still no answer, huh, kid?" asked Eberstadt as Jim Lowry came back to the car parked in front of Flythe's apartment after trying Elaine Albee's telephone number again.

"We didn't actually have a date," said Lowry. "I said something this morning about a movie, but nothing definite."

He settled back in the seat disconsolately. They had missed Flythe at his office and it was beginning to look as if the Graphic Games rep had his own plans for the evening.

"Let's give him another twenty minutes and then call it a day," suggested Eberstadt, rummaging in the bottom of the bag which had held their greasy cheeseburgers for the last stray french fry. His kids were teenagers, his wife on half a dozen church committees, so he was in no hurry to get home; but he remembered how it used to be.

Even as he spoke, they saw Ted Flythe swing down from a city bus on the corner and head toward them, jingling his door keys.

They got out of the car. "Mr. Flythe? NYPD. About the Maintenon case."

"Yeah?" He stood with his key ring dangling from his index finger. "I remember you guys. What's happening?"

"We wondered if we could ask you a few more questions."

"Sure. Come on up."

Flythe's apartment was not all that different from his, thought Jim Lowry, looking around. A little bigger maybe, a little neater, but definitely the space inhabited by a man living without a woman. He'd never quite understood why a woman's apartment differed from a man's. It was the same sort of furniture, the same rugs on the floor, and sometimes the same stacks of newspapers and magazines and dirty dishes piled just as high; and yet there was always something. Lamps maybe? Light always seemed softer in a woman's place.

"How about a beer?" asked Flythe from the kitchen.

"Sure," said Eberstadt.

"Nothing for me, thanks," said Lowry, prowling the living room restlessly. Should he call Lainey again? It wasn't like her not to leave a message.

"So, gentlemen," said Flythe as he opened their beers. "What would you like to know?"

"More routine," said Eberstadt, co-opting the most comfortable chair in the room. There were no coasters on the end table, so he used a magazine for his beer can. "Just getting the loose ends straight. This was your first tournament with Graphic Games?"

"Right." Flythe blotted the foam from his neat Vandyke beard and repeated what he'd told them before: how long he'd been with Graphic Games, a bit of his previous history. He seemed almost as relaxed as Matt Eberstadt.

Jim Lowry was still roaming the room and he paused before a framed diploma over the stereo. "Carlyle Union College," he read, then peered closer at the faded ink. "June 1967."

"You were probably just entering grade school," said Flythe. "You sure I can't get you a drink?"

"No, thanks. We were wondering about Sunday morning."

"What about it?"

"Did you know the kid that was killed? Pernell Johnson?"

"Not by name. I'd seen him around all weekend though."

"Talk to him much?"

Flythe shook his head. "No need to. Miss Baldwin and the room steward— What's his name? George? They kept that side of the tournament running smoothly. I'll say that for the Maintenon.

Graphic Games got its money's worth. Lucienne Ronay runs a class operation. Those fancy ballrooms.''

"We heard you liked the bedroom, too," said Eberstadt, with a slow wink that was like a visual nudge.

Flythe gave an airy man-of-the-world wave of his hand. "No point letting opportunity knock and not get up to answer," he grinned.

"The last time anyone seems to have seen Johnson alive was about the middle of the break on Sunday morning," said Lowry. "About 10:41. Did you run into him after the break began?"

"Nope, can't say that I did." Flythe drained his glass and looked at Eberstadt's. "Ready for another suds?"

"No, thanks. Let me get this straight, now. When you left the tournament, you went out the back exit, right?"

"Right. There's an elevator behind the one in the lobby and I took it up to my room. Had to change my shirt because of one of those ditsy kids. I didn't even know she was there. I turned around right after the break started and she had one of those goddamned permanent markers in her hand—getting ready to make someone a new name tag she said—and put a black line three inches long right across the front of a new forty-five-dollar shirt. And don't think *that* didn't go on the expense account I turned in yesterday."

"Did the girl go up with you?" asked Eberstadt, with an insinuating smile. "Help you find a fresh shirt or something?"

"Naw. I didn't have time for a long hunt." He laughed.

"So in fact," said Lowry, "you were away from the Bontemps Room from, shall we say, 10:25 to 10:55? With no one to confirm your movements?"

"Hey, wait a minute! What the hell are you playing at?"

"Oh, we're not playing, Mr. Flythe. Pernell Johnson was killed sometime between 10:41 and eleven o'clock A.M. and you can't seem to prove where you were."

"Jesus H. Christ!" groaned Flythe. "I'll show you the goddamn shirt!"

Lowry followed him to the bedroom, his hand inconspicuously close to the gun under his jacket. But Flythe rummaged through a basket of dirty laundry and came up with a crumpled shirt. It did indeed have a long black ink stain across the front.

"You think I'd lie about a dumb thing like this?"

"I don't know," said Eberstadt from the doorway, where he stood with the framed diploma in his big hands. "You lied about a dumb thing like a college, why not murder?"

"What the bloody hell—?"

"Knock it off, Flythe," said Lowry impatiently. "Alfred Theodore Flythe—the *real* Alfred Theodore Flythe—graduated in 1907. If you look closely, you can see where you changed the zero to a six. You never went to Carlyle. Why did you lie about it?"

Ted Flythe sank down on his unmade bed and put a pillow over his head. They heard a steady string of muffled heartfelt curses, and they waited till he started repeating himself.

"Who's Alfred Theodore Flythe?" asked Eberstadt.

Flythe sat up. "Me. And my grandfather. I was named for him. Look, you gotta understand: every job you go into today, doesn't matter how sharp you are, how much chutzpah you've got, the first thing they want to know is, have you got your college degree? You think it takes a college education to handle a bloody cribbage tournament? So I tell 'em I graduated from this little college that went bankrupt in the seventies, show 'em the old sheepskin, and I'm in. They're never going to look it up. They don't really care. They're just checking off boxes on their questionnaire."

They went back into the living room. Eberstadt accepted another beer and they turned Flythe inside out, but got nothing further out of him. He insisted that he'd never seen John Sutton before that first chance encounter last Wednesday and that the only place he'd gone during the Sunday morning break was straight upstairs to his room for a fresh shirt and back down again.

It was only seven o'clock when they gave up. Lowry borrowed Flythe's phone and rang Elaine Albee's apartment again.

Still no answer.

CHAPTER XXIX

Vassily Ivanovich had been on his way out of his apartment near the UN when Elaine Albee and Alan Knight caught him. The big Russian invited them back inside for a glass of rosé.

"No more vodka or slivovitz," he apologized. "Now I am having to watch my blood pressure."

He explained he was on his way to the hospital. "Molly

Baldwin and me, we have long talk yesterday and she explains to me so much foolishness for her job. She cries very hard when I tell her it is foolishness. All is understood now and last night they let me see T.J. This morning I go, and tonight I go. Next week I go home."

"To Russia?"

"*Da*. To Russia. My delegation here is finished."

He did not take offense when they questioned him again about his movements Sunday morning. It was almost as if he did not realize he could be seriously considered for the murders. Asked why he was late getting back to the tournament after the break, he said he'd made a phone call to a member of his trade delegation and had been put on hold for longer than he'd anticipated.

It was not something they could easily check, but Elaine remembered another possibility, the theft of the cribbage board, and asked, "Did you work on Thursday, Mr. Ivanovich? Between noon and three, say?"

"Thursday? *Da*. We meet with export group from Georgia. We have same state. In our south, too," he beamed at them. "They want to sell us new fish they make there. Crawdudes."

"I think you mean crawdads," said Alan Knight with a perfectly straight face.

"We meet at ten, have lunch at one, make first agreements at four."

"And that's something I *can* check out," said Knight as he and Elaine left Ivanovich's apartment in Tudor City, that enclave of pseudo–French-Gothic buildings on the East River across from the UN.

They strolled north along a tree-lined street that was so quiet they might have been in one of the outer boroughs of the city. Lights glowed softly behind the leaded glass windows around them and midtown bustle seemed far away. As they paused on the bridge above Forty-second Street to watch the early evening traffic pass below them, the night breeze off the river was cool with a lurking undertone of coming winter.

Alan bent his fair head to Elaine's and his drawl was as warm as a summer night in Georgia. "I know a little place down in Chelsea where they make a shrimp tempura that's almost as good as chicken-fried shrimp back home. Do you like Japanese food?"

"Ye-ess," she said slowly.

"But what?"

She looked at her watch. "I half-promised Jim Lowry—"

"If it's not a whole promise by five, it doesn't count."

"Is that the way it works down South?" she dimpled.

"Oh, we're much more formal in the South. Half-past three's the cutoff point for half-promises."

"Tell the kids I like the pictures," Tillie said, looking at the crayoned drawings taped to the wall beside his bed.

"You sound better tonight," said Marian's warm voice in his ear.

He positioned the phone more comfortably on the pillow beside his head. "I am. I ought to be. Sleeping through your visit this afternoon. You should have waked me."

The three older kids got on the phone then and talked a few minutes—Chuck about football, Shelly about a drawing she would make of Chuck in his uniform, and Carl about Halloween, still two weeks away. At three, this would be his first real trick-or-treat experience and he was both fearful and excited about the scary costumes and all the candy he could eat.

One-year-old Jenny hadn't quite got the hang of telephones yet, but Marian reported that she was smiling after he'd spoken to her and he could hear her "Da-da-da-da!" in the background.

"Get a good night's sleep, darling, and I'll see you tomorrow," said Marian.

"I will," he promised and hung up.

Not sleepy yet, he reached for the folder Lieutenant Harald had brought the day before.

Piers Leyden stood in front of one of his large figure paintings regaling critics from *Art News* and *The Loaded Brush* with his scatological anecdotes. This one was about a reclining female nude painted larger than life size which somehow wound up sharing a rotunda at Vanderlyn College with a retirement tea for a dean's secretary.

"So the president's secretary called the art department's secretary and said my picture would have to go. The only place their refreshment table would fit was against the same wall and they didn't want to chance pubic hairs falling in their silver punch bowl!"

Sigrid had heard the story earlier, in the spring when she investigated that murder in the Vanderlyn art department, but she laughed again with the rest because Leyden had a lusty delivery.

Leyden's work was nowhere near as firmly established as

Nauman's, but a growing interest in the "new realism" had jammed his opening with fellow artists, critics, dealers, students, friends, and groupies. There even seemed to be a serious collector or two in the crowd. His dealer had talked him into hanging a couple of already-sold works which they had red-dotted as a sort of pump-priming tactic, and several other pictures already sported little red dots of their own.

An orange-haired woman in a short blue dress, oversized olive sweater and army boots stood talking to a platinum blonde with black lipstick and black fingernail polish and a thin young man, closely shaved and barbered, who wore an immaculate white dinner jacket and matching white sneakers trimmed in rhinestones.

"Buntrock at the Friedinger told me they were ready to make a move toward the new realism soon and that I'd better get in while I could," the orange-haired woman announced importantly.

"*I* told you that months ago," retorted white sneakers with a covetous glance at Leyden's wonderful "Nude on a Cerise Rug," which his friend had just purchased. "If you'd acted when I told you, you could have picked that up for two thou less."

Sigrid found herself swept on and pushed up against a chalk drawing on pale blue paper. Amid curved lines vaguely suggestive of rounded blue clouds was a single small dark circle with soft lines radiating from the center, rather like a child might draw a starburst. Stylized stars? From a realist like Piers Leyden?

"You have to step back a few feet to get the full impact," said Nauman's voice behind her.

Obediently Sigrid stepped back and it became immediately obvious that the small dark circle was an anal view from pointblank range.

"Oh," she said, and turned to Nauman with a smile.

"You cut your hair."

She felt self-conscious again. "Yes."

"Earrings, a real dress, even silk stockings."

"They tell me gentlemen prefer Hanes," she said, striving for lightness.

"Very nice," he said, but there was an odd quality in his voice.

"Don't you like it?" she asked, puzzled.

"Oscar Nauman!" cried a jovial little Frenchman. "Tell me, *mon frère,* what do you think of Kissie Riddle's new abstracts?"

"Innocuous awning stripes," Oscar said sourly. "Vuzak."

They passed into the gallery's crowded middle room where

Doris Quinn, Leyden's inamorata, presided over the wine punch and toasted brie with a proprietary air. Lovely as ever, she wore a russet-colored jumpsuit and lots of heavy gold bracelets and chains. (In the picture behind her, she knelt on an oriental rug her late husband had given her for an anniversary present and wore nothing except a knowing smile.)

"Lieutenant Harald?" she exclaimed. "Why, I almost didn't recognize you. You look stunning!"

Praise from Caesar was praise indeed, thought Sigrid. She accepted a glass of the wine punch with murmured thanks while the little French gallery owner continued to badger Nauman for a kind word about the show he had currently mounted.

All around them swirled the darting glances, the languid handshakes, the empty kisses, the knowing faces mouthing profound judgments and invidious comparisons between Leyden's current show, his past shows, his future:

"He's ready to take off."

"What a rich complex of architectonic imponderables."

"Notice the resonant ambiguities in the reds."

"His strategies *work*, darling."

"What panache!"

"What presence!"

"What energy!"

"What crap!" muttered Nauman as he was carried off by a group that included Elliott Buntrock, perhaps the hottest curator in town at the moment.

"Now, Oscar," Buntrock said sternly. "Stop calling it crotch art and tell me: who mentored Leyden? You?"

Nauman gave a bitter laugh. "Bob Guccione probably, but neither of them will admit it."

While Nauman was trapped, Sigrid drifted around the gallery, conscientiously looking at Leyden's new pictures. She didn't know the right catch phrases and she didn't care for very much on the current scene, having long since given her heart to the clean, uncluttered purity of the late Gothic.

A craggy Hans Baldung head, for example, spoke volumes more to Sigrid than any Piers Leyden full-figured odalisque.

"Ready to go?" asked Nauman, abruptly reappearing on her second circuit of the rooms.

He was silent in the elevator going down, but once they were out on the sidewalk, he made a great show of looking up and down the street. "What? No battlecruisers to sail you away tonight?"

Sigrid gazed at him a long moment; then it came to her and she was incredulous. "You're jealous!"

"You're damn right I'm jealous!" he scowled. "For six months! Didn't I know? A swan hiding under all those prickly gray feathers. Didn't I say? And you fighting every attempt— No matter how much bread I scattered on the water—"

His angry metaphors outran his tongue. "Then little Sammy Sailor comes floating by and hey, presto!"

Others had descended from the Leyden opening and Sigrid became aware of curious faces. "Stop it, Nauman," she said. "You're making a scene."

"And what about Knight? Did he make you beautiful or did he just make you?"

"You're insulting," she said icily. "If there hadn't been a half-bottle of wine to a gallon of soda in that punch upstairs, I'd say you were drunk."

"An excellent suggestion!" he said and stomped away.

CHAPTER XXX

Sigrid changed her mind as the taxi cruised down the avenue. She didn't want to go home to Roman's curious face, she wasn't hungry enough to have dinner out, and there was no movie she wanted to see. Headquarters might have been an alternative, but dressed like this she would provoke even more curious looks. What she really wanted was a quiet, nonthreatening person who would talk about common unemotional things until she quit feeling as if she wanted to burst into tears.

Half of any solution lies in formulating the problem.

She leaned forward and asked the driver to take her to Metro Medical.

Visiting hours were not over until nine o'clock, so the hospital was still abuzz with daytime chatter, snatches of television music and the rattle of juice carts.

Sigrid had decided that if Tillie were asleep, she wouldn't disturb him. Happily, she found him awkwardly endeavoring to replace the telephone on the bedside table and his mild blue eyes registered surprise as he recognized her.

"Lieutenant! But he said— I just tried to call you. He said you were out."

"I am," she said dryly.

"I'm glad you came by," he beamed, waving a piece of paper.

The expression on his bruised face was one that Sigrid had come to expect whenever he discovered a significant bit of data that everyone else had overlooked.

"What is it, Tillie? What have you found?"

"You said it would be easier if you knew for sure who the bomb was meant for, right?"

"Right." Sigrid knew he savored the telling, so she did not spoil his enjoyment by rushing him.

"Well, look at this pairings roster you got from Graphic Games. Look at Wolferman."

Sigrid looked. "Zachary Wolferman, Number 101," she read.

"Now the commander."

"Commander T. J. Dixon, Number 102."

"And me?"

"Charles Tildon, Number 102."

"Now look at Professor Sutton."

"John Sutton, Number *161?*"

"Somebody must have changed the six to a zero. You still have the seating chart from Friday night, don't you?"

"The one that was on that little easel affair? I'm sure we do. It's a bit smudged and crumpled though. It got knocked over and stepped on a few times."

"You should still be able to tell. Somebody had to change Sutton's number to 101 and somebody else's to 161. One of those two numbers ought to be visible."

Sigrid grasped his point. "And that'll tell us if the killer made the change on the pairings print-out or after the hotel's artist had finished making the display chart."

Tillie leafed through the folder till he found a rough sketch of how the tables had been set up and numbered. "Number 161 would have been at Table 7," he said, passing it over to her.

"Right in the middle of the room. It would have done a lot more damage if the bomb had gone off there," Sigrid mused. "I thought the killer had a total disregard for human life, but it would appear I was wrong."

She smiled at her partner. "So we finally know that John Sutton's the right jack. I don't suppose you found his killer in those notes and papers?"

"Not yet, but I'll keep working on it. Looks more than ever like Flythe, doesn't it?"

"He may be the killer, but he isn't Fred Hamilton," she said and brought him up to date on her trip to Mantausic and the interview with Victor Earle.

They talked until Sigrid saw the weariness in Tillie's face and stood to go.

"I'm glad you stopped by, Lieutenant, and I like the way you changed your hair."

Her whole appearance seemed to register for the first time— her wine-colored dress, the high-heeled shoes, the musky scent of perfume.

"You look very nice tonight," he said wistfully. "You must be going someplace special."

"I did," she smiled. "I came here. Sleep well, Tillie."

"Good night, Lieutenant."

By the time Sigrid got home a little after nine, Roman Tramegra was totally exasperated. He had wanted to experiment with a new guacamole dip but the telephone had driven him to distraction.

"So _there_ you are! Oscar's been calling every twelve minutes for the last hour. He sounds frightfully upset."

Roman had been out when she came home to change earlier, so this was his first view of her new appearance and his hooded eyes widened in appreciation.

"My _dear_ Sigrid! I never _dreamed!_ That color is _you._ And your eyes—your _hair!_ Words simply _fail_ me."

Sigrid immediately wished that they would.

The telephone began to ring. "If that's Nauman, tell him I'm not back."

"He'll only call again," Roman grumbled, but did as he was told. "No, she isn't home yet," he lied irritably. "No, you certainly may *not* come over and wait. Oscar, I *promise* you—the very *minute* she walks in, I'll have her—''

He paused and looked at the receiver. ''I say, old chap. Are you quite sober?''

When at last he got off the line, Roman asked crossly, ''What on earth is this all about?''

''Nothing important,'' she said airily, leaning over to dip a tortilla chip in his guacamole.

It was delicious and she suddenly remembered that she'd had nothing except a glass of dreadful wine punch and a nibble of almond-toasted brie since lunch.

''Don't add a thing to that for the next three minutes,'' she urged, slipping out of her shoes and down to the bedroom.

There, she changed into a soft yellow robe and switched on her answering machine. The kitchen extension, which was also on her line, began to ring as she came back along the hall.

''Don't answer it,'' she called and the ringing stopped as the machine took over.

There were two more attempts on her line before it finally went silent. Sigrid sampled several versions of the dip and had a long relaxing conversation with Roman about the effects one might achieve with cosmetics. As usual, he added to her knowledge from his fund of inexhaustible trivia.

One of the things the Mantausic beautician had sold her was a tube of green lipstick. Sigrid was intrigued with the way it turned red on her lips, but Roman was less impressed.

''The Chinese have had rouge like that for *ages*. Made from safflower, I believe. It used to be sold on little cards and had a brilliant metallic green luster; but as soon as it was moistened and applied to the skin, it turned a delicate pink.''

''Nothing new under the sun,'' she said, which led to Cleopatra's kohl eyeliner and Elizabeth I's attempts to stay the calendar with henna rinses.

''What newswoman was it who said men get grayer with age while women get blonder?'' Sigrid wondered.

''Up to forty, only your hairdresser knows for sure. After forty, it's a safe assumption.''

''Is it?'' asked Sigrid, thinking of Doris Quinn's natural-looking daffodil yellow at the gallery tonight.

''My dear Sigrid, I'm delighted by your new interest in this field—may one assume it's connected with Oscar's agitation?—but do *not* be led down any primrose path. There is no fountain of youth in your little jars and tubes.''

"Makeup can take off years. Everyone says so."

"At a distance perhaps, or in *very* subdued light; but it's only an illusion, my dear. Only an illusion."

"What about Lucienne Ronay? She's fifty, almost as old as Mother, yet she looks ten years younger."

"Every rule has an exception, although if you stood quite close to her, I'm sure you'd detect wrinkles even there. The Dixon woman you described—"

"Commander Dixon?"

"Yes. Now you *said*—"

The telephone's abrupt ring made them both jump.

Roman looked at her reproachfully. "Don't you think you should set his mind at rest?"

Sigrid considered.

"No," she decided and switched off the bell.

They put away the food and cleaned up the kitchen, but every now and then, from his quarters beyond the kitchen door, they could hear the plaintive bleat of Roman's telephone.

When Sigrid fell asleep that night, she hugged to herself for the very first time in her entire life the blissful and deliciously feminine knowledge that she was making someone crazy.

CHAPTER XXXI

Alan Knight was not at headquarters when Sigrid arrived there the next morning, but Elaine Albee was. "He called and said he'd be here by ten," she reported.

Both women pretended not to notice Jim Lowry's sullen expression this morning as Albee reviewed the meeting with Ivanovich.

"Lieutenant Knight's checking with the Georgia Crayfish Association."

"Is there really such a group?" asked Sigrid, amused.

"Apparently."

Everyone was interested to hear of Tillie's discovery that the tournament pairings had been changed. They unearthed the smudged seating chart that had been trampled underfoot during the confusion Friday night. Despite the damage it had sustained, a close examination did reveal that the middle digits of the numbers 101 and 161 had been altered.

"That's exactly what Ted Flythe did with his grandfather's diploma," Eberstadt pointed out. "Changed 1907 to 1967."

"But *why* kill John Sutton?" Albee wondered aloud. "What did it gain?"

More material had come in over the Police Intelligence Network during the night. There was sketchy confirmation of Flythe's background and something interesting on the room steward: Raymond George, a.k.a. Amiri Attucks, had been a member of a Black Panther chapter in Sacramento where he was twice arrested for unlawful demonstrations in 1970 and was briefly detained in 1972 for the murder of a fellow Panther before his release for lack of evidence.

"Peters' invisible man!" said Eberstadt. "Who would be less noticeable than a hotel employee who had every right to be there?"

The three detectives argued it back and forth until it gradually penetrated that Lieutenant Harald was listening almost absentmindedly. Something had begun to niggle around the edges of her mind, something as nebulous as a stray hair that one brushes at unconsciously.

"Um?" she said, as she became aware of their questions. "Yes, he would certainly have the opportunity."

She took her arm out of the sling, flexed it gingerly, then spread across her desk all the photographs that had been taken at the Maintenon over the past weekend. What was beginning to coalesce and take shape was so unlikely that she couldn't voice it and what she sought in the pictures didn't seem to be there.

"Albee, were you there when I interviewed Flythe Saturday and those young women on the Graphic Games crew kept coming over to him with questions?"

"No, I was still rounding up witnesses, why?"

"We kept being interrupted and finally Flythe told one of them if she had any more questions to go ask one of the crew members with more experience. Barbara, he said."

"I think I talked with her," said Matt Eberstadt, pawing through his notes. "A Barbara Freeman."

"I don't see her in these pictures. Wasn't she older than the others?"

He nodded. "In fact I got the impression she thought she should be running the tournament instead of Flythe."

He pointed to a stocky figure with her face only partially in view.

"Oh, yeah," said Albee. "I remember her."

"How old is she?"

"Twenty-eight or thirty," Eberstadt hazarded.

"More like thirty-three or thirty-four," said Albee.

"I'd like to know for sure. You interviewed her, Eberstadt? See if you can get her exact birth date. And as long as you're at it, check the ages of everyone on the Graphic Games crew. Take Peters with you and try not to be too obvious about what you're looking for."

Eberstadt shook his head in puzzlement. "What exactly *are* we looking for, Lieutenant?"

"A thirty-seven-year-old killer," she said bluntly.

Alan Knight arrived after the others had left—Peters and Eberstadt for Graphic Games, Lowry and Albee for the Hotel Maintenon. They were to question Gustaffason, the hotel's staff artist, about the pairings list, and they also planned to ask Molly Baldwin which of the maids might have entered the d'Aubigné Room Wednesday morning. Their final chore would be to see that Mr. George was available when Sigrid arrived later that morning.

There was paperwork that could wait no longer for her attention, but it received only half her mind while the other half zipped among the possibilities.

Her telephone rang just as Knight finished reporting that the Georgia Crayfish Association had confirmed Vassily Ivanovich's presence at an all-day meeting on Thursday.

"Lieutenant?" came Albee's breathless voice. "I think Victor Earle just came in the hotel."

"What?"

"He looks exactly like you described Earle: bald, enormous moustache, really creepy stare."

The creepy stare convinced her. "I'm on my way."

Sigrid slammed down the phone. "Is Schmitt downstairs with your car?"

"Yeah, but I've got to tell you—"

"Tell me later," she said, grabbing up the case folder with its papers and photographs.

Followed by a protesting Alan Knight, she darted down the stairs and out the wide front entrance, spotted Petty Officer Schmitt, and raced toward the station wagon.

"Hurry up!" she told Knight. To Schmitt she said, "Hotel Maintenon as fast as you can."

"Yes, ma'am!"

Almost immediately they were careening uptown with as much speed as any New York cabbie ever made on a Wednesday morning.

"You aren't listening to me," said Alan. "I've been pulled back to my own office. My C.O. asked for a report this morning and he agrees with me that Commander Dixon wasn't the intended victim, so—"

"The Navy can have you back this afternoon," said Sigrid, easing her arm back into the sling. "In fact, they can have you back as soon as you drop me at the hotel. Victor Earle just turned up there."

"The hell you say!"

For the first time, Sigrid began to believe that Alan Knight might be halfway competent in an investigation. Certainly he could add two and two.

"The little bastard!" he said softly. "So he *did* spot something in those pictures. I wondered. But what?"

He almost tore the folder from Sigrid's grasp and began turning the photographs rapidly.

Sigrid stopped him at a long view of the room and pointed to the figure of Barbara Freeman. "Elaine Albee thinks she's about thirty-three or thirty-four."

"Huh?"

"A woman usually lies about her age. What if she's really thirty-six or -seven?"

"I don't get you."

"No?" Sigrid riffled through the pictures and touched another face as the car jounced over a bone-rattling pothole and zoomed around a stalled delivery truck. "Don't tell me I'm out of my mind. Just remember what that lying Victor Earle told us about Fred Hamilton."

The car swerved in toward the curb in front of the hotel and Sigrid had the door open before it came to a complete stop. Alan Knight was right beside her as she dashed into the luxurious lobby and looked around for Lowry or Albee, ignoring the startled looks of several hotel guests.

Elaine Albee signaled from across the lobby. "We just lost him," she moaned as they hurried over. "We knew he was watching for someone by the elevators—he made a call on the house phone—but the woman didn't get off; just held the door open while she spoke to him and then he got on and the doors closed before we realized what was happening.''

"How old was she?" asked Knight.

"Old? I don't know—thirty-nine or forty maybe. Why?"

They reached Lowry at the elevator bank, Sigrid flashed her ID at a nearby attendant while Albee commandeered another elevator and the two men watched to see where Earle's car would stop.

"NYPD," Sigrid said. "There was a man just here. Short, bald, large moustache. He met a woman on the elevator—"

"Mrs. O'Riley," he nodded.

"The car's stopped at thirty," said Lowry.

"That's where she works," said the attendant. "Up in the office there."

They piled into the next elevator; but without a key to turn it into an express, they were forced to pause twice along the way.

On the thirtieth floor, they stopped a startled secretary and said, "Quick! A Mrs. O'Riley. Where does she work?"

"Th-there!"

They burst through the double doors into a quiet executive office. A woman with lightly frosted hair looked up from behind a nameplate which read Susan O'Riley.

Sigrid had her ID out again. "Police, Mrs. O'Riley. You were just seen with a man, Victor Earle. Where is he?"

"May I ask what this is all about?"

"There's no time to explain. Whose office is this? Where did you take him? Through there?"

"Now just a minute!" said Mrs. O'Riley, rising from her desk. "You can't go in there!"

She was too late. They'd already flung open the door.

It was a corner office with tall windows from floor to ceiling and a magnificent view of midtown Manhattan's spires and towers. It was also quite empty.

"Is this Madame Ronay's office?"

"Yes," cried the bewildered secretary.

"Where is she?"

"I don't know! I thought she was here with him. He said he had something that belonged to her husband."

She trailed them across the office as they found a rear exit to a private elevator. There were no floor indicators in sight. Sigrid pushed the button.

"Where does this go?" she asked.

Mrs. O'Riley hesitated and Sigrid turned on her fiercely. "Can't you understand the danger? Someone could get killed."

Mrs. O'Riley took a deep breath and became the very capable executive secretary that she was.

"There are only three stops: this floor, her penthouse, and the basement where her car is garaged. You can get to the garage from any of the elevators outside, but this is the only one that goes directly to the penthouse. I'll get my keys."

"Albee, you and Lowry take the garage; Knight and I will try the penthouse."

Mrs. O'Riley was almost bowled over as they shot past her. She hurried back and inserted a key in the slot and within seconds, the door slid open. Less than a minute later, they were pounding on the door of Lucienne Ronay's penthouse.

Mrs. O'Riley was fumbling through the key ring, but Sigrid nodded to Alan Knight and he smashed the flimsy lock with one solid kick.

Just as they broke down the door, they heard Madame Ronay scream for help, then a deafening explosion. Through a wide arch, they glimpsed two figures struggling, then a gun fell to the floor, and a split-second later Victor Earle crumpled and fell on top of it.

Madame Lucienne Ronay stumbled toward them, her face ashen. "*Grâce à Dieu!*" she sobbed hysterically. "*Quelle horreur!*"

"What happened?" cried Sigrid, rushing past her to check Earle's vital signs.

"*Je ne sais pas.* This man. He calls me and says he has something that belongs to my beloved husband. Then, when we are alone, he points at me his gun and forces me here. I say to him '*Que voulez-vous?* Tell me and I will give you anything—money? jewels?' But he does not say, just looks at me with those horrible eyes. When he hears you, for *un petit moment* he looks away and I grasp his arm and we fight and then—"

She covered her face with her hands.

"Oh, Madame, how awful!" said Mrs. O'Riley. "Shall I call your doctor?"

Sobbing, Lucienne Ronay nodded gratefully.

Sigrid straightened from the dead man's body.

"At this point," she said icily, "I think your lawyer would be more helpful."

"Lawyer?" asked Madame Ronay in a trembling voice.

"Because a man who would kill me is himself killed? *Quelle absurdité!*"

"Nevertheless, these are your rights," said Sigrid and quoted them to the letter.

"Lieutenant!" cried Mrs. O'Riley, appalled. "How can you? After what she's just been through."

"Lieutenant Knight, please describe the scene you witnessed as we entered this apartment."

As Knight began, Jim Lowry and Elaine Albee, escorted by an elevator attendant with a key, rushed into the penthouse. "The garage man said no one—"

Albee fell silent when she saw Madame Ronay huddled on the couch and Victor Earle's body beyond.

"Continue, Lieutenant Knight," said Sigrid sternly.

"Very well. As we entered, I heard a woman scream for help, followed almost immediately by a gunshot. An instant later, I saw two figures struggling, then the gun fell from Madame Ronay's hand, and Victor Earle followed."

"Not my hand—his!" insisted Lucienne Ronay. "He tried to kill me."

"Blackmail you, perhaps, but not kill," Sigrid said. "He told your secretary he had something of your husband's. Which husband, Brooks Ann Farr? Maurice Ronay or Fred Hamilton?"

CHAPTER XXXII

It was late afternoon and Victor Earle's body had long since been taken away, but police technicians continued to process the apartment.

They had found the pseudo-Frenchwoman's hidden cache of chemical compounds, enough to level the hotel, in a concealed compartment built into the floor of her closet. Another hiding place in the paneled ceiling of her dressing room revealed a tin box that confirmed what Sigrid had already reasoned out: pictures of Farr/Ronay with Fred Hamilton and a yellowed news clipping from a French newspaper, the obituary of Lucienne Duval, *orpheline*, born in Lyons in 1938.

Thanks to her Swiss prep school, Brooks Ann spoke flawless French, so it would have been simple to obtain a birth certificate and step into the identity of a dead woman with no relatives. Had anyone continued to look for Brooks Ann Farr, they would surely look for someone born thirty-seven years before.

It was a stroke of genius, an inspired adaptation of Poe's purloined letter, to hide her past in the public eye. She had lost weight, lightened her hair, and learned to create a glamorous persona with cosmetics, but any woman might do those things.

What made her disguise so flawless, thought Sigrid, was her brilliant realization that since most women pretend to youth, the best camouflage was a pretense of age. To speak constantly of one's approaching fortieth birthday while still in one's twenties. To be vocally rueful about nearing the half-century while still in one's thirties.

She was ferociously strong-willed and intelligent, and somehow she had captured the whimsical fancy of an elderly French millionaire. They would probably never learn if he had known her true background. Somehow, Sigrid doubted it. On the other hand, Maurice Ronay was said to have had eccentric tastes.

Absently smoothing her hair, Sigrid turned through the souvenirs that Farr/Ronay had chosen to keep of her former life.

Someone cleared his throat and she turned to see Oscar Nauman in the doorway.

"How did you talk your way past the guards and reporters downstairs?" she asked.

"You know my methods, Watson," he said vaguely.

And she did. It could have been Susan O'Riley; it could have been Ronay's personal maid; it could even be one of her own police officers. She'd quit being surprised at the odd assortment of people Nauman knew.

"I've just come from Val's," he said.

Sigrid waited.

"So much for the observation of an artistic eye," he said dejectedly. "I thought John was trying to place that Flythe man and all the time it was really Ronay. Val said John used to feel sorry for her; spent a lot of time listening to her problems with Fred Hamilton, so she must have recognized him immediately and was afraid it would soon be reciprocal."

"Is Val bitter about that?"

"Right now. Eventually, she'll realize that's what made him John."

"Ronay was safe as long as she stayed away from people connected with Red Snow," said Sigrid, absently massaging her wounded arm. "Not hard to do with everyone except Earle either dead or involved in middle-class pursuits. John Sutton was probably the only member of McClellan's SDS ever to walk into the Maintenon and he might not have given her a second glance if he hadn't been immersed then in his book and lectures of the period."

"Did the busboy see her switch the boards?"

"I doubt it. I think what happened is that young Johnson saw Ronay on her way to check on the d'Aubigné Room and followed to offer his assistance. Raymond George said he was going to recommend Johnson for a bonus because he reacted so quickly to the fire, but Johnson had his immediate goal set on becoming a waiter in the Emeraude Room. The boy probably made some innocent remark about not wanting money for what he did Friday night, but a promotion."

Nauman nodded reflectively. "And she interpreted that as a blackmail threat that he'd seen her switch the boards. If I'd been paying attention last Wednesday—"

"Don't heap all the blame on yourself," Sigrid said sharply. "I should have caught it sooner myself, realized that she ordered the ashtrays changed to muddy the waters. I even had a witness tell me on Saturday that Madame Ronay was the one who bumped into the altered seating chart and trampled it underfoot. She probably hoped we wouldn't notice that Sutton's number had been changed to put him where the bomb would do the least damage to her precious ballroom."

Nauman looked around, mentally cataloging the paintings over the bed and on the opposite wall. What sad dim parodies they were of those exquisite entertainments of Watteau and Fragonard, and how suited to the surface image of Lucienne Ronay.

He glanced at Sigrid and found her regarding him with a quizzical expression. Her new bangs wisped softly over her strong forehead but she'd eaten off most of her lipstick. Her bare lips made him feel strangely tender.

"You finished here soon?"

"I'm finished now. Let me tell the others I'm leaving."

"Why don't you ask Knight to join us for a drink?" It was the nearest he could come just then to an apology.

"Alan? Oh, I sent him off with Albee an hour ago."

"You did?" Some of Nauman's old preening masculinity

crept back into his smile. "Look, Siga—take off a few days and come to Connecticut with me this weekend."

Sigrid tilted her head.

"You ought to give your arm a chance to heal properly," he coaxed. "I promise I'll behave myself."

Sudden mischief quirked her lips and danced in her gray eyes but her tone was innocent as she asked, "Want to bet?"

ABOUT THE AUTHOR

Margaret Maron lives with her husband, an artist, on the family farm in North Carolina. THE RIGHT JACK is the fourth in her Sigrid Harald series.

Kinsey Millhone is . . .

"The best new private eye." —The Detroit News

"A tough-cookie with a soft center." —Newsweek

"A stand-out specimen of the new female operatives."
—Philadelphia Inquirer

Sue Grafton is . . .

The Shamus and Anthony Award winning creator of Kinsey
Millhone and quite simply one of the hottest new mystery
writers around.

Bantam is . . .

The proud publisher of Sue Grafton's Kinsey Millhone
mysteries:

50 YEARS OF GREAT AMERICAN MYSTERIES
FROM BANTAM BOOKS

Stuart Palmer

"Those who have not already made the acquaintance of Hildegarde Withers should make haste to do so, for she is one of the world's shrewdest and most amusing detectives." —*New York Times*
May 6, 1934

- ☐ 25934-2 THE PUZZLE OF THE SILVER PERSIAN (1934) $2.95
- ☐ 26024-3 THE PUZZLE OF THE HAPPY HOOLIGAN (1941) $2.95
- ☐ 26334 THE PENGUIN POOL MURDER $2.95
- ☐ 26150 THE PUZZLE OF THE RED STALLION $2.95

Barbara Paul

- ☐ 26234-3 RENEWABLE VIRGIN (1985) $2.95
  "The talk crackles, the characters are bouncy, and New York's media world is caught with all its vitality and vulgarity." —*Washington Post Book World*
- ☐ 26225-4 KILL FEE (1985) $2.95
  "A desperately treacherous game of cat-and-mouse whose well-wrought tension is heightened by a freakish twist that culminates in a particularly chilling conclusion." —*Booklist*

For your ordering convenience, use the handy coupon below: